W9-BFJ-583

Praise for the Kendra Ballantyne,
Pet-Sitter Mystery series

Nothing to Fear but Ferrets

"Linda O. Johnston has a definite talent for infusing humor in just the right places . . . Pet lovers and amateur sleuth fans will find this series deserving of an award as well as a place on the bestseller lists." —*Midwest Book Review*

"Another clever foray into the life and crime-beset times of Kendra Ballantyne . . . Be sure to read this pet lover's dream of a book . . . You won't regret it."
—*Mystery Lovers News*

Sit, Stay, Slay

"Very funny and exciting . . . worthy of an award nomination . . . The romance in this novel adds spice to a very clever crime thriller." —*The Best Reviews*

"A brilliantly entertaining new puppy caper, a doggie-filled who-done-it . . . Johnston's novel is a real pedigree!"
—Dorothy Cannell

"Pet-sitter sleuth Kendra Ballantyne is up to her snake-draped neck in peril in Linda O. Johnston's hilarious debut mystery *Sit, Stay, Slay*. Witty, wry, and highly entertaining."
—Carolyn Hart

Berkley Prime Crime Books by Linda O. Johnston

SIT, STAY, SLAY
NOTHING TO FEAR BUT FERRETS
FINE-FEATHERED DEATH

Fine-Feathered Death

Linda O. Johnston

BERKLEY PRIME CRIME, NEW YORK

THE BERKLEY PUBLISHING GROUP
Published by the Penguin Group
Penguin Group (USA) Inc.
375 Hudson Street, New York, New York 10014, USA
Penguin Group (Canada), 90 Eglinton Avenue East, Suite 700, Toronto, Ontario M4P 2Y3, Canada
(a division of Pearson Penguin Canada Inc.)
Penguin Books Ltd., 80 Strand, London WC2R 0RL, England
Penguin Group Ireland, 25 St. Stephen's Green, Dublin 2, Ireland (a division of Penguin Books Ltd.)
Penguin Group (Australia), 250 Camberwell Road, Camberwell, Victoria 3124, Australia
(a division of Pearson Australia Group Pty. Ltd.)
Penguin Books India Pvt. Ltd., 11 Community Centre, Panchsheel Park, New Delhi—110 017, India
Penguin Group (NZ), Cnr. Airborne and Rosedale Roads, Albany, Auckland 1310, New Zealand
(a division of Pearson New Zealand Ltd.)
Penguin Books (South Africa) (Pty.) Ltd., 24 Sturdee Avenue, Rosebank, Johannesburg 2196,
South Africa

Penguin Books Ltd., Registered offices: 80 Strand, London WC2R 0RL, England

This is a work of fiction. Names, characters, places, and incidents either are the product of the author's imagination or are used fictitiously, and any resemblance to actual persons, living or dead, business establishments, events, or locales is entirely coincidental. The publisher does not have any control over and does not assume any responsibility for author or third-party websites or their content.

FINE-FEATHERED DEATH

A Berkley Prime Crime Book / published by arrangement with the author

PRINTING HISTORY
Berkley Prime Crime mass-market edition / May 2006

Copyright © 2006 by Linda O. Johnston.
Cover illustration by Monika Roe.
Cover logo by axb group.
Cover design by Rita Frangie.
Interior text design by Stacy Irwin.

ISBN: 0-425-20374-3

BERKLEY® PRIME CRIME
Berkley Prime Crime Books are published by The Berkley Publishing Group,
a division of Penguin Group (USA) Inc.,
375 Hudson Street, New York, New York 10014.
BERKLEY PRIME CRIME and the BERKLEY PRIME CRIME design are trademarks belonging to
Penguin Group (USA) Inc.

PRINTED IN THE UNITED STATES OF AMERICA

10 9 8 7 6 5 4 3 2 1

To bird lovers everywhere, and especially our thanks to the West Valley Bird Association for letting Linda enjoy a meeting and a macaw. Thanks also to Tiana Carroll, who entertained Linda and let her ask lots of questions at the bird show at the Las Vegas Tropicana.

And to Fred, through love and adversity, forever. This is mostly from Linda, but Fred has grown on Kendra, too.

—*Kendra Ballantyne / Linda O. Johnston*

Chapter One

THE SHRIEK SLAMMED into my ears. It radiated through my slouched, nearly sedentary body. My fingertips jerked on the computer keyboard, and the legal brief I'd been writing was suddenly full of gibberish.

Maybe it was already full of gibberish. Who knew? But the sudden surfeit of extraneous letters made it all the more incomprehensible.

Like my thoughts. Who'd screamed? Why? Where?

It was nearly ten o'clock at night. No one else was nuts—er . . . dedicated—enough to still be around the law offices of Yurick & Associates.

Or so I'd assumed an instant earlier.

The scream had sounded like someone inside this building. Someone incensed. Someone in pain. Someone hurt . . . dying?

Heck, there'd been too many murders around me lately. The usual person soars through her entire lifetime without encountering even one, but several had orbited my existence in the last few months. No wonder my imagination lent emotions to a sound that was probably in my head.

But I was a lawyer. What imagination I had was devoted to dreaming up winning legal arguments for clients, not screams in the night.

I couldn't ignore the noise.

As if my shaking body would let me.

I stood, listening to the now utter silence, except for the rapid thud from my overly excited heart.

Should I dial 911? I reached for my purse, stashed in a desk drawer, and snatched my cell phone from it. I pushed in the numbers, but wouldn't hit "Send" till I was sure something was wrong. Maybe someone had programmed some jarring mechanical gadget to turn on at this hour. Or I'd heard squealing tires outside on Ventura Boulevard, unidentified thanks to how intensely I'd been concentrating on my brief. Or—

I was rationalizing. What I'd heard wasn't electronic, and it unequivocally emanated from inside. My shivering finger pressed "Send." I prepared to identify myself, Kendra Ballantyne, attorney-at-law.

Except no one answered; a recorded message insisted that I hold. How could all 911 operators be busy? What if someone were dying?

I didn't know that nobody *was* dying. Or worse, was dead by now.

What if someone had actually been attacked here? The assailant could still be around, intending to silence— permanently—whoever'd heard that scream. I hissed in my breath and held it . . . as I hung up, stuffed the phone into a pocket, and slipped carefully from my office, my ears on full alert.

Not for the first time, I wished I'd brought Lexie along when I headed back to work this evening. My Cavalier King Charles spaniel would have let me know if there was something to bark about.

At least I was dressed down that day, in a shirt tucked into casual slacks that wouldn't restrict running should I seek to escape. Better yet, my blessedly quiet walking shoes didn't make a sound as I slipped through the one-story office building.

I'd left lights on in the hall, which could be a bad thing if someone lurked in one of the darkened rooms whose doors opened off it. The offices of Yurick & Associates squatted in a structure that had once been a restaurant, and small, private offices had been built along the outer wall, with open cubicles for paralegals and secretaries in the center.

Outside the door to my comfy corner office, I stood still for an instant and held my breath. Heard nothing. Saw nothing that shouldn't be in the hall. I started slowly along it, preparing to flee first, ask questions later.

I stopped when I reached the door three down from mine—a closed door. A rustling sound emanated from inside, like someone shuffling papers.

The office belonged to the firm's newest associate— Ezra Cossner, who'd joined us just yesterday. Not that senior citizen Ezra was new to the practice of law. Heck, no. At thirty-five, I was about half the age of most of Borden Yurick's new brain trust of attorneys.

Should I call out? What if Ezra was under siege from someone who'd hurt him? Would that person start shooting through the door?

Obviously I'd seen too many action films and cop-filled TV shows. Still, I edged away, my back along the wall. I pulled out my cell phone, preparing to send my distress call again—and ready to pray that a real person picked up this time.

More shuffling sounded from beyond the door. But no more screams. A good sign—wasn't it?

I took a deep breath, steeling myself for what was to come. Then I called out, "Ezra? Are you in there?"

No response. No shuffling either.

"Ezra?" I tried again.

Still silence.

I scanned the closest cubicles for anything that might double as a weapon, should I need to protect myself. Sharp pens for stabbing skin? Computer keyboards for bopping heads? How about a stapler, to fasten my frayed nerves back together?

And now, after calling out, I'd even lost the edge of surprise.

Heck, Kendra. Are you a woman or a wimp?

Before I could berate myself with the best answer— both—I wrapped my fingers around the doorknob. Turned it. Shoved the door open.

And gasped at the immediate shrill string of squawks that accosted me.

I blinked. I grinned. I hurried inside, and flicked on the light.

Near Ezra's empty desk crouched a huge cage. And in it was a beautiful, mostly blue macaw.

A COUPLE OF minutes later, I was still there, taking a break and talking to the bird. We were, after all, kindred spirits, the only living creatures occupying the Yurick law offices at this ridiculous hour.

And my relief that nothing was wrong, that no one was mortally wounded, made me giddy.

"I heard rumors that Ezra owned a macaw," I remarked during a rare respite from her raucous cries. "No one mentioned that he might bring you here, though."

This time, the bird talked back. Her dark-colored tongue appeared between the top and bottom of her sharply curved and perilously pointed black beak. "Gigi, gorgeous girl, gorgeous girl," she rasped in her rough voice. She repeated it. And repeated it. And repeated it.

"Glad to meet you, Gigi," I said over the din, assuming she was asserting her own name. "Can you say anything else? How about Kendra? Can you say 'Hi, Kendra'?"

"Gorgeous girl," she grumped, and I doubted her goal was to compliment me. Instead, she stopped speaking and stared suspiciously through the brass-toned spokes of her cage with one eye, then turned her head to glare at me with the other.

The dark gleam in those small black eyes was emphasized by the discrete field of small white feathers surrounding each of them. Her chest and belly were plumed in gold. And though I could certainly term her back blue, that was as descriptive as calling a rainbow an attractive arch. The feathers fluffed about the back of her head were lighter than the deep royal blue of her body and the dark navy of her long tail.

My clothes paled in comparison, which was no wonder, since they were beige and bland. Months ago, my hair had returned to its basic, blah brown when I could no longer afford to have it highlighted blond and beautiful. It now just skimmed my shoulders. My face? Okay after I added makeup, but even so, essentially ordinary.

Gorgeous girl? Hah!

I took a seat in an uncomfortable antique chair beside the beautifully hued bird. Ezra apparently liked old stuff, since the desk, outsized for the cramped quarters, was a big, carved monstrosity. Even Gigi's huge cage appeared antique. Fortunately, it crouched on wheels, since carrying it would doubtless be difficult.

Beside it stood a large metal doodad that I discerned must be Gigi's official perch when she wasn't pent up in her cage. The edges of Ezra's office were lined with neatly labeled cardboard crates that confirmed he hadn't fully settled in yet.

"When did Ezra bring you here?" I asked Gigi. "I was around most of the day, and I'd surely have heard everyone talking about you. Did you come in earlier this evening, when I was out doing my pet-sitting rounds?"

Her only response was to shift her weight from one of the claws gripping her perch to the other.

"You know, I work as a pet-sitter on the side these days. I've never had a bird like you to tend. If you became my client, would you tell me how to take care of you?"

She opened her beak, and the sound she made was rude by human standards.

"I'm really pretty good at pet-sitting," I protested. But I doubted she'd care if I explained the origin of my alternate career. See, I'd been accused many months ago of serious breaches of attorney ethics—which, believe it or not, isn't always an oxymoron. Though ultimately I was able to prove I'd been framed, the State Bar had nevertheless decided I had to pass the MPRE—Multistate Professional Responsibility Exam—before my suspension from the practice of law was lifted.

As a consequence of the initial allegations, my career had been put on hold, along with my income. I'd had to file for bankruptcy, with no means of making ends meet. My good friend Darryl Nestler, owner of the Doggy Indulgence Day Resort, had suggested that I take up pet-sitting so Lexie and I would be able to eat in the interim.

To my surprise, I'd enjoyed it—enough that I still indulged in pet-sitting, even though I had recently resumed practicing law.

Fortunately, Borden Yurick, a partner in my former law firm Marden, Sergement & Yurick, had decided around the time I'd gotten in trouble that he'd rather have fun practicing law than hang around the stuffy firm. That had caused his uncomprehending and unforgiving partners to assert he'd had a nervous breakdown.

After a cathartic globe-circling expedition, Borden opened this office, where he'd promised his newest associates, mostly old-time attorneys, that they'd enjoy what they did for a living. He'd invited me to join them, agreeing I could continue pet-sitting if I wished. I could even take on pet advocacy cases. In fact, I could pretty much practice law as I pleased, as long as I assisted him on cases he chose to handle.

"It was definitely a good deal for me," I related aloud to Gigi. She bobbed her blue head twice, as if she'd read my thoughts and agreed.

I laughed. And then I looked at my watch. "Sorry, my friend, but I need to finish part of a brief I was working on, then head home. My dog Lexie's waiting for me. So's her friend Odin, the Akita we watch when his owner's out of town."

That owner would be Jeff Hubbard, a private investigator and security expert who also happened to be my sometime lover—when he wasn't withholding important facts about his background from me.

"Anyway, I'll see you around, okay?"

Gigi regarded me skeptically but said not a word.

I did hear some words, though, as I exited the open office door. Nothing as sinister as I'd interpreted Gigi's earlier shriek, but definitely human voices, drawing near from the reception area.

Raised human voices.

I wondered if I was wrong about the nonsinister part.

I soon recognized who was shouting. Unsurprisingly, one was Ezra Cossner. I'd figured he wouldn't simply leave lovely Gigi by her lonesome all night. He was probably here to take his pretty pet home.

The other voice was female, and also familiar. It belonged to Elaine Aames, another senior-citizen law associate Borden had hired to have fun practicing law. She didn't sound as if she was having fun now. Her voice remained too distant for me to make out what she said, but its shrillness suggested fury.

They came into view in the hall. Ezra, somewhat

stoop-shouldered, had a partially shiny pate and wore a light sweater over baggy slacks. Elaine was shorter and slighter, with neat silver hair and a shocking pink blouse beneath a subdued suit.

Ezra's shout was angry and audible enough to make my ears ring—and cause Gigi, inside her cage, to flutter her long blue wings and start squawking in response. Disconcerting.

Disturbing.

And definitely menacing.

Over Gigi's noise, Ezra yelled, "You'll buy that house over my dead body!"

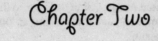

Chapter Two

SURE, THAT THREAT can be a simple figure of speech. Only sometimes it's not so simple—like when someone sincerely means it.

Okay, maybe I'm a little sensitive lately, having had so many murders mushrooming around me. But still—

Both Ezra and Elaine spotted me at the same time. Elaine smiled—sort of. A classy older lady who adored her specialty of estates and trusts, she was in her late sixties, with laugh lines that suggested she spent a lot of her life in mirth. She dressed like an old-school ladylike lawyer, usually clad in skirted suits. We were of similar height, but she wore her five-foot-five so much more elegantly.

"Why are you here so late, Kendra?" she asked. Whatever her gripe with Ezra, it was gone from her voice as she spoke warmly to me. The look she shot him from the edge of her eye suggested strongly that they keep their disagreement to themselves.

Which was fine, as far as I was concerned. Except that I was curious.

"I was working," I responded with a smile of my own. "Until Gigi gave me a start. I didn't know she was here." I sure did now, though. Her cries continued, carrying raucously through the open doorway.

Ezra apparently didn't like the noise. He approached his office and shouted inside, "Shut up!"

The bird complied . . . for all of two seconds. And then she started up again.

Ezra repeated his ignored order, then slammed the door shut. He was well into his seventies. I'd heard he'd had health problems a decade ago that he'd fought off like an embattled homeowner exterminates ants. They'd left him with stooped shoulders and, I'd imagined, added to the forest of wrinkles on his wizened face, but he seemed healthy to me.

Now, arms folded, thin brown brows flexed and head angled back, he stared with suspicion from the bottom part of his bifocals, as if he could read the awful answers about me on my face. Well, I'd emerged from his office, but I had good reason to be there. And I thought my explanation was self-evident, especially after his attempt to silence his still-squawking bird.

Even so, he sputtered, "What were you doing in there?"

Though I'd met Ezra only yesterday, his reputation had preceded him. Borden had warned us all that it wasn't easy to warm up to the eccentric, edgy Ezra, but that he was a damned fine attorney—and he was bringing a damned fine portfolio of clients who'd stuck with him when he was forced to retire from his prior firm.

Clients who apparently saw through his grumpy side to his lovably successful lawyering.

"Oh, I just used Gigi as an excuse to snoop through all the boxes in your office," I said with a smile.

Elaine's eyes widened. She shook her head slightly, as if in warning. Maybe no one who knew Ezra well dared to tease him.

I held my breath for an instant, awaiting the inevitable explosion. Instead, to my surprise, he smiled back. Then he opened his flat lips and guffawed.

I glanced at Elaine. Her grin looked more relieved than riotous.

Feeling on a roll, I continued, "I didn't find anything of interest, though, darn it. Except for your bird. She's beautiful, Ezra—even if she likes to hear herself talk. And screech." Which she still did from behind the door, ad nauseum. "She said her name was Gigi. Is that right?"

"Sure is. And don't be so hasty about saying you didn't find anything of interest. Borden said you work on matters for other attorneys in this firm, and that you'd help *me*. In fact, I expect to use your services on one big bugger of a case I'm involved in right now. Maybe more, if you do a good job with this one." He stood up straighter, as if to point out that he was several inches taller than me and many years my senior, both in age and in experience.

My smile sagged as I waited for the punch line, but the smugness settling into the lines on his skinny face told me there wouldn't be one. Hmmm. That would teach me to tease a guy with a cantankerous reputation.

"Er . . . what kind of case?" I inquired.

"I'll tell you about it when it's not so late."

Good entrée to change the subject. "Why are you here at this hour?" I asked.

"Elaine and I lost track of time over dinner." Ezra shifted a telling look toward his companion, only I couldn't read what it told her. "We're old friends. We got to talking and— Well, never mind."

"So I heard," I blurted.

I watched Elaine's pale face flush pink. "Sorry," she said. "No one was supposed to hear our little disagreement."

"I figured," I replied, my gaze on Ezra. He reddened, too. "What house were you talking about?"

"No big deal." I admired how airily Elaine attempted to

talk, though the rapid way she respired suggested that it was, indeed, a big deal. "I'm selling the condo where I've lived since I was widowed ten years ago, and only recently found a house I'd like to buy. Ezra doesn't like it. He says it's too big, too San Fernando Valley. Too architecturally ordinary. Just too . . . *too*. But it's my decision."

"Of course," I agreed, though I had the distinct impression, from the tomato tint to Ezra's complexion, that he wasn't used to anyone disputing his demands.

"Not that it's any of your business," Ezra growled.

"Right," I agreed, staring daggers back at him. And this guy wanted me to work with him on a legal matter?

"We'll talk tomorrow about my case," he continued, his tone not a lot lighter, "since I need you to dig right in."

I wouldn't tell him to go pound sand till I'd talked to Borden, who was, despite his easygoing approach to practicing law, my boss. But work with this ill-mannered ass of an attorney? Unlikely.

Besides, I had cases of my own to complete.

I equivocated. "I was here late working on a brief I have to file tomorrow," I told him. "And until—"

"Fine," he interrupted. "File it. Then talk to me."

Suddenly, the exhaustion I'd been setting aside all evening seemed to settle into my weary mind. "Let's discuss it tomorrow," I said, stifling a yawn.

Maybe, by then, I'd have thought of a good excuse to evade Ezra's case.

AFTER GOODNIGHTS TO noisy Gigi and silent, unsmiling Elaine, I headed home.

Rather, I aimed my nine-year-old BMW toward the Mexican ranch-style house in Sherman Oaks where I was hanging out this week. And had been for a lot of weeks, on and off. It was the place I'd been invited to move into. Permanently. I had even considered it . . . briefly.

Before I'd found out that my dog-sitting client, host, and would-be live-in lover, Jeff Hubbard, had lied to me.

Okay, an exaggeration. He simply hadn't told me the whole truth.

I pulled my Beamer into Jeff's driveway and parked, turned off his security system, and slipped into his house, where I was greeted effusively by my little furry tricolor Cavalier King Charles spaniel, Lexie, and by bigger, sleeker white and red Odin, an Akita.

Gad, did that ever feel good, to have the dogs go wild just because I was there. I stooped and hugged them. "How 'ya doing, guys? I'm glad to see you, too."

If they'd spoken English, I was sure they'd tell me about their evening, since I'd walked and fed them earlier, before finishing my day's pet-sitting rounds and heading back to the office. They'd probably complain that I hadn't stayed home to snuggle with them on the sofa and watch TV.

After I accompanied them on their final constitutional of the night, and just before I prepared to plant my exhausted bod in bed, the phone rang. It was Jeff.

"How are things?" he asked.

"Other than being nearly scared to death by a scream in the night, just fine."

My smile at his initial silence felt deliciously evil.

"What—?"

I didn't let him get far before I explained about Gigi.

"Glad it all worked out, darlin'. I'll be home tomorrow, so think about me in bed tonight."

It was a way he often ended our conversations when he was traveling—which was a lot of the time. The hell with my ambivalence about the guy. I grinned as I hung up, and the dogs leapt on me. We roughhoused for a full five minutes, till my exhaustion told me I'd better head for bed or I'd wind up sleeping with the pups on the floor.

I felt damned good, thinking about Jeff after I lay down.

Until my Ezra dilemma popped back into my head.

No matter. I'd handle him just as I'd handled all of my many problems as of late.

I hoped.

AS ALWAYS, WEEKDAY or workday—heck, for me there was no such thing as a non-workday—I awoke early the next morning, showered, dressed, and lovingly tended to Lexie and Odin. I spent extra time walking them in the friendly, flat residential area where Jeff lived. After all, the likelihood was that I'd have another long lawyering day.

I was clad in nice slacks and a sweatshirt over a pink blouse dressy enough to throw my suit jacket over if, despite my most negative druthers, I wound up meeting one of Ezra's clients. Despite the dampness, I took my time as I let Odin and Lexie sniff around Jeff's street.

Rain threatened to intrude into the Los Angeles basin. That meant I was likely to get wet. My canine clients, too.

I still enjoyed my pet-sitting gig. Still appreciated how it had helped me over the indignity of having no income. Sure, I'd agreed to the temporary suspension of my law license—that, or go to trial and risk a longer loss. Like, permanent. My alleged infraction? Leaking a strategy memo to the other side in a complex lawsuit I'd been defending on behalf of a corporate client. The plaintiff to whom I'd purportedly handed the memo, a lunatic named Lorraine, had been so incensed over its contents that she had murdered the head of my client corporation.

I subsequently cleared myself. Someone else had leaked that memo. But I'd kept pet-sitting because I liked it.

Now, since I was again practicing law, I had less time to sit, so I had fewer pet-type clients. Once I settled Lexie and Odin back in Jeff's house, I reviewed my list to ensure I remembered to visit all my charges. I'm a confirmed lista-holic. Few events in my life avoided being stuck on sheets of paper in the order of priority I gave them. I relied on lists in both of my revered careers: pet-sitting and attorneying. And I'd lately developed a pet-sitting contract for client owners to execute. It detailed my duties and limited my liability. I was, after all, a lawyer.

Once I knew what I was doing that day, I headed for the home occupied by Alexander the pit bull, one in my stable of pets to sit.

After taking excellent care of Alexander, I was off to tend the remainder of my morning charges, spending all the time each dog needed for eating and walking. I would also make certain each cat on my route was equally well tended, though they didn't demand as much attention.

At the moment, all my charges were canine and feline, though I'd also tended rabbits, a pot-bellied pig, and a ball python.

I adored every one of them.

I savored my twice-daily dose of the bittersweet when I visited the newest addition to my client list: Beggar, a beautiful Irish setter. He belonged to Russ Preesinger, who sublet my very own leased-out mansion. My prior tenants were on location in another state, shooting yet another reality TV show.

Eventually, my morning chores were completed. I shoved my Beamer's nose farther out in the Valley, toward the Yurick offices. I had a feeling I would have more shit to contend with there than I'd already managed this morning.

"Sure, Kendra, Borden's in," chirped Mignon, the Yurick & Associates receptionist—an adorable, effervescent twenty-two-year-old who seldom spoke without singing. She sat at a big, file-littered desk in the office suite's entry, where a hostess once awaited diners at this former restaurant. "Want me to let him know you're on your way?"

"No need," said a high-pitched male voice from behind me. I turned, and there was the very man I'd intended to chat with as soon as possible. "Morning, Kendra."

Borden Yurick was a slender senior citizen with a soupçon of a paunch, big trifocals, and an adorably lopsided smile. These days, he favored wearing Hawaiian-print shirts. Because this was January, though, and a little chilly in L.A. for short sleeves, he'd donned a bright red sweater, and only the collar of his pink-and-green floral shirt peeked out.

"Hi, Borden," I said. "Have a minute?"

"Sure. Let's go to my office." Since he was senior partner and founding father of the firm, his office was, appropriately, the biggest, in the corner at the far end from mine. That meant we made a ninety-degree turn, passing cubicles of paralegals and legal assistants on one side, and attorney offices on the other.

Ezra Cossner's closed door, three past mine, was shoved open as we approached. Ezra appeared, holding the door open as if attempting to usher someone out.

A short, stocky man wearing a shirt, tie, and scowl stood just inside. His glare at Ezra appeared explosive enough to ignite the older guy.

I was beginning to know the feeling.

From inside the office came a chorus of "No, no, no, no," followed by a series of clamorous squawks. I recognized Gigi the macaw's raucous ripostes.

On top of that, the stranger spat stridently at Ezra, "You haven't heard the end of this. Stealing clients is unethical."

Before Ezra could shout a retort, Borden stepped between them and stuck out his creased hand toward the stranger. "Nice of you to visit, Jonathon. And I'm sure any clients Ezra brought with him haven't been coerced to allow us to do their work. It's because they're fond of Ezra and the results he gets. Right, Ezra?"

"Yeah." Ezra's eyes were as angry as his accuser's, but his voice stayed smugly soft. "They like me. They really like me." He laughed. "Tell the other partners that they'd have been better off if they hadn't let you convince them I was suddenly too old to practice law—which we both know wasn't the real reason you got rid of me. Do you have enough clients left to keep the place running?" He didn't pause for a response. "See 'ya sometime, Jonathon."

He stood back, and the man named Jonathon edged around him and stamped his furious glare on everyone nearby—including me. Mostly me. Maybe he'd given up on Borden, since his next comment was definitely aimed in my direction. "You really want to work with this guy? You'll be damned sorry. Believe it."

I already did.

But he wasn't through. "He ruins everything he touches. Of course clients love him. He lets them run amok, do whatever they want, even if it's illegal."

Before I could ask for an explanation, he stomped down the hall toward the exit.

"You okay, Ezra?" Borden asked.

"Never better, partner," the snide senior said, then glanced at me. "So, Ballantyne, ready to work on my matter this morning?"

I blinked, definitely uncomfortable to be suddenly put on the spot like this. I'd intended to broach the bumpy subject with Borden before talking again to Ezra about it.

"I need to finish the brief I was working on last night," I said. "And I want to discuss it with you first, Borden." I hoped my stare spoke enough exclamatory sentences for Borden to understand what I really needed to talk about.

It did. But spending twenty minutes immersed in the matter with Borden's door closed behind us, I knew what I'd feared was the fact. Like Ezra, Borden had cadged his own caseload of clients from the firm where we both had formerly worked, Marden, Sergement & Yurick. He'd had a huge workload, which was why he'd wooed me to join him here.

He'd also hired a growing stable of his own old cronies—stress the word "old." His caseload was now adequately staffed with aging but agile attorneys who'd do a great job with them.

The pet law matters I'd begun to bring in were still fairly few, and in any event weren't likely to be lucrative.

As a result, taking on Ezra's clients would help assure my own longevity at the Yurick firm, since Borden wasn't apt to want to boot out his aging buddies if the business dwindled. Seniors would have harder times finding other law jobs. At my age, more numerous doors might open to me. Supposedly.

So much for Borden's promise that we'd all have fun here, practicing law. The practicality of it was that, if I wanted to hang around, I needed Ezra's meat-and-potatoes legal platter to keep myself employed.

Ezra needed help. Borden wouldn't order me to provide it, although we both knew that I owed him.

But I couldn't help cogitating on what Jonathon had said. Did Ezra act unethically? Counsel his clients to ignore the law?

Even though I'd been exonerated, I didn't need further ethics insinuations interfering with my legal career.

I returned a couple of calls, then made the interoffice approach I'd dreaded. "Ezra? This is Kendra." I knew I'd phoned the right office since I heard Gigi screeching in the background even louder than I heard her from down the hall. "I'd like to talk to you about the matter you want me to work on in, say, fifteen minutes?"

"Make that bird be quiet!" he shouted, though his voice sounded muffled, as if he'd covered the telephone receiver with his hand. Who was he talking to? Not me, surely. In a second, he said, "Ah, yes, Kendra," loudly enough that I knew he was speaking directly into the phone. In fact, I heard his silent yet victorious chortle as he said smugly, "I'll be ready."

Chapter Three

WHEN I ENTERED Ezra's office a little later, he wasn't alone. Gigi was there, of course, loose and perched on the pedestal outside her cage. She was squawking rhythmically as usual, this time bobbing her blue-and-white head along with her chosen cadence. Making noise wasn't all she'd been up to—I noticed some gnawing on the edges of Ezra's antique desk.

Uh-oh.

Ezra sat silently behind that desk, a yellow knit shirt emphasizing his thin, stooped shoulders. Judging by the grumpy grimace on his wrinkly face, he wasn't happy—which seemed to be his perpetual mood. Next to Gigi stood a short, slightly overweight woman with pale skin, a broad double chin, and unnaturally bright red hair.

"Kendra, meet Polly Bright," Ezra said, surprising me with my own perspicacity. I'd already thought of the word "bright" upon noticing her—and that included her clothes. "Polly, this is Kendra Ballantyne, one of the firm's partners."

"Glad to meet you, Kendra." Polly proffered her hand in greeting, and we shook soundly. Speaking of bright, her nails were tipped in scarlet as vivid as her lipstick, a hue that clashed with the artificial shade of her shiny hair. "I'm a bird psychologist and trainer," she continued. "I've worked with a friend of Ezra's who owns another member of the parrot family. Macaws are a type of parrot, you know. Isn't that a hoot—a bird trainer named Polly Bright?" She said it lightly with a laugh, and it sounded like a well-used refrain. "Here's more information about me." She slipped a flyer from the pocket of her flowing orange coat and handed it to me. It depicted the covers of half a dozen books on bird psychology—all written by Polly. "I'm known everywhere for my expertise on parrots, you know." Her eyes lowered in a modicum of modesty before she again met my gaze. "Ezra called and said Gigi needs counseling," she continued, "so here I am."

"Yeah," Ezra grumbled. "But so far you haven't even been able to get her to calm down."

"Patience!" Polly commanded. "You disrupted this poor creature's routine by adopting her. Then, before she could even get used to you, you moved her from your home to this office." Like everything else about her, Polly's dress beneath her jacket was bright—a long patchwork, peasant-style thing in blues, greens, and yellows. I'd have considered such a getup garish on almost anyone else, but on her it somehow worked.

"I brought Gigi home with me last night, then here again today," Ezra said, aiming his habitual scowl at the parrot psychologist. "I figured she'd be better off going back and forth, having company, being wherever I am. Aren't you, gorgeous girl?" This last was said in a soft and gushy tone. The bird stopped bobbing as if aware she was being sweet-talked. "Did you know she's a Blue and Gold Macaw, Kendra? They're smart and trainable, and Gigi already knows a lot. Don't you, girl?"

"Gorgeous girl," Gigi gargled demurely to her aging male owner. Amazingly, his attitude toward Gigi today indicated to me that, despite most appearances, Ezra Cossner had a modicum of humanity. I found myself almost liking the guy.

"I like having Gigi around," Ezra said. "But she can't hang out here if she's noisy all the time. And I can't have her eating everything, whether here or at my house."

"Well, I'm glad you called me to come here, rather than to your house," Polly said, peering around. She caught my eye and gave a grand, teeth-revealing smile. "There are lots of people around this office. It's not lonely or eerie, like so many places I have to go." She shuddered delicately, making her colorful coat shimmer. "I never refuse, of course, when a bird needs me. I simply take precautions if I must, and I have learned many. I have been all over the world, teaching people, enriching the lives of birds of so many kinds." She tossed her head back dramatically, apparently pleased she had found an audience in me, though I couldn't imagine why.

"What about Gigi?" I asked, attempting to redirect her back to her reason for coming to this particular piece of the world. "How can we help her?"

"She's like a four-year-old child," Polly replied with a much more mundane shrug. "She needs a schedule. She needs stability."

"She needs discipline," Ezra shouted. Then, slightly more calmly, he hissed to Polly. "You're the bird shrink. Tell me what to do so we can make this work."

Polly appeared both haughty and hurt as she took several sweeping strides toward Gigi's perch. Gigi squawked even louder and stretched out her huge blue wings. Above the din Polly demanded, "Let me have a few minutes with her. Alone."

I wasn't sure what magic she would attempt on the macaw, but I, for one, was willing to let her try.

"Come on, Kendra," Ezra said. "We'll talk in your office."

Before we exited, Ezra's phone rang. He listened for a minute, and I wasn't sure what he heard over the continued clamor from Gigi. "Yes," he ultimately roared. "I get it. And I'll figure it out before tonight. Count on it."

When he hung up, he glared at me as if whatever he'd heard wasn't good—and he'd set the blame squarely on me. "Let's go," he commanded. "We've got even more trouble than I thought."

BORDEN HAD DELIGHTFULLY furnished my digs here with items both ergonomic and eye-catching: a chair adjusted to hit my back and buns in the most comfortable spots, a functional oak desk with deep drawers that doubled as file holders, wooden file cabinets to match, and compatible oak client chairs upholstered in brilliant blue.

Ezra plunked himself down with no preamble on one of the comfortable client chairs. "Damn!" he exclaimed.

"What's wrong?" Of course he expected me to ask, but I complied only because I was curious.

"Word's already gotten out. Damn!" he said again. He stroked his pointed chin, and his facial wrinkles seemed even deeper in the brighter light of day pouring in through open vertical blinds at my windows.

"Word about what?" I asked with an inward sigh. This conversation was already degenerating into a depressing game of Twenty Questions, and I had no idea yet if we were discussing animal, vegetable, or mineral.

"You know any good investigators?" he countered.

"Sure do," I replied. "The best. And he's due back in town"—I looked at my watch—"five minutes ago."

I might often be ambivalent about my personal feelings toward my foremost pet-sitting client and sexy-as-hell lover, Jeff Hubbard, but I knew he was a damned good P.I.

"Good. Let me tell you what's going on, then I need you to call the guy. We need answers fast. Before tonight."

"Well, okay . . ." I equivocated. "I'm sure if anyone can find answers, Jeff's your man. But—"

"Here's the deal," Ezra said. "I represent a major real estate developer. *We* do now—Borden's firm, including you. You may have heard of the company: T.O. Properties. The initials stand for 'Tomorrow's Opportunities.' T.O's putting together a nice piece of prime property in Vancino and plans to construct a mixed-use development there."

Vancino was the new name of a mature section of the San Fernando Valley. Because some areas, over time, develop a reputation of being run-down or rough, concerned commercial property owners and residents sometimes chose to have their neighborhoods secede and assume different names. Thus, parts of ill-reputed North Hollywood were now Valley Village. Portions of seedy Sepúlveda were now North Hills.

Vancino had been part of Van Nuys, an area whose status had taken a nosedive. Its property owners had decided to take advantage of their proximity to nearby prestigious Encino. Hence, Vancino.

I had never heard of T.O. I opened my mouth to ask about the company and its legal needs, but Ezra beat me to the punch. "That call in my office? It was from Brian O'Barlen."

"No kidding." Despite myself, I felt impressed. O'Barlen was an impresario of L.A.'s real estate scene. Was he involved with T.O.? If so, that made this deal decidedly real. High powered. Most likely hugely financed.

"The deal's in trouble—the one I need you to work on. We were papering it—drafting purchase agreements, helping to obtain building permits, that kind of thing. But the shit's hit the fan. Local property owners just found out what T.O.'s planning, and they're up in arms. Everything's been handled quietly, with affiliated and subsidiary companies doing the buying to avoid a local brouhaha before all pieces of the site were obtained."

And to prevent the last owners of whatever parcel they were aggregating from knowing enough to charge premium prices, I thought, but zipped my mouth shut. Hey, it was business. And it wasn't my business to sympathize with those who'd sold early on at what would later seem rock-bottom prices.

Even if I'd hate to be in their shoes.

"I'd been planning a meeting to introduce you to the T.O. guys and get you started with whatever paperwork they needed."

"But I'm a litigator," I protested. Transactional types papered deals, not me. I handled cases in court. After my recent problems, I mostly argued motions these days but hoped to take on a trial again soon.

"And a good thing," he said, staring at me grimly. "First, we need to find and plug the leak, though that may not do much good now. I need you to get your investigator on it right away. Next, we'll make it clear that T.O.'s doing this development, no matter what other area owners think. That may mean litigation. You ready to sue the pants off everyone involved?"

Inside, I sighed. I'd excelled in law school where I'd learned to think like a lawyer, so I now could fashion fabulous legal arguments for either side of an issue. And having Brian O'Barlen as a client was an incredible inspiration for dreaming up invincible arguments. But I'd argued cases where public opinion rested with the opposition, and no matter how much the law was on your side, those were damned difficult cases to win.

Well, hell. It had been a while since I'd had a truly wonderful challenge. I was up to it. I would win! I hoped.

"According to O'Barlen," Ezra continued, "the local property owners formed an association when Vancino first became a discrete area. It's called VORPO: Vancino Residents and Property Owners. They've been fairly inactive—but they plan to meet tonight in an emergency session. We're going to be there representing our client's interests. You up for it?"

"Absolutely," I exclaimed.

EZRA LEFT MY office soon afterward. I accompanied him to his own environs as I was curious how Polly Bright was faring.

Not that I had much doubt about the answer. As far as my aching ears could tell, Gigi hadn't ended her screams.

"Damn!" Ezra muttered.

"Yeah," I agreed.

He opened the door. Polly still stood beside Gigi's perch, stroking her brilliant blue back and whispering to her, but her bright, red-outlined smile seemed more than a little frazzled.

From the doorway, I stuck my fingers into the sides of my mouth and issued my loudest referee tweet, aiming it at Gigi.

She stopped shrieking—for a moment, at least.

As soon as she started up again, I instinctively grasped for something—anything—to divert her attention once more.

Now, no one had ever accused me of having a civilized singing voice. In fact, in grade school, when children were supposed to carry tunes to the standard nursery songs, I'd croaked, and cried when other kids laughed. It didn't improve as I got older, so I confined my singing to showers when no one could possibly hear. Until now.

It seemed that something outrageous might be the only method to distract Gigi. And so I approached, hands raised and outstretched like an endowed opera diva and began singing—assuming you could call such off-key clatter a song, "Ninety-nine bottles of beer on the wall, ninety-nine bottles of beer . . ."

Damned if Gigi didn't stop and stare at me. But would it last? I kept on belting and didn't stop until I got to "Eight-five bottles of beer . . . ," which was when otherwise-silent Gigi began speaking in her inimitable rasp: "Bottles of beer. Bottles of beer."

"Hey!" Polly exclaimed excitedly.

Ezra initiated applause.

I laughed and tossed a wave behind me to them both as I exited the office.

BACK IN MY own digs, I made the call I'd both promised and anticipated with pleasure. I reached Jeff on his cell phone practically the moment he stepped off the plane, or so he informed me.

"I've been eager to talk to you, too," he said in a sweet, suggestive tone, morphing my mounting doubts about our relationship into a sizzle of sexy ashes. For now, at least.

"Hmmm," I said. "Hold that thought. This is business." Quickly I filled him in on Ezra's issue. "I'm committed to work with the guy," I finished, "and if you find the answer about who caused the T.O. leak before the Vancino meeting tonight, I should score a lot of points with him."

"As long as you let me score," Jeff replied, a laugh in his lustful voice.

"You've got to earn it," I retorted.

"You bet," he said. "See you soon."

Chapter Four

THAT EVENING, I wished there were two of me. I mean, my pet-sitting agenda wasn't overwhelming, but I didn't want to cheat any of my charges, and tending to each took time.

I eventually hustled to Jeff's, knowing he wasn't home. As requested, he had pitched himself headfirst into our high-priority assignment. His whole team of trained investigators, too. He would meet us at the VORPO meeting that night.

With Jeff in town, I took care of Odin, then hurriedly hied Lexie back to my apartment and changed clothes before heading off, ignoring my pup's perturbation at being alone. "I'll be home soon," I told her. And this way, I wouldn't have to worry how the wind blew in my sometime relationship with Jeff.

The VORPO session was to convene in the Vancino High auditorium, a fitting place only a couple of blocks from the chunk of real estate that was the focus of this night's assembly. Ezra, Jeff, and I had decided to convene quickly in the parking lot just before the meeting to conclave about our strategy. Ezra's clients would meet us there, too, so we could all sit harmoniously together inside in a show of interest—and strength.

Jeff was waiting when I arrived, sitting in the driver's seat of his big, black Escalade. My reservations about our relationship evanesced—at least for this instant—the moment he opened his door and jumped out.

Jeff's about six feet worth of sexy male. He's got a buff bod, and his looks are more than memorable: an angled face in which his teasing blue eyes fit just fine, light brown hair and lots of it . . . okay, I'm still smitten, despite the disputes we've had over his ex-wife Amanda's reappearance in his life.

"Hi," he said in that deep voice that never failed to get my hormones humming. He was clad in a dark buttoned shirt and black slacks, dressy enough for a client meeting.

"Hi, back," I replied as I melted momentarily into his arms. All qualms about this evening were shoved to the farthest recesses of my distracted mind as we shared one heck of a sensuous kiss—

Until I heard an irritated harrumph from behind my head. Reluctantly, I stepped back and spun around. I tried unsuccessfully to obfuscate the fuzziness in my tone. "Hi, Ezra. I'd like you to meet the private investigator I told you about, Jeff Hubbard. Jeff, this is Ezra."

They eyed each other warily.

"Hi, Kendra," said a softer, cheerier voice. Elaine appeared around the side of Jeff's SUV. "I decided to come, too."

"Welcome," I said fervently. Maybe she would temper Ezra's irritability. Maybe not.

As always, Elaine wore a pretty and professional suit. I introduced her to Jeff.

"We spoke on the phone earlier today," Elaine said with a smile, shaking Jeff's hand. "I'm always happy to put a name with a face."

The parking lot was already crowded. We didn't have much time, so I immediately initiated our discussion. "I realize it was short notice," I said to Jeff, "but were you able to find out anything about the leak—how VORPO members found out T.O. is behind the property purchases on Vancino Boulevard?"

We'd talked often this afternoon, and I'd given him what background I could. I'd put him in touch with Ezra and others in the Yurick firm who might even inadvertently have information, including everyone who lived in the San Fernando Valley. Sometimes neighborhood rumors resulted from reality.

"I sure did." Jeff aimed at me one of those irrepressible smiles that always tossed a twinkle into his blue eyes. He opened the Escalade door and pulled out an expandable file filled with papers. "My assistants and I checked out all the names and information Kendra gave me," he said to Ezra after closing the car door. "When I spoke to Elaine, she inadvertently gave me the key clue." He smiled at her again.

"Elaine's the source?" Ezra's voice was so strident that some people walking by jumped as they glanced toward us.

"No," Jeff countered, his tone low as if to set an example and his gaze on the obviously troubled Elaine. "The situation's more ironic than that." Before Ezra could interrupt with another inquiry, Jeff continued, "Elaine's broker is Bobby Lawrence, a big wheel with a small mid-Valley office of Nessix Realty."

Elaine nodded.

I'd heard of Nessix. Who hadn't? It was one of the largest real estate outfits in the country, with lots of local offices.

Jeff continued, "He apparently wasn't at all pleased that Elaine, after a week of negotiations on a house, decided to back off—without much explanation. That house is in Vancino."

I hadn't known that—but I suspected Ezra did.

I also had a sneaking suspicion of what Jeff was going to say. I swallowed and set my shoulders, ready to cringe.

Jeff continued, "Apparently Bobby Lawrence decided to see why someone wouldn't want a home in perfectly lovely Vancino."

"I told him I'd simply changed my mind," Elaine protested. "Why would he think something was wrong with that?"

"He didn't say," Jeff said. "He mentioned he'd contacted a chum at a title company, who searched recent records for properties near that house and unearthed that a lot of sites along one side of Vancino Boulevard had changed hands lately. Some heavier snooping, and he learned that one company was behind all the purchases. Bobby himself lives around there, so he reported what he'd found to VORPO. I talked to him and confirmed that his discovery is why they've called an emergency meeting tonight."

"Damned interfering—"

Jeff interrupted Ezra. "Elaine told me you'd insisted that she not buy that house. Her backing out was the reason Bobby Lawrence started snooping. So, Ezra, you're indirectly the reason VORPO learned of T.O.'s involvement in the lot purchases."

As I'd feared, Ezra erupted immediately. "Don't you accuse me, you damned fool!"

His earlier shouting had snapped up some attention, but his latest outburst attracted a larger crowd.

"Let's discuss this later," I urged quietly, gesturing downward to suggest softer voices. Of course I was ignored.

"You have the nerve to accuse me of acting contrary to my client's best interests?" Ezra demanded.

Though the blue in Jeff's eyes started to blaze, his hands rose in a gesture that appeared placating. "That's not true. What I said was—"

"Don't you contradict me." Ezra's voice elevated again. "T.O.'s going to be facing an angry owners' association, and with all your interfering questions, you've undoubtedly made it worse. And you have the nerve to accuse *me* of ruining things."

"I asked around after this meeting was already scheduled," Jeff insisted. "The harm was already done."

"And did you try to fix it?" Ezra blasted. "Did you try to at least put a helpful spin on it? No. You were hired on behalf of T.O. *You're* the one who acted in a way that could damage the client. And I'm going to make damned sure that you never act as an investigator for any attorney again."

"That's not fair!" I interjected.

"You have a conflict of interest, young lady," Ezra shouted. "This man's obviously your lover, so keep out of this or I'll report you to the State Bar for a breach of ethics."

Cringe? Heck, I recoiled.

"Let's go inside, everyone," I said insistently, ignoring how my voice quaked. "And instead of shouting recriminations, let's remember we're on the same side."

"Yeah, remember that," Ezra said irritably, and then his face unexpectedly lit up as he looked over my shoulder. "Brian, hello." I turned to see an overweight, silver-haired dragon descending on us. Brian O'Barlen. I recognized him from infinite newspaper articles in which he'd played a featured role. Had he heard what was going on here?

"You remember Elaine, I'm sure," Ezra continued. "I'd like you to meet my young associate, Kendra Ballantyne, an attorney at my new firm who's going to assist on your property dispute." He didn't mention Jeff. Just as well, considering the kind of introduction he was likely to give.

O'Barlen was shorter than I'd expected for such a renowned entrepreneur. He looked like an angry undertaker in his dark suit and even darker scowl beneath fuzzy gray brows. Three smaller men, similarly attired, stood behind him, and I assessed that they were his sycophants.

"Hello, Kendra," he growled, holding out his hand. His grip was firm but cold—though not as cold as my internal organs as I observed how Ezra and Jeff continued to eye each other.

"I'm delighted to meet you, Mr. O'Barlen," I gushed. "Now let's go inside and stake out where we'll sit. This promises to be an interesting evening."

To say the least.

AS WITH MANY schools in the L.A. Unified District, the main building of Vancino High had aged none too gracefully, with worn edges on the entry arches and damp spots darkening the otherwise attractive granite façade.

The auditorium was brightly lit and filling fast. I spied an empty set of seats at the front facing stage left. With a wave of "Forward, ho," I led my silent entourage toward that section. I planted myself firmly between Ezra and Jeff, who still watched each other wrathfully. Elaine sat on Jeff's other side, and O'Barlen on Ezra's.

Almost immediately, someone rapped on the onstage microphone. The guy standing on the dais wore a lime green sweatsuit and a huge smile. "Take your seats, please. It's time to begin . . ." *The takedown of T.O.,* I finished in my head. "I'm Flint Daniels," he went on after people had time to settle down. "President of VORPO. We're here tonight because some interesting information just became public. Bobby, please explain."

A man on the podium behind Daniels rose.

"Everyone, this is Bobby Lawrence." Flint Daniels danced away from the microphone so the broker could take over.

Real estate agents often got the same bum rap as attorneys in the public eye: sleazy, money-hungry, and only marginally ethical. That was an incorrect assessment of lawyers—most of us, at least. I didn't know Bobby Lawrence, but if I had to guess, I'd figure he lived up to boorish broker reputation. His smile revealed white teeth that sparkled in the sparse stage light. His slicked-down black hair also shone. His denim jeans and jacket were designer casual—if I had to guess, I'd say Banana Republic or Armani Exchange. He all but kissed the microphone in his effort to embrace the audience.

"Hi, y'all," he started in a drawl that proclaimed his area of origin as the South. "Just wanted you to know what I found out today. A client of mine changed her mind about buying a house without giving a reason. Won't name names." But big surprise, his eyes shifted toward us and lit for a second on Elaine. "I got to thinking, talked to a friend at a title company, and dug up some info on the 16300 block of Vancino Boulevard. Turns out most commercial properties on the south side have changed hands over the past two years—and all the buyers are affiliates of T.O. Development Company."

Angry murmurs surged through the audience. Livid stares lit on the T.O. group.

"Now, I don't know about y'all, but I like to know what's going on in my neighborhood. Right?"

Cries of "Yeah!" "Yes!" and "You bet!" resounded everywhere.

I noticed then that an audience member was marching up the side steps to the stage. I knew her! It was Millie Franzel, owner of Pamperville Pet Place. It hadn't occurred to me before, but Pamperville was situated right on the subject block.

Uh-oh.

I loved Pamperville. Back when I'd had money to spend on expensive doggy paraphernalia, I'd adored dropping in to pick out special puppy playthings for an appreciative Lexie: designer collars, cookie-shaped biscuits . . .

I suddenly had a genuine conflict of interest, one I hadn't known about. An internal one, at least.

Millie took the mike. She was a little older than me, slim, dark-haired, and poodle-pretty, with slightly buck teeth and a narrow, long nose. "Now I get it. I was approached a few months back by a nice man who said he wanted in the worst way to buy my building. He offered a lot of money, said he'd help me move my business anywhere I wanted. He claimed he was from the East, heard of Vancino, and wanted to open his steak house there. It seemed odd, so I just told him I'd think about it. And I did—for maybe five minutes. He kept calling, trying to change my mind. I finally said I'd call the cops if he kept it up, and I haven't heard from him since." She glared from the podium toward Brian O'Barlen. "Does he work for you?"

O'Barlen stayed blank-faced. Ezra pinkened as if prepared again to steam.

"No matter," Millie said. "I'm not selling to anyone. No matter how good the offer." Her words were met by a huge round of applause and animated cheers.

I admired her. Deep inside only, of course.

She stomped down from the podium as people stood and slapped her back.

I almost gasped in shock as Ezra rose and approached the stage. Oh, heavens. What was the irascible attorney up to? Would he blow his own client's case?

I was amazed as he calmly addressed the spectators. "Good evening. I'm Ezra Cossner, an attorney representing T.O. Development. We want you all to know we understand your concerns. Yes, T.O. has been quietly acquiring property along Vancino Boulevard. Their intent is to build a mixed-use development to benefit everyone in the area. There will be upscale retail and residential sites, and the project will increase the area's tax base, which will provide money to pay for school improvements and more. They'll offer sufficient street improvements, signalization, and parking so traffic will only be minimally affected. They'll—"

"They'll ruin the neighborhood," yelled an audience member.

"Why weren't they up front about it?" shouted someone else.

The full house erupted into a fracas of shouts and accusations as a myriad of vicious VORPO people confronted Ezra.

Was he up to it? Of course. It was *Ezra* standing there, once more turning red. Losing his temper.

Speaking of eruptions, I almost saw a plume of smoke and a flow of lava as the man suddenly seized the microphone and shouted, "Now, listen, all you fools. Don't you understand how much good this will do you? Are you so stupid that you can't—?"

I was beat up to the stage by Brian O'Barlen. Wresting the mike from Ezra, he spoke soothingly. "We'd like to meet with your representatives. Show them what we're talking about and get your input. You'll see it's to your benefit, all of you, to let T.O. enhance this important Vancino block."

He was edged aside by a man who'd sat on the stage but hadn't spoken before. "Excellent idea, Mr. O'Barlen. I'm Michael Kleer, VORPO's attorney." Really? He hardly looked old enough to be out of law school, let alone representing a vocal and volatile group like VORPO. "Let's set up a time for Flint Daniels and me to meet with you and your counsel. We'll see what you have in mind and present it to the group. Of course, the more input you allow us in your project, the less opposition we'll have."

"Fine," said O'Barlen, his teeth gritted in a forced grin.

"Fine," repeated Ezra.

And with that, they left the stage—and the whole T.O. group, including me, left the auditorium.

We regrouped twenty minutes later at the Yurick offices—in what used to be the bar. Borden had left that room intact, with its large wooden bar and high-backed booths. It lent charm to the law offices and provided a larger meeting area than any individual office.

The principals spouted recriminations, Ezra in particular. His accusations encompassed everyone imaginable—especially Jeff.

"Brian, this bozo of an investigator dared to say I was the one to make your purchases public. All I did was to tell Elaine that I didn't like the house she was zeroing in on that happened to be in the vicinity. I'll bet the questions he asked got that Lawrence character to start poking around and make this mess."

"You're full of shit, Cossner," Jeff countered angrily. "That makes no sense. I investigated because Lawrence was already poking around."

"Yeah? Well, I'll have your license for your ineptitude."

Before I could step in, Ezra started another attack elsewhere. He seemed to suggest that O'Barlen himself, and his tsking toadies, had a lot to do with the night's fiasco. "Secrecy is a great scheme at first," he snorted, pacing the length of the unstocked bar, "but what it all boils down to is that you should have beat them to the punch by going public first."

"So that's why you spilled the beans?" O'Barlen countered with a sneer, standing beside the booth where he and his staff sat. "Because you decided someone you like shouldn't buy property in that area since it might be devalued by our project? Some advocate you are."

"I'm a damned good advocate," shrieked Ezra. That's where Gigi must have learned her stock scream.

The free-for-all continued for a few more minutes. I finally stood and said, "It's late, everyone. We're all upset about how that meeting went. Let's go home. We'll touch base tomorrow and set up a strategy session. Okay?"

Surprisingly, everyone agreed. And cleared out. Fast. Jeff and I, too.

When we departed, only Elaine and Ezra were left. Oh, and Gigi, too, in Ezra's office. She'd started squawking once the shouting exploded. Without asking Ezra, I'd allowed Jeff a brief peek to behold the mighty loud macaw.

"Are Lexie and you coming to my place tonight?" Jeff asked later, eyebrows lifting suggestively as we stood between the Escalade and Beamer in the firm parking lot.

Not a bad idea, even if it did mean I had to go home so late to retrieve my little spaniel first. Some human warmth along with the canine company sounded excellent.

Until Jeff's phone sang out its tune: a unique sound, the theme song of *Magnum P.I.,* a 1980s TV show now in syndication and on DVD about a guy more or less in Jeff's profession. His company's chief computer geek, Althea, had recently programmed it in as a joke, but Jeff liked it, so it stuck.

He responded to the tune, and I could tell by his contortions as he shifted his head and body away from me that it was Amanda. His ex-wife.

His tone was sweet and consoling to her.

And drew blood from me.

Before he could say anything else to me, I was in my Beamer, heading home. Alone.

Okay, I confess. My night was long and lugubrious. At least Lexie kept me from being too lonely.

The next morning, I awoke early and tried to keep my thoughts on just about anything but Jeff—which meant it settled on last night's VORPO fiasco. Not good either.

Thank heavens that I had mood-settling pet-sitting rounds to focus on.

Except . . . just after I'd hugged Alexander and settled the pit bull back into his home, my cell phone rang. These days, I still had it programmed to play Bon Jovi's "It's My Life," which was an excellent tune to focus on that morning.

I recognized the number: the Yurick office. "Hello?" I said.

"Oh, Kendra, I'm so glad I reached you. This is Elaine." She sounded way strung out—and no wonder. "I got to the office first this morning and . . . and . . ."

"And?" I prompted.

"It's Ezra. I think he's been shot. He's dead."

Chapter Five

I WASN'T SURE whether Elaine had chosen to call me as a result of my reputation of running into dead bodies, or whether I was simply on her list of Yurick firm personnel needing notification in case of emergencies.

In any event, after obtaining Elaine's assurance that she'd already called 911, I stuck Lexie in the Beamer and headed toward the office, using surface streets. I wasn't too far away, but it was still the A.M. rush hour in L.A. The freeways would be at a standstill, like the blocked arteries they were.

Arteries reminded me of blood, which reminded me of Ezra. As if I'd forgotten him.

Stopped at a light, I reached over to stroke my sweet Lexie, who stood on the passenger seat sniffing out the window. I hadn't wanted to leave her alone at home all day after so much time in Odin's company, so she'd accompanied me on pet-sitting rounds.

Besides, I'd been curious how my good-natured, normally quiet Cavalier would react to the screeching macaw.

Only now, I wasn't sure how anyone would react to anything today. Not with Ezra lying dead in the office, and the whole place subject to a police investigation.

Poor Ezra. Not that I was best buddies with the guy, but he'd occasionally grown on me during our short acquaintance. He obviously cared for Gigi. And he had a sense of humor way down deep inside that even sometimes emerged.

We finally reached the office, and I pulled into an empty parking space. There weren't many—not with all the emergency vehicles around.

I lowered a couple of Beamer windows enough for Lexie to stick out her inquisitive nose, and I exited the car.

Unsurprisingly, Mignon stood outside the open building door. The usually effervescent receptionist appeared pale and unperky. "Oh, Kendra, did you hear?"

I nodded, though it was hard to hear anything. Gigi screeched from somewhere inside. Plus, unfamiliar voices raised a ruckus, not the rule for the generally sedate law office. And several secretaries stood around, sighing and speaking loudly about being kept in the dark on this bright January day.

A somber-looking lady in a gray pantsuit approached, holding a clipboard. "May I have your name?" she asked.

"Kendra Ballantyne. I'm an attorney with this firm. And you are . . . ?"

"Detective Schwinglan." She proffered L.A.P.D. ID.

Not Ned Noralles. He was the detective who'd investigated the other murder cases I'd been involved with.

But then, this was Encino. The others had been closer to the North Hollywood Police Station. I wasn't sure which station would have jurisdiction here, but not that one.

"Do you know yet what happened?" I asked.

The detective, who was half a foot taller than me, lifted one edge of her slim lips in a droll grin. "That's what I need to ask you." She edged me several feet away from

Mignon by a movement of her shoulder and a follow-me stride. When we were separated from the others, she said, "Tell me what you know."

I told her how I'd received a call from Elaine Aames, and that I knew Ezra had been hurt. "Is he alive?" I asked.

"Sorry, no." She shook her head, barely moving a strand of the hair pulled to the back of her head and fastened with a clip.

"Well, what about Elaine? Is she here? Is she okay?"

"I believe she's still being questioned. And as I said, I'm the one who needs to ask the questions."

But before she did, I heard a familiar, raised voice call me by name. "Ms. Ballantyne. This is becoming a habit."

I winced and turned. "Not one I enter into willingly, Ned," I said. The L.A.P.D. detective approached up the walkway.

Ned Noralles was a tall, solemn African-American, a good-looking dude with a job that I assume jaded most cops. Not only had he tried and failed to prove me guilty of a couple of murders, but he had also been the detective-in-charge when my tenant was accused of killing an acquaintance right in my leased-out house.

I'd helped to prove his theories wrong in both instances. He nevertheless remained cordial—more or less.

"What are you doing here?" I asked him. "This isn't your jurisdiction, is it?"

"As I told you, Ms. Ballantyne," Detective Schwinglan said, "I'm supposed to ask the questions." She faced Ned. "Like she said, Detective. What are you doing here?"

"Let's talk," he said, giving a brisk sideways nod signaling her to follow him. They strolled far enough off that I couldn't hear the conversation they held with their heads together.

Was Noralles here in an official capacity? If so, how had he managed to get involved here, out of his typical territory?

Whatever he said must have satisfied the other detective, since she nodded, then headed back inside the office building.

Ned stayed outside with me. "So, what do you know about this one?" he asked. As always, he wore a dark suit. He seemed especially skilled at staying expressionless, but right now his dark eyes overflowed with irony. I suspected he didn't much like that I was likely to stick my own, rather ordinary nose in one of his cases again.

Unless, of course, he'd taken on this case expressly to take *me* on.

"I don't know anything," I told him truthfully. "What happened?"

"I think you know," he said. "Another murder, Ms. Ballantyne. And somehow, you're involved."

I sighed and said, "So you're not just visiting? You're one of the detectives on this case?"

"I'm assisting on this investigation."

"How—" I could see by the way his dark eyebrows rose that he wasn't going to tell me.

"We'll talk later," he said. "Right now, I need to see the scene."

"One thing I should warn you about," I told him, then mentioned Gigi, whom I still heard shrieking in the background. "She's highly excitable."

"That's the noise I hear?" Ned asked.

I nodded. "I'm afraid she'll hurt herself, especially if you have Animal Services haul her off. Can you please just leave her here? There's no reason to have her removed, let alone 'humanely euthanized.' "

I used the term I'd learned before when referring to animals who'd supposedly caused a crime—like some ferrets I'd met during the last situation I'd sunk my teeth into that involved cops. Of course, ferrets are illegal in California to begin with, and those particular ferrets were considered murder suspects.

Fortunately, the ferrets hadn't been euthanized, humanely or otherwise. They'd found a new home. Well, not necessarily new, but . . . Heck, no need to get into that, since its result might not have been fully legal.

In any event, Gigi wasn't to blame here. All I knew from Elaine was that she thought Ezra had been shot.

"Please, just let some of us here continue to take care of her," I finished. "Okay?"

"We'll see," he said, then stomped inside.

Since this had once been a restaurant, there was a paved patio to one side of the entry where patrons must have been sent to await their tables. I checked often on Lexie in the car, of course. Those who'd arrived so far all milled around the patio.

"Poor Ezra," Mignon chirped sadly, in the middle of a group of support staff. "He wasn't the nicest man, but he still—"

"Kendra!" Ned Noralles called from the door. "Come here."

I couldn't help swallowing hard in consternation. Being shown up as an awful amateur detective didn't faze me . . . much. But what if Ned had decided to handle this homicide in the hopes he'd finally pin one on me after all?

I nevertheless obeyed his command and came near him. "What's up?" I asked, striving to sound confident.

"You want to save that bird? Then you calm her down."

"Is she okay?" I asked.

"She's screaming, beating her wings, and . . . can you help?"

I considered my first contact with Gigi and her shrieks in the night. Her continued squawking and how it had driven Ezra nuts. I thought about the visit from the expert Polly Bright yesterday, and how Gigi had responded to my whistle and singing—if you could call it that—better than to her macaw shrink stuff. "I can try," I said slowly. "No guarantees. But you still promise to let her stay here?"

"If you don't promise, I don't. But come on." Noralles gestured, and I followed him inside the building that still bustled with crime-scene investigators, then down the hall.

"Is Gigi still in Ezra's office?" I asked, my anxiety increasing.

"Yeah. So's the body. You okay with that?"

Not hardly—but I nonetheless responded, "More or less."

In moments, that's where we were. I tried not to face the part of the floor where investigators snapped photos and foraged for clues—where Ezra lay, on the floor beside his desk. Identification numbers were scattered about, each signifying where some piece of evidence had been removed. Judging by the number of numbers, there'd been a lot of clues.

Gigi was secured in her giant wire cage, screeching and flapping and shifting around as if she wanted to soar out of it. Ezra must have put her in it last night to take her home.

Only they hadn't gone.

Elaine had been the only one with them when Jeff and I left . . . but I didn't see Elaine as Ezra's killer. I'd only say what I saw to Noralles if he asked. After all, he'd undoubtedly be interrogating Elaine anyway, since she was the one who'd found Ezra's body.

"Do something!" Noralles shouted, his expression perplexed and even a little pleading. His tone grew commanding, though, as he insisted, "But don't get too close. And don't touch anything. We're almost ready to let the coroner remove the victim, but this crime scene is still under investigation."

What I wanted to do was to cover my ears, but instead approached Gigi. I stuck my fingers in my mouth and whistled.

She hardly looked at me as she continued her crazy movements and even crazier screams. If she kept it up, she'd not only deafen the investigators but also upend her cage and injure herself.

Sighing because I was undoubtedly about to make an ass of myself in front of the dour detective and his assemblage of investigators, I started singing at the top of my voice, "Ninety-nine bottles of beer on the wall . . ."

No change. She didn't even start repeating her vocal repertoire about bottles of beer.

I went through a couple of choruses before giving up. "I think we'd better call in the expert," I finally said.

FORTUNATELY, POLLY BRIGHT made fast emergency office calls. She promised to be there in half an hour.

I'd looked in again on Lexie, still locked in my car. It was January and overcast, so I hadn't had to find her some shade. I could also see her from my office window and all seemed well. I knew her ears were sensitive, though, so I wondered whether they were being assailed long distance by Gigi's endless cries.

I spent the time waiting for Polly in my office, an investigator in attendance, as soon as Noralles gave me the go-ahead. I was permitted to pull some of my files to work on outside the Yurick offices while the investigation continued.

Speaking of Yurick, Borden had arrived, too, and stood out on the patio with other attorneys—William Fortier and Geraldine Glass, both senior citizens who'd joined up with Borden after retiring from other firms. Also the rest of the secretaries and paralegals, including Corrie Montez, who'd come with Ezra from his former firm. All had been initially interrogated by Noralles and his investigators, I learned when I went outside with Ned at my side. I believed that all those who'd finished going through the wringer had been permitted to leave for the day. Corrie, crying softly, had stayed.

I considered fleeing, too, but figured someone who'd met Polly ought to greet her. I only wished I could plug my ears, even as I stood outside.

Eventually, she arrived. By then, I'd gone back to my office. A cop poked his head inside and asked me to meet her in the reception area—and not to touch anything on the way.

I joined Polly there. Her plumage—er, clothing—seemed equally colorful as yesterday. She wore a multicolor neon scarf over her brilliant green blouse and matching peasant skirt.

Her eyes were huge, her skin pale. "Ezra's dead?" she rasped, as if she somehow hadn't believed what she'd been told.

I nodded. "And Gigi's going nuts. I was told one of the crime-scene investigators tried to take fingerprints from her cage and she stuck her beak out between the wires and bit him. Fortunately, he saw it coming so he wasn't hurt. But the poor bird hasn't stopped shrieking."

"I noticed." There was a slight wryness now to Polly's tone. "Let's go see her."

I was glad to discover that Ezra was no longer in his office. Noralles was, and I introduced him to Polly. The parrot expert approached the rocking cage that contained Gigi and began speaking softly. Unsurprisingly to me, Gigi didn't calm.

"First thing, let's remove her from these surroundings," Polly said. "But not too far. Please help me move her to someplace quiet in these offices. Any suggestions?" she asked me.

"Well, there's what used to be the restaurant kitchen. We still use it as a coffee-and-lunch room. It's fairly remote and we can keep people out of it."

"Sounds perfect."

I looked at Noralles. "Is that okay?"

"Yeah. It looks like the homicide took place in one location. The victim wasn't chased around the building, so his office is our main focus. The kitchen's been checked already for evidence, and we've conducted some interrogations there."

"Good," Polly said. "But we'll need a little help." She

looked pointedly at Noralles. "A strong police officer to push her cage would be just the thing."

Meekly—for him—Noralles followed her orders. A burly uniformed officer pushed the large wheeled cage containing the upset macaw down the hall and around a couple of corners.

The kitchen was quiet and dimly illuminated from a window with miniblinds till we turned on the lights. There were gleaming metal counters containing a sink, coffee-maker, and microwave. There was also a full-sized re-frigerator. The room had already been preliminarily probed for evidence, so no one was likely to bother Gigi here. Once tables were pushed out of the way and the macaw's cage slid into the center of the room, everyone left except Polly and me. Was it my imagination, had my eardrums at-rophied, or was the bird finally crying less loudly?

This time, when Polly started speaking to Gigi, she sounded more persuasive, as if this was a training session. She commanded the macaw to say, "Gigi, gorgeous girl. That's you. Now say it, Gigi."

Amazingly, after half a dozen reiterated orders, Gigi stopped squawking and started talking. "Gigi, gorgeous girl, gorgeous girl."

"You did it!" I exclaimed softly, forbearing from giving Polly a great big hug.

The parrot pro turned to me and smiled proudly.

BEFORE POLLY LEFT, I made sure she, the expert, in-structed Noralles that Gigi was not to be shuffled off to an animal shelter.

"This bird will undoubtedly get even more upset in wholly unfamiliar surroundings," Polly assured Noralles. "I know she was present at a murder scene, but in the inter-est of keeping her as healthy as possible, she must stay in a soothing environment. Like this kitchen."

"I'll allow it for now," Noralles said irritably, but the way he hazarded a reluctant glance at Gigi, I suspect he was relieved he had an expert's directive to allow him not to deal much with the emotional bird. "But I'll still have to clear it with Animal Services."

Of course, Noralles used the sudden quiet to remember that he hadn't finished interrogating me. I told him all I knew about Ezra, his friends, acquaintances, and enemies—that latter including, after last night, the entire community of Vancino.

Eventually, Ned released the Yurick gang. He insisted that we stay out of the building for the rest of the day while the Scientific Investigation Division dudes concluded their scrutiny, but said he'd try to have everything but Ezra's office cleared for use again tomorrow.

I figured that Lexie and I would head for home-sweet-garage—our apartment on the grounds of the big, beautiful house I now leased to Beggar's owner.

But there was somewhere else I wanted to stop first.

KNOWING THAT BOTH Lexie and I could use a little TLC—Tenderness, Loyalty, and Canines—I aimed my Beamer for the Doggy Indulgence Day Resort, a day-care facility on Ventura Boulevard in Studio City owned by my dearest friend in the world, Darryl Nestler.

Thin, lanky Darryl was at the front desk of the domain over which he reigned as alpha male, despite his beta-sweet demeanor.

As I walked in the door, Darryl gave me one of his big, open grins. As usual, he wore one of his signature Henley-style green shirts with the Doggy Indulgence logo on the pocket. "Kendra! Lexie! I'm glad you're here."

As I headed into his outstretched arms and accepted a well-needed hug, I saw the sideways glance and eye roll from one of his canine caretakers: Kiki, a blond bombshell and starlet wannabe.

"Glad to see you, too, Kiki," I said. "Lexie sure is." I'd let my Cavalier off her leash, and she leaped on the reception counter, as if asking permission to peel off to one of the resort's multiple play areas for pets—including a corner containing all sorts of doggy toys, and another with lots of people furniture to veg out on.

"Come on, Lexie." Kiki walked with my Cavalier over the shiny, spotless pine floor toward the area where employees were engaged in endless games with ecstatic doggy charges.

"Believe it or not, she's one of my best employees," Darryl said.

"I believe it," I acknowledged. "She might be awful to owners, but she's great with the dogs. Have time for a chat?"

"About the latest murder?"

"You heard?"

"It's on the news—a lawyer at your new firm. Soon as I was assured it wasn't you, I wondered how you were involved."

I sighed. "Yes, I do seem to be a murder magnet these days. Wish I could figure out a way to demagnetize myself."

"Come into my office," Darryl said. "I want to hear everything."

I tailed him into his domain with its cluttered desk, and dumped my dejected self into the plush chair facing it. I gave Darryl a rundown of all that had happened starting from yesterday, omitting complications that could be considered attorney-client privileged.

As I finished talking about how Gigi finally quieted down, this time thanks to the advice of macaw maven Polly Bright, Darryl said, "Do you read mystery novels? Or watch detective shows on TV?"

I blinked. "Who has time?"

"Well, something struck me as you were talking. If your life was fiction that had taken these turns, know what?"

"What?" I was decidedly peeved and sounded it, since I knew Darryl was building up the drama. But heck, he was my friend. If he wanted to have some fun with my frazzled psyche, why not?

"If this was a novel, and a parrot was in the room where a murder was committed, all you'd have to do is to keep asking the bird some questions. In mysteries with parrots, they always reveal the clue that gives the killer away."

Chapter Six

I WASN'T SURE whether Darryl was pulling my leg. On the other hand, he hadn't said that birds of the parrot persuasion truly provided solutions to murders they'd witnessed, only that certain creative mystery authors asserted they did.

Might actual avians similarly repeat sounds, even words, they overheard in excessively emotional circumstances? As absurd as it sounded, it was an avenue I couldn't omit exploring.

The hour was too late to leave Lexie in the excellent paws of Doggy Indulgence, so she and I headed off to my pet-sitting visits. I made sure to lavish ample attention on each of my charges. It wasn't their fault that my mind churned around traumatic topics like Ezra's untimely, ugly death, the dissatisfied client whose work I'd at least temporarily take over—and whether macaws might in actuality be able to disclose the identities of murderers.

As soon as I'd seen to my last canine customer, I aimed my auto back toward my office. "I hope that's okay with you," I said to Lexie. "But I really need to see Gigi as soon as I can." Lexie wagged her tail and woofed her approval, so I felt guiltless as I drove westward.

It was nearly eight at night, so I figured no office staff would be around. But since we'd been promised access to the office building tomorrow, crime-scene investigators could still be there en masse. I doubted Noralles would still be around, nattering all night about how all nuances of the investigation should go. But without his otherwise un-welcome presence, I couldn't be positive I'd be permitted inside.

I'd elicited parrot-care instructions and a cache of food from Polly before she'd pranced out of there, so I'd known what to feed the then-placid Gigi before I'd left. But I was still concerned about her. Blame the pet-sitter part of me.

I wasn't surprised, when I arrived at the Yurick offices, to see lights on inside the onetime restaurant building. Or cars in the parking lot, too. Two.

No black-and-white cop cars, though, or L.A.P.D. Sci-entific Investigation Division vehicles. Nor were vans carrying media vipers still around. Thank heavens. Re-porters of all meddling types had appeared soon after I had this morning. They'd hung about all day, trying to get someone to give them the scoop on the slaying inside the law office. I'd listened to some of the results on the radio while in my car. Lots of hype and innuendo—of course. But there'd been no hints of any eyewitnesses at all, let alone one with wings.

Somehow, I couldn't buy that I'd get Gigi to testify about what she'd seen. In any event, the lights inside and cars in the lot proclaimed that others were present. The ve-hicles were familiar, so I doubted they were unmarked wheels of investigators. Plus, the entryways were unen-cumbered by crime-scene tape or dire keep-out caveats. Maybe the structure had already been released back into the law firm's hands.

But who was here? Someone else concerned about

Gigi? Or had some of the firm's senior citizen attorneys grown guilty about being behind in billable hours?

Turned out to be kind of a combination of the two—and the second involved a paralegal, not a lawyer.

After assuring Lexie I wouldn't be long and as always enlisting her unsurpassed skill in guarding our car, I headed inside. When I rambled behind the reception area toward the kitchen, my ears were once again bombarded by a blast of screeching emanating from that direction, so loud that I nearly missed hearing the soft, soothing sounds in the background.

The former, not unexpectedly, originated from Gigi. The quieter voice belonged to Elaine Aames. She stood outside Gigi's cage, talking to the macaw, her shoulders hunched beneath the bird's brow beating. "What are we going to do with you, gorgeous girl?" she said. Gigi didn't slow her squawking as she hopped from one claw to the other. "You'll need a new home now," Elaine continued, "and I'd love to offer it to you, but I can't unless you calm down." Even that amazing invitation didn't quiet Gigi. Elaine raised her voice. "Please, girl. You've got to—" Elaine shook her head in apparent disgust, and mid-shake she spotted me. "Hi, Kendra," she called. "What are you doing here?"

I motioned her out into the hall, where, after I closed the door, Gigi's screeches were somewhat muted. "I was worried about Gigi. I wanted to make sure she was okay for the night."

"She'd be a lot better if she simmered down, but she's safe and away from the worst of the excitement, at least."

"Maybe," I acknowledged. "And how are you doing?"

The older attorney seemed to have aged a lot more since Ezra's departure. She was still well dressed in a white blouse and navy blue skirt, but both were rumpled, and her suit jacket was somewhere else. The exaggerated wrinkles wedged around her eyes and mouth looked like anything but laugh lines tonight. Her silver hair, usually with seldom a strand out of place, had wilted as if water-soaked.

I figured that Detective Ned Noralles or an equally insistent crony had put the poor older lawyer through the wringer with one of their nastier inquisitions. I might not have looked as wilted after something similar, but I was around half Elaine's age. Or maybe I *had* looked as bad and had deluded myself otherwise.

"I was worried about Gigi, too," Elaine said. "And myself, if I can be candid." She sighed as I nodded my encouragement to her openness—while wondering what I was letting myself in for. "I spent most of the day at the West Valley Police Station, answering questions about my relationship with Ezra, my argument with him over the house, how I found him dead . . . But I figure you know how that goes. Borden told me over the phone how you were unjustly accused of murder a few months ago, and once he mentioned it, I remembered hearing about it in the news."

"That's right," I said. "Fortunately, the truth came out. Of course, I had help. I hope you had a good criminal attorney with you." I was wondering whether Elaine was yet another suspect to whom I'd need to refer my good friend Esther Ickes, who'd helped me not only through my State Bar proceedings and bankruptcy, but also when I was suspected of murder. I'd suggested her to my tenants, too, when they were unjustly accused of aiding and abetting fatal ferrets.

Elaine assured me she'd had someone with her from her former firm—an attorney I'd never heard of, but she was satisfied with the young guy's representation and counseling concerning cops.

"Anyway, after I checked with Borden and he said most of the building had been released by the police, I came to pick up my briefcase and other things I'd left earlier," Elaine said. "And of course, to look in on Gigi. She was quiet, but when I put my hand on her cage, she immediately tried to bite my fingers. Then she started screaming again."

Hmmm. If Darryl's suggestion was sound, might that mean Gigi had seen Elaine bump off Ezra? But the bird started shrieking so often, and for no obvious reason, I couldn't use that as a clue to suppose the worst of Elaine.

"I talked to Polly Bright," Elaine continued. "She promised to stay on call and help us get Gigi through this terrible situation. She mentioned she had been here earlier today. I asked her to stop by again tomorrow, if she could."

After my discussion with Darryl, I itched to ask Elaine, who'd spent at least part of this evening in Gigi's company, if the bird had said anything at all that smacked of significance—like whom she'd seen slay Ezra . . . again assuming it wasn't Elaine herself.

In the interest of discretion, though, I said, "I heard you tell Gigi you might want to adopt her."

"For Ezra's sake," Elaine said, nodding as she winced once more at Gigi's continued shouts from behind the kitchen door. "I might have fought with the guy, but I really cared for him." She lifted her thin, wrinkled hands as if to stave off anticipated amazement. "Yes, I know he was abrasive and even nasty at times, but inside he was really quite sweet—once you got to know him." Tears suddenly flooded her eyes. "And now you never will."

I was slightly surprised when I grew similarly misty. But heck, I had seen another side of Ezra Cossner now and then. Maybe he *would* have grown on me even more had he lived.

"Anyway," Elaine sniffed, "Ezra hasn't much family left, and he was mostly estranged from the remaining ones." Big surprise. "I don't know whether he made arrangements for Gigi after his death—even if he didn't anticipate it happening so soon, macaws can live a long time—but I'd love to adopt Gigi if I could get her to be more friendly with me. If I can't even touch her cage, though, let alone move her outside it to a perch, I don't think it would work for either of us. And those noises . . ."

As if on cue, Gigi's screams seemed to intensify. Was she about to make some huge revelation about what she'd seen? I nearly yanked open the door. But then she started into a medley of "Gigi, gorgeous girl, gorgeous girl," combined with wolf whistles. I sighed. If that was some kind of clue, I, for one, didn't get it.

"Hi," said a voice from around the reception area, loud enough to be heard over Gigi's continued chorus. "I didn't know you were here, Kendra. Is everything okay?" I turned away to see Corrie Montez standing there. She was clad in a sweater and jeans and a slew of file folders. Well, maybe the folders weren't part of her outfit, but in the few times I'd seen the youthful paralegal since she'd joined the firm along with Ezra a few days ago, she'd always seemed to be clad in a bunch.

Corrie had short black hair, huge brown eyes, a largeish nose, and a small, ever-lipsticked red mouth. Ezra had stolen her from his former firm—another reason for them to be peeved with him.

I thought about Jonathon Jetts, the partner who'd shown up here yesterday and assailed Ezra for waltzing away with his former firm's clients. Coming here with Corrie could have provided icing on the ill-willed cake. Could Jetts have been mad enough to murder Ezra?

"Everything's as fine as it can be for the moment," I assured Corrie. "We were just talking about Ezra, of course."

"Of course," Corrie repeated with a raw sigh. "I only wish . . ."

"What?" I encouraged.

"Well, I think Elaine really knew him." She aimed a brave smile at the older woman, whose tears now tumbled down her cheeks. "But most people didn't. He was a good guy, deep down. He really was." Her stark stare at me both dared me to deny it and pleaded with me to believe it.

"I didn't get to spend much time with him," I told her tactfully, "and he seemed under a lot of pressure about the T.O.-Vancino matter, so he didn't get a chance to show me much of his softer side. But I saw he really cared about Gigi. And I got a hint of his sense of humor."

That sent both of Ezra's former friends into sheer sobbery. And I have to admit it was contagious.

A shriek startled us out of our sobs. No more singsong chorus from Gigi. I opened the door to look in at her and found her flapping her wings—as much as she could within the confines of her cage. She screamed three times more, and I didn't stop my hands from enveloping my aching ears. And then she started shouting out, "Ezra, Ezra, Ezra," in her own squawking voice.

It didn't provide any clue as to who killed him, but it sure got all three of us girls gooey again.

ELAINE LEFT BEFORE I did, but Corrie remained, though she'd soon apologized her way out of the kitchen and back to her own office, near Ezra's. She'd mentioned that many of Ezra's files were confiscated by the cops as possible evidence in his murder—at least those boxed in his office at the time. I wouldn't know, since his door was still sealed shut by yellow crime-scene tape—the only room still off-limits in this small building.

Fortunately for the firm, Corrie had some of her own files, and a lot of her own knowledge, about clients Ezra had carried from their old firm. She was, at Borden's phoned request, making as reliable a reiteration as she could, logging clients and their concerns so this firm could step in and take over for Ezra.

Assuming the clients stayed with us.

I managed a few minutes alone with Gigi. Amazingly, she'd quieted down somewhat. "Anything to tell me, girl?" I asked. "What did you see last night?"

"Ezra, Ezra, Gigi, gorgeous girl," she squawked in reply. "Bottles of beer." And then she started additional screaming and flapping around her cage, as if she wanted to get out and fly off. I couldn't get her to stop. Corrie couldn't get her to stop.

In desperation, I resumed an encore chorus of "Ninety-Nine Bottles of Beer," but it only made her screech all the more. I finally gave up. So did Corrie. We turned out the kitchen lights with Gigi still flailing and vocalizing.

"I hope she doesn't hurt herself," I said.

"Me, too," Corrie agreed. "I'll be here a little longer, so I'll check on her."

I was glad Corrie hadn't stayed so long last night, or maybe Ezra would have had company in extinction. Unless Corrie . . . Nah, why would she have killed her boss? Because he'd brought her to the Yurick firm?

Or—

My cell phone rang. I'd just climbed into the Beamer beside an excited Lexie. I noted the number on caller ID: Jeff's.

"Hi," I said. We hadn't spoken much that day, although I'd called first thing to inform him about Ezra.

"Hi," he repeated. If I could read his mood behind that one quiet word, I'd have said he sounded exhausted. He soon confirmed my calculated guess—and the reason behind it. "It's been a hell of a day, Kendra. I've spent most of it in the new building at one of my old haunts—the West Valley Station." Jeff had been an L.A.P.D. cop before he became a P.I. Long story, but it had involved a game of one-upsmanship with his former friend and current foe—who just happened to be on my list of least favorite people, too: Detective Ned Noralles. Jeff had won the game but his victory had resulted in his resignation from the force and commencement of his successful career as a private investigator.

"Why were you there?" I asked, shivering a smidgen as I anticipated his answer.

"Being interrogated by the lead detective on the case, Candace Schwinglan, a pleasure I owe to her temporary volunteer assistant from a fellow Valley Bureau station, Ned Noralles." His tone suggested he'd ingested something extremely distasteful—like crow. "He heard about my argument with Ezra—and he made it clear to Schwinglan that I'm number one on his suspect list."

Chapter Seven

OKAY, SO I'M a big softy. Or perhaps my sex drive was stuck in overdrive. Regardless of the rationale, Lexie and I spent the night at Jeff's. And not in his guest room. His bed is much cozier. So are his arms. And the rest of his body? Well, he certainly knows how to use each and every erogenous part.

And I tactfully kept to myself my interminable testiness about his ex-wife Amanda's intrusions into his life.

Not that Jeff and I indulged only in fun and games. The next morning, after our habitual hound walk with Lexie and Odin, we dissected all we knew about Ezra's murder over our usual breakfast of eggs and toast.

"I've already started my list of suspects," I said as we sat at the round wooden table in his small, functional kitchen. Jeff knew my penchant for producing lists. I handwrote a copy for him, and he vowed to have his chief computer geek Althea check out each person in his P.I. firm's boundless databases. I'd included Jonathon Jetts, the vocal people at the VORPO meeting the night Ezra was snuffed, and even Elaine Aames and Corrie Montez, who'd known him prior to working for Borden.

"What about Borden himself?" Jeff asked. When Lexie and I showed up at his doorstep last night, he had looked as spent as he'd sounded, his blue eyes bleary, his six-foot-tall body bent a bit in dejection. This morning, though he'd not gotten a lot of sleep, he appeared more optimistic. Hopefully, I had something to do with that.

"Include Borden if you want," I said, "but we know a lot of what Althea's likely to find on him anyway. He's a prior partner at my old firm Marden, Sergement & Yurick. His supposed mental breakdown was manufactured by unforgiving former partners to explain his defection from what they considered the perfect law firm. But if she can find anything about prior connections between Borden and Ezra, she might as well try. Although Borden's enough of a sweetie that I can't imagine him offing Ezra. Especially when the guy was in some ways saving our overstaffed firm, or at least some of the staff"—mostly me—"by boosting the client base. There's no guarantee the new clients will hang around now that Ezra's gone."

"Any other ideas?" Jeff asked.

"If I had any, they'd be on my list. But it's absolutely expandable, and I intend to keep eyes and ears open." And to ask lots of questions of anyone likely to have answers. And as a litigator, I was one hell of an interrogator.

One thing I'd resolved not to reveal to Jeff was Darryl's theory that the macaw might hold a clue to the murder. Although his suggestion might work well in fiction, it was implausible in real life. Of course, if Gigi happened to drop a clue, along with whatever else she dropped in her portable cage . . .

I glanced at my watch. "Time for me to go." I stood, and so did Lexie. "I have pet clients waiting." Not to mention people clients who'd need my legal skills later at the law office.

"Will you be back tonight?" Jeff asked. For a big, strong guy who was almost always supremely self-assured, he sounded a smidgen plaintive. Poor P.I. Being a murder suspect did awful things to the ego. As I well knew.

"That depends," I said, not committing to another delightful night despite my hormones hounding me to shout, "Hell, yes!"

"On what?" he asked.

"On Lexie." I looked at the Cavalier in question. "Want to hang around to keep Odin company?" Her response was to wag her tail and wriggle in glee. Of course it was a loaded question. My enthusiastic Lexie acted equally excited about each iota of attention I administered to her.

Still, using my beloved Cavalier as a convenient excuse to come by later didn't necessarily mean we'd stay the night.

I bent and hugged the pups adieu, then turned and gave Jeff a hug, too, followed by a heck of a kiss to remember me by for the rest of the day.

Then I left to start pet-sitting rounds.

THE YURICK & ASSOCIATES offices were as hushed as a ghostly graveyard when I arrived a while later—a too-apt analogy, I thought with a sigh. When Mignon whispered a greeting as I entered, I realized the silence was so noticeable because our resident macaw was uncharacteristically quiet.

"Is Gigi okay?" I said softly to the young receptionist. Elaine had alleged that no one in Ezra's family wanted anything to do with him alive, but I suddenly wondered if an heir had appeared and absconded with his pet.

"Kind of," Mignon said, "but she's gnawing on her cage and snapping at everyone who enters the kitchen for coffee."

I ventured that direction for my own caffeine fix—also

an excuse to check on the mad macaw. Gigi was indeed silent, but I was graced with the sight of her attempting to spring herself from her cage by breaking it apart with her beak.

"If you stay calm," I told her, "I'll see how soon we can put you on your perch in Ezra's office, okay?"

She stopped only long enough to stare at me for an instant before returning to her thankless task.

As I passed Ezra's office, I noticed that the yellow crime-scene tape was gone. "Are the cops already done in here?" I inquired of Corrie, who, file-laden as usual, edged into the office door.

"Yes, they said it was okay to start cleaning the room. They even recommended a crime-scene cleaning company. Of course, they haven't given back any files they confiscated. Borden said he's going to talk to you about getting a court order to get them returned, on grounds of attorney-client privilege."

"Can I get you to research the issue?"

"Absolutely," she agreed.

I went to see Borden after putting my purse into a desk drawer in my office. "It's going to be a hell of a day, Kendra," he said after greeting me. He looked tired as he peered blearily over his bifocals. "Not as bad as yesterday, of course. But we need to get the client files the cops took returned as fast as possible."

I assured him I'd spoken with Corrie about it and that she'd start the research.

"Then there's that whole T.O. fiasco. I need for you to speak with Brian O'Barlen and find out his schedule. Then contact that attorney for VORPO—what was his name?"

"Michael Kleer," I said. "Both those calls are on top of my to-do list for today. I'll set up a meeting to learn what VORPO really wants. We'll see if there's any common ground around that Vancino property to avoid litigation over T.O.'s proposed development."

"I knew I could count on you, Kendra," Borden said with an optimistic smile almost lighting up his sad, skinny face.

I only hoped his tune wouldn't degenerate into a critical dirge as the day wore on.

MY PHONE WAS ringing as I reached my office. "This is Kendra Ballantyne," I answered in my formal lawyerly voice.

"Michael Kleer," responded the male voice at the other end. Ah! VORPO's attorney. This would save me from making the topmost call on my to-do list.

"First, let me extend my condolences and those of my client on the passing of Mr. Cossner," Kleer continued somberly. "That said"—his tone shed its sympathy—"we want to discuss the issues raised at last night's VORPO meeting as soon as possible. Since you were present, can I assume you'll take the lead as T.O's legal counsel regarding its proposed development in Vancino?" He emphasized the word "proposed," verifying—as if he needed to—that VORPO was dead set against it.

Hmmm . . . another exceedingly appropriate phrase. Was someone in VORPO so dead set against the development that he or she had been willing to render Ezra dead in an attempt to preclude it? If so, it might have been better to eliminate O'Barlen—not that I wished such a miserable fate on the man.

"I'll need to verify with our client that my handling of the matter is acceptable," I replied to Kleer in my stilted professional tone, crafting my customary notes on a yellow legal pad as I spoke. "As far as this firm is concerned, though, my involvement has been confirmed."

"Good." Was Kleer merely being polite, or was he pleased I was involved? The only reason for one lawyer to welcome the opposition of another is because he assumes a

successful conclusion for his client, as opposed to his op-
ponent's. If that was Kleer's cogitation, there'd be one
monster of a massive surprise looming in his future . . .

Hey! I grinned. Was my once well-deserved litigator
self-confidence finally returning after its utter retreat during my prior troubles? Hallelujah!

"I know this is short notice, Ms. Ballantyne," Kleer continued, "and perhaps not appropriate considering your firm's
recent loss, but if at all possible, my client has requested a
meeting this afternoon with a representative of T.O."

"I'll check with my client and get back to you." I jotted
down the particulars: his name, phone number, e-mail address, and a doodle I hadn't done in ages: a snide smiley
face with a sweetly evil grin.

After we hung up, I quickly called Brian O'Barlen and
recounted Kleer's call. "I know this is short notice, Mr.
O'Barlen, and realize you might want to hold off for a few
days after losing your trusted lawyer, Ezra. My suggestion,
though, is that you meet with the VORPO crowd sooner
rather than later. Learn what they want you to know about
their opposition to your project. That way, we can leap
right in to research what they're not saying. If they think
they can extort a fortune from T.O. in exchange for not
contesting your development, we'll put a strategy in place
to make them weep for the privilege of letting you do exactly what you want. And if they assume they'll be able to
abridge your rights in the property you've already acquired, we'll take care of that, too."

"I like your style, Ms. Ballantyne," O'Barlen said, causing me to cringe.

Was the long-awaited hint of my returning confidence
causing me to slather on promises way too thick? Could I
deliver the rosy future I'd begun to paint, or was this client
doomed to deal with the black-and-white starkness of
court pleadings?

"We've been discussing what to do about our legal

representation now that Ezra's gone," he continued, "but for now we'll stay with your firm. And yes, I can gather my people together for a meeting this afternoon. How's three o'clock? We'll arrive a little earlier to talk over our approach."

"Perfect," I purred, though inside my engine sputtered. Could I deliver?

How could I not?

THE T.O. CONTINGENT met first with Borden in his office, where he assured O'Barlen and his team of toadies that I'd stay assigned to their matter, and that the firm would do all it could to assure a smooth transition now that Ezra was gone.

I'd invited the VORPO side to meet with us here, and when they arrived, they were shown into the area of the offices that had once been the restaurant's bar. It was, after all, the building's biggest conference room.

Unfortunately, at three o'clock, the acknowledged time for our meeting, Gigi, still in the kitchen, apparently awakened and started her usual screams.

I had to explain it first thing to the people on both sides of the table. "It's poor Ezra Cossner's pet macaw," I said. "She's taking his loss very hard."

"I can understand that," sighed Millie Franzel. Yes, Millie, owner of the best pet boutique I knew of, was one of the VORPO representatives at the table that day. "I've had a parrot or two in my shop, and they're definitely emotional at times. That poor bird—losing her best friend in such a terrible way."

Damn, but I liked Millie—except that, at this moment, she sat on the wrong side of the table.

I closed the door to mute Gigi's cries as much as possible.

Flint Daniels was present, too, which was no surprise.

He was introduced as the group's president at last evening's meeting.

And then there was Michael Kleer. VORPO's legal counsel was definitely clear, living up to his name as he laid out their list of demands.

First was that no mixed-use development be built on the critical block. "There are homes along the streets behind Vancino Boulevard," Kleer said. The boyish lawyer with the baby face looked too young to be taken seriously. Almost. His hair was deep brown and wavy. His eyes were huge and guileless—those awful, insincere orbs. "The residents like things as they are. They don't want a bunch of apartments to be built near them, especially above the area's commercial establishments."

Which was the essence of mixed use—stores, offices, and apartments constructed to coexist harmoniously in the same neighborhood. One use was often stacked on top of another.

I glanced at Brian O'Barlen. His round face had grown red beneath his flowing silver mane, and I almost anticipated seeing flames shoot from his flaring nostrils. "What else?" he growled.

"I don't like the fact that you own nearly all the other property along Vancino Boulevard," Millie Franzel piped up. Her dark hair poofed up on top even more poodle-like than I'd ever seen it. But her similarity to canines was more pit bull than snugly pet, in the way she aimed for the T.O. jugular. "I think you should be forced to sell it all again."

"You'd change your tune if we offered to buy you out at an outrageous price," O'Barlen baited her through gritted teeth.

"What are you offering?" asked Kleer, baring a boyish smile.

"Its appraised value," O'Barlen barked. "Not a penny more."

"Whose appraiser?" countered Kleer. "Yours or ours?"

I held up my hand. "We won't resolve anything at this rate," I reminded them. "Let's have each side describe what it wants so we can see if there's any common ground."

There wasn't. The meeting adjourned less than half an hour later. It had become clear that VORPO couldn't be bought. Or so they wanted T.O. to think at this point. In any event, the meeting had dissolved into mush.

I was a litigator at heart. As a result, that same heart should have sung, since it appeared we were destined to take this dispute to court.

But as one who wanted the best possible deal for her client, I felt depressed.

Once everyone had left, I ducked into the kitchen to see Gigi. The beautiful mostly blue macaw did nothing to shriek my own blues away.

"Scream a few for me, gorgeous girl," I said, then headed toward my office for my purse. I was more than ready to commence the evening's pet-sitting.

At this moment, I was ecstatic that I had an alternate career. Despite my temporary rally this afternoon, I had a sad, sneaking suspicion that my lawyering days were numbered—as in, perhaps, three.

Or would it even take three days before T.O. told Borden to can me or face the loss of a potentially lucrative client?

Chapter Eight

TO MY SURPRISE, when I got to the Yurick firm parking lot, Millie Franzel was still there. She stood beside a black minivan with a sign on the side that said PAMPERVILLE PET PLACE—THE BOUTIQUE FOR THE VALLEY'S MOST PAM-PERED PETS.

"Hi, Kendra," she said. I'd been a lucrative enough cus-tomer in the past, when I was a well-paid litigator, for her to remember me.

"Hi, Millie." I beelined straight for my Beamer, not wanting to stop and talk. It wouldn't have been ethical. She was represented by another attorney, and I hadn't gotten his consent to chat with her.

"Kendra, wait," she said. She was an attractive entrepre-neur with her poodle-pretty hair and otherwise well-enhanced looks. Her makeup was applied skillfully enough to draw attention to her sloe brown eyes and away from her longish nose and lightly protruding teeth. I hadn't noticed when she was seated at the conference table, but she was

clad in black, satiny pants and very high heels. I'd mentally
remarked upon her white-and-rose-striped blouse with its
line of schnauzers marching along the neckline. It was undoubtedly one of the products she sold at her store—for
people, not their pets.

I stopped expectantly, my hand on the Beamer's door
handle. Though I'd dressed nicely in creased khaki slacks,
a brown blouse, and a light wool sport jacket, I wasn't
nearly as dressed up as she. "How've you been, Millie?" I
asked neutrally. Even if I couldn't chat about our respective
sides in the legal matter looming between us, I abhorred
the idea of acting antagonistic.

"I've been better." Her dark, arched brows slumped into
a scowl. "I'm sorry about what happened to Ezra Cossner,
Kendra, but I despised how he came across at the VORPO
meeting. Now that you're representing T.O., I thought
things would improve, but after the meeting we just had,
I'm losing hope."

Did she dislike Ezra enough to do something about him
and slip me into his negotiating shoes? I hated to think
such a thing about someone I knew and liked . . . but it was
entirely possible that someone I knew and liked had slain
Ezra, whether or not it was the bowwow boutique owner
before me.

She hadn't stopped speaking. "How can you represent
that creepy Brian O'Barlen? I don't care how much money
he has. He shouldn't think he can buy—"

I lifted my hand from the Beamer and waved it to cut
off her chatter. "Sorry, Millie. I can't discuss the dispute
between T.O. and VORPO with you."

She seemed shocked. "Why not?"

"Because I'm an opposing attorney, and you're represented by counsel. It's unethical for me to discuss the
case with you unless your lawyer is present or otherwise
okays it."

Her brown eyes narrowed to sly slits. "But I've read

about you, Kendra. Ethics isn't exactly your middle name. And surely you see our point. Our block on Vancino Boulevard is fine the way it is. You've been to my store and seen how great it is. The other establishments around there are nice, too. And . . ." Her talk trailed off as she met my gaze, and she suddenly stepped backward. It was her turn to touch the Beamer, but in her case it was for balance. Those high heels of hers wobbled woefully as she gaped at me. Was it fear I saw on her face?

Well, good. Not that I'd really pop the pet-store owner in the puss, but my mind had stalled on an earlier sentence in her speech. I'd drawn myself up to my full five-five height, not nearly as tall as she in my flat shoes, but my anger must have been obvious. "Ethics is, in fact, my middle name, Millie," I hissed. "If you'd read all the articles about me, heard everything that happened, you'd know that all the accusations against me were proven false. I'm a damned good and ethical lawyer." And again I didn't suggest that those two words might present an oxymoron in many people's minds. "Now, let me repeat: I can't discuss this matter with you. Ask your own counsel, Michael Kleer. You know how much I enjoy your store, but—" Oops. I was slipping into dangerous waters by even bringing up her boutique. "Have a pleasant evening," I ended, shining a contrived smile at her.

"I'm sorry, Kendra," she said, and she truly looked contrite. "I wish we weren't on opposite sides."

"Me, too, Millie," I admitted, then ducked quickly into my car before I could say anything else.

A few seconds after I'd exited the parking lot, my cell phone sang, "It's My Life."

I groped inside my purse and grabbed my phone as I navigated Ventura Boulevard toward the freeway. I barely scanned the screen to see the caller ID: Darryl.

"Pooper-Scoopers Anonymous," I quipped. "We pick up what your pet puts down."

"I'll remember that next time one of our guests has an accident," Darryl said dryly. "I'll call you first."

"No thanks. How're things?"

Darryl nearly never called just for the heck of hearing my voice. I figured he had a reason.

I only hoped it was one I wanted to hear.

He apparently aspired to shoot the breeze first, though. "How's your malcontent macaw?"

"I'm just leaving the office. Yes, I know it's late," I inserted to stave off his inevitable comment. "I needed to be around for a negotiation. I checked on Gigi just before I left. She made a lot of background noise during the meeting, but after snapping her big beak at me, she quieted down a little. Elaine's going to feed her later."

"Did you ask Gigi what she saw during Ezra's murder?"

Of course that was why he'd inquired. "Sure. She described in detail exactly who came in with the gun and killed him. She's a little shy, though, and refuses to testify to the police."

"You're pulling my leg."

"Yep, the left one. It's my favorite."

"What's wrong with the right one?"

"It's even skinnier than the other." I smiled as I let the Beamer barrel up the freeway on-ramp.

"No way," Darryl said. "So, bird's help or not, have you solved the murder yet?"

"Not hardly," I replied with a sigh. I didn't have to ask why Darryl would make such an inquiry. Sure, I had two genuine careers these days: pet-sitter and lawyer. I'd also, inadvertently and unintentionally, taken on another: amateur sleuth, since I'd solved two murders of which I'd been accused, plus one that had been heaped on my tenants.

Would I now figure out who'd ended Ezra's life, too? Not if Detective Ned Noralles had anything to say about it.

But I found myself yet again in the thick of a miserable situation. I could more easily ask questions without anyone knowing exactly what I was up to.

"Don't be surprised if I do solve it," I answered Darryl.

"I figured. Anyhow, that's not why I called. Now that you're a big-time lawyer again, I know that the fact that tomorrow's Saturday doesn't mean you're not going to the office, but do you have an hour to meet with someone I'd like to refer to you—a lady with a dog-related legal problem?"

"Another unneighborly bite situation?" That was the basis for the brief I'd been writing—to support a summary judgment motion in a pet law dog bite matter that involved one of my pet-sitting clients, Lester the basset hound. Darryl had referred me as a sitter to Lester's owner, so I'd kept Darryl informed about the nonconfidential side of the case.

"No, this one's about an inheritance."

Though the VORPO thing could take a lot of time, I'd found that practicing pet law, like that dog chomp case, was of particular pleasure to me, although I wouldn't know if this one was something I could help with till I heard more about it.

"Can I count on you?" Darryl asked.

"I'll come and discuss it," I said. "No promises I'll take it on."

"I think you will. See you around three?"

My curiosity churning, I said, "I'll be there."

Traffic was abysmally slow, the common state these days on local L.A. freeways. I got off soon and maneuvered even more rapidly along local streets toward the pets I was sitting.

Once again I anticipated Alexander the pit bull's eager need for exercise, walking him for an extra mile in his owner's neighborhood. I saw another couple of canines who craved food and attention. Then, I visited Harold Reddingam's place to ensure that his feline friends Abra and Cadabra were well fed and that their litter boxes were raked to suit their finicky fancies.

I had only one more pet client to visit—Beggar, who made his home these days in the mansion that was more or less mine. At the moment, though, I was nearer to Jeff's Sherman Oaks abode than the house I rented out, so I decided to stop by and pick up Lexie before heading back.

And if I happened to run into Odin's good-looking, sexy owner . . . well, that would hopefully only provide me with incentive to finish my pet-sitting pronto and hurry back for another memorable night.

Only . . . yes, Jeff was home with Odin and Lexie. But the three of them weren't alone.

I realized that the moment I curbed my Beamer in front of his pseudo-Spanish-style hacienda and stared at the driveway. His Escalade was blocked in by a cherry red Camry that looked way too familiar. It belonged to Jeff's ex-wife, Amanda.

I'd never quite figured out how blood could chill all icy when nerves around its vessels were steamed, but that's exactly how my body reacted.

Well, hell. I knew Jeff needed juicing up because he hated being under the microscope as a murder suspect. Had he sought sympathy from the woman who'd asked that he use his security expertise to save her from a supposed stalker?

I was just irritated enough to ask.

I purposely put myself on the firing line by using the key he'd given me to provide free access to his home during his frequent travels. "Hi, Jeff," I called. "I'm home."

I heard the scuffling of small claws on tile as the pups raced toward me from the kitchen. I also heard low murmurs from the same direction suddenly stop.

Soon, I was surrounded by leaping Lexie and her pal

Odin . . . and faced with two too-cheerful faces, Jeff's and Amanda's.

"Well, hello, Amanda," I said, as if surprised to see her. I turned as if to stare out the front door. "Is Leon out there?" That was the name of her post-Jeff ex-boyfriend who had allegedly decided to tail her day and night. Mostly night. He apparently hoped that one day he'd get to spend all his nights with her. Or so she said. And what did I think? Well, even though there actually seemed to be a bona fide bozo named Leon whom she'd dated, I suspected that he'd given up following her long ago, except in her overactive and ingenious imagination.

I mean, what better way to get one's old ex, who happened to be both a private investigator and a security expert, back into one's life than to cry on his shoulder about unending danger?

And the fact that Jeff fell for it? Well, yes, that made him seem the champion of truth, justice, and the American way that all heroes strove to be.

And since I knew Jeff wasn't a stupid person, his accepting her tale suggested to me that he didn't completely want Amanda to exit his life, either.

Which left me out in the cold, this January evening in L.A.

"If it's really any of your business," Amanda answered me haughtily, "I don't know where Leon is, but he called me this afternoon and I needed Jeff's advice. Leon said—"

"I'd love to hear about it," I lied, meeting Jeff's eye. He'd managed to maneuver an apologetic expression onto that susceptible and sexy face, but I wasn't buying it. "But I've got one more pet-sitting stop to make tonight that can't wait. I just wanted to pick Lexie up to join me. Ready to go, girl?"

Of course she was.

"Enjoy your talk," I said sweetly, and then Lexie and I were gone.

LEXIE TOOK ME at my word when I wailed, "I don't want to talk about it," once we were in the car. She didn't demand any explanation, but I found myself following up nonetheless. "It's not as if we have a real relationship." I let the Beamer take a corner a little too quickly, and that elicited a concerned blink from Lexie as she scrambled not to slide off the seat. "It's business. I pet-sit for him and he does occasional investigations for me. In between, during the rare times he's in town, we take advantage of our mutual admiration of each other's bodies." And how!

Jeff and I had decided a few weeks ago to continue seeing one another despite my prior retreat when Amanda insinuated herself back into his life. We'd determined to just see how things progressed.

I suspected that progression was now past history.

"I've never professed to have good taste in men," I reiterated to my long-suffering pup as I pushed the button to open the gate to the grounds of my house. Electric lights lit the yard. I aimed the Beamer toward the empty space beside the garage—over which was the apartment where Lexie and I resided.

I allowed Lexie the relief of relieving herself before climbing the steps and entering our home. "Now, you stay here," I told her, "while I go take care of Beggar." Since I'd left the lovely Irish setter till last on my pet-sitting list tonight, I wanted to lavish some extra individual attention on him.

And maybe roughhousing with a larger dog than Lexie would help me settle down for my solo evening. Hopefully, I wouldn't have to converse with any convivial neighbors as I walked Beggar. I'd seen a lot less of the local residents since my party-tossing tenant Charlotte moved out.

Lexie whined while I shut our apartment door behind

me. I skipped down the steps and onto the driveway, maneuvering myself toward the mansion that was mine by title but occupied by a subtenant. I didn't know Russ Preesinger nearly as well as I'd come to know Beggar, since the guy traveled a lot, which suited me fine.

Although it was January in L.A., this week had been dry. Last week was a different story, and the lush vegetation constituting my landscape—now maintained by the subtenant as part of his lease obligations—had grown a little wild. Birds of paradise, roses, and shrubbery lined the path to the main house's front door. I used my key to enter and flicked on the lights to the large, multilevel entry, expecting Beggar to greet me as he usually did.

He didn't.

"Beggar?" I called. He didn't come.

Which gave me an eerie feeling. I'd entered homes before where the pets avoided me, and sometimes that was because they were guarding their owners, who'd been brutally murdered.

In this very house, I'd discovered the body of a reality television star only a couple of months ago.

Damn! After Ezra's death, obviously my imagination had erupted into overtime.

But where was Beggar?

I held still for an instant, listening.

And heard something from upstairs.

Swallowing, I crossed the rustic tilework—fortunately now denuded of the ugly rug my tenants had formerly draped over it—blinked up at my favorite crystal chandelier, and started up the stairs.

I heard murmuring from somewhere. "Beggar?" I whispered, wondering why I didn't feel right shouting for the dog. He wasn't the one doing the murmuring. It sounded like some low voice . . .

At the top of the steps, I stared down the hall. The walls held no pictures. The rug remained the same pretty beige plush I'd had installed. Nothing appeared even remotely menacing.

Yet I was damned anxious.

Should I call the cops? But why? For all I knew, sub-tenant Russ Preesinger had arrived home early and had forgotten to let me know. That would explain Beggar's for-bearance from greeting me at the door.

Holding my head high, I headed down the hall. "Russ, are you here?" I called. "Beggar?"

The Irish setter suddenly bounded out of a bedroom. "Hi, boy," I called.

Then someone screamed . . . and so did I.

Chapter Nine

THE SCREAM THAT had instigated mine was nothing like a macaw's screech. I saw its source immediately: an obviously frightened young female who emerged from the bedroom down the hall.

I stopped screaming first. "Who are you?" I demanded.

"I live here," she said without identifying herself. "What are *you* doing here?"

This kid seemed a teen, if my age assessment was anywhere on target. I suspected that the hugeness of her big brown eyes was natural and had little to do with how she'd apparently been startled by my appearance. She would appear waiflike with her short, shaggy black hair if not for the way her lips pouted petulantly.

"I own this place," I replied, then rebutted, "And you don't live here. Or at least you'd better not."

"Why not? It's my dad's."

Ah. That constituted a clue. "Your dad is Russ Preesinger?"

She gave an emphatic nod, then scanned those big

brown eyes up and down my person as if assessing me. "I'm Rachel. And you're not his girlfriend," she asserted.

"No, I'm not. I told you, I own this place. Your dad"—assuming she was telling the truth—"sublets this house from my tenants."

"Whatever." She shrugged a skinny shoulder beneath a tight, short T-shirt that barely reached her midriff. The slight curves the shirt hugged suggested adolescence, but I suspected she was slightly older than that.

The heat wasn't on in the house, so it was chilly in here, maybe mid-sixties. I considered how cold I would feel had I been dressed similarly and shivered slightly beneath my comfy wool jacket. At least her gray, baggy slacks with mid-thigh pockets on the sides were full length. But how she could walk in those ugly platform shoes . . .

"My dad likes women who are prettier than you," she continued snidely as she bent and threw her arms around Beggar, who'd sat down calmly beside this young intruder. His apparent acceptance of her suggested she told the truth. At least the Irish setter seemed to know her. She peered up from beside the pup. "He likes blondes, mostly. Ones younger and thinner than you, like those he meets when he's working on a film location."

That did it. The kid obviously was attempting to feed my inferiority complex. And after all I'd gone through in the last year, my complex had reason—at times—to feel inferior. I'd thought I'd nearly shed the uncertainty. I didn't need anyone to recall it now. Icily, I said, "I came here this evening because I'm in charge of taking care of Beggar, and that's what I'm going to do. As soon as I've fed and walked him, I'm calling Russ Preesinger, who may or may not be your dad."

That seemed to startle her, for she stood and stared at me. "Of course he's my—"

I didn't let her finish. "If he assures me you're who you say you are, then you may stay until he gets back. There is nothing in the lease that allows another person to live here, so I'll most likely throw you out at that time. Is that clear?"

Those huge eyes of hers grew even greater in diameter and dampened. She nodded slowly.

"Did Russ give you a key?" I asked.

"No," she replied.

"Then how did you get in?"

The sudden stubborn set to her jaw suggested this would remain her secret, at least for now. Which didn't give me much confidence in my home's recently refurbished security, despite the perimeter gate.

Maybe I'd have to consult my security expert again. Jeff Hubbard came to mind . . . and I immediately hurled him out.

"Come here, Beggar," I ordered. The pretty red setter stood. He looked along his long muzzle, first at the girl, then at me. And then he obeyed. Together, he and I headed down the stairs. I wasn't sure whether it was a good idea to turn my back on Rachel, but nothing battered my behind except, I felt certain, her evil glare.

I took good care of Beggar, making sure to spend the extra time with him that I'd previously allotted. When I was done, I brought him upstairs to my apartment so Lexie and he could exchange the obligatory doggy sniff while I searched for Russ Preesinger's phone number. I brought it along when I returned to the house with Beggar, and my cell phone as well.

I stood in the brightly lit downstairs entryway when I called Russ, speaking loudly enough that Rachel would know what I was up to. When I explained the latest events to my subtenant, there was an explosion from the other end of the phone. "Yes, I have a nineteen-year-old daughter named Rachel," Russ exclaimed.

"This girl looks younger," I contradicted.

"I know, but she's nineteen. And Rachel looks the way you've described her: large eyes, snappish mouth, too thin, and no common sense." Ah, it did sound as if we were talking about the same girl. "She's supposed to be with her mother, my former wife, in Arizona, going to college there. Let me call my ex and find out what's going on, and I'll get right back to you."

I mounted the steps to assure myself that Rachel was indeed eavesdropping. I smiled at her disagreeably. "Mr. Preesinger is calling his ex-wife to see if his daughter is there."

"I told you—" She started to shout, but then my cell phone sounded, "It's My Life," and I lifted its cover to respond.

"She ran away from her mother, the brat," Russ Preesinger shouted into my ear. "Kendra, I know it's a huge imposition, but please let her stay for now. I'll try my damnedest to get home tomorrow and talk to her. Just keep an eye on her for me."

"I'm a pet-sitter, not a people-sitter, Russ," I reminded him, aghast at the very thought of becoming responsible for a runaway teenaged adult.

"I know. And it's not fair of me to ask. Tell you what. Put her on the phone."

I did so gladly, thrusting my phone at the pouting teen. Rachel wasn't so glad. I could tell from the gripes I overheard.

I felt my eyes bulge and my anger build as she blurted to him how she'd happened to get into the house. She'd gotten a ride here from a friend early this morning and slipped in when I stepped out to walk Beggar.

I did need to secure Jeff's further advice on security, damn it!

Rachel soon sullenly handed the phone back to me. She continued to glare as I spoke once more to Russ.

"I told her I'll be there as soon as I can," he informed me hastily, as if assuming I'd want to hang up on him. The thought had crossed my mind . . . "I also told her that if she doesn't stay there and behave, she'll have to start earning her own living immediately. Her mom and I have both had enough."

Something I could certainly understand . . . especially since, when I hung up from speaking with Russ, Rachel immediately exploded into a tirade against both parents.

"Good night," I shouted before she could get very far. "Since he's in my care, I'll be back to see to Beggar in the morning. Early." And after a hasty hug to the setter in question, I hurried back to the haven of my apartment.

THE NEXT DAY was Saturday, and I greeted it rather grumpily.

Thank heavens Lexie was the only one with me. After last night's disastrous confrontations with Rachel Preesinger plus Jeff and his ex, I had no interest in seeing anyone remotely connected with the human race, at least not too soon.

I brought Lexie along on pet-sitting rounds, then drove us both to the Yurick offices. I wanted to check on Gigi, even though she wasn't one of my pet-sitting charges. I also intended to be present for Elaine's ten o'clock appointment with parrot expert Polly Bright to hear any bright suggestions about how to care for the traumatized bird.

Plus, I intended to produce a strategy memo to pass along to Brian O'Barlen and his T.O. clan, to suggest how best to salvage the Vancino situation.

I was surprised to find the firm parking lot as car-filled as on weekdays. When Lexie and I entered, no receptionist greeted us, but as I approached my office, I found that most firm attorneys and paralegals were present that day. So much for eschewing company. At least, when Elaine saw me, she confirmed that I could sit in on her session with Polly Bright.

Leaving Lexie inside my digs, I ran into senior citizen attorneys William Fortier and Geraldine Glass in the kitchen getting coffee as they pretended to ignore the big bird occupying the cage in the middle of the floor.

Gigi's schtick today was to moan mournfully. Had she picked that up by listening to Ezra's last gasps? I shuddered at the thought, even as I tried cheerfully to ignore her, too, while bantering with the older attorneys.

"Does that creature have to stay here?" demanded Geraldine right in Gigi's presence. Geraldine had curly brown hair and a thick neck, and constantly wore reading glasses clipped to the end of her nose.

"Yes," I asserted firmly. "She's had a hard time, losing her owner that way, and at least for now she needs to be in familiar surroundings."

"Gigi want a cracker?" chirped plump and well-preserved William as he stuffed a sliver of English muffin between the cage bars. Gigi barely eyed it before grabbing it in her sharp, black beak and making short shrift of it— then returning to her sorrowful sounds.

"She could at least say thank you," Geraldine said with a sniff, then slipped from the kitchen holding her coffee mug.

Borden was in his office, and I shot the breeze with him for a short while. "I'm going to suggest that T.O. put together a dog-and-pony show to wow the Vancino opposition," I told him. "Anticipate their every complaint and address it first, like noise, parking, upscale businesses and residents the development will attract, mitigation measures to propose to the city to secure building permits—such as low-income housing units—everything. Once the plans are complete, we'll let the media meddle in it, too. Obtain as much public opinion on our side as possible. Then, if we go to trial, we'll insist on a jury, and most members will have seen a discussion of the best points about the project in the papers."

"Will that work?" Borden asked.

"Who knows? But we'll also make it damned clear that even as T.O. tries to accommodate VORPO's reasonable requests—assuming there are any—they're ready to commit a fountain full of money to fight. Of course, they're willing to use it as sums for settlement instead of enriching their attorneys. Money sometimes works where words don't."

Borden grinned his agreement. "Sure, but *we're* their money-hungry attorneys, so let's not toss away those fees too fast." He frowned. "The police have questioned me a lot, Kendra, about how well I knew Ezra. I thought I knew him well. I liked him. I told the detectives that, but they seem to think I could have killed him."

"It's their job to think that anyone who knew a victim could have killed him," I assured the senior partner. "They're probably not serious about you. Unless . . ." Okay, I had to ask. As I've said, circumstances over the last few months had set me thinking like an amateur sleuth. "Was there any animosity between Ezra and you? Anything the cops could latch on to as a motive for you to have murdered him?"

Borden's eyes grew horrified behind his bifocals. "Of course not." He hesitated. "Although . . ."

"Although?" I prompted.

"I gently suggested to Ezra that he act a little nicer to people around here. He responded by telling me I could either let him be or rely on my own stable of clients to keep everyone busy."

"It sounds as if he'd have left willingly if you'd told him to. I don't see that as a motive for murder."

"Me, neither." Borden's shoulders visibly relaxed beneath this day's Hawaiian shirt. He even sent me one of his lopsided smiles.

I didn't suggest that it *would* have been a motive for murder if he'd decided to keep Ezra's clients while dumping his difficult personality by disposing of him more direly.

Back in my office, I spent the next hour at my computer listing scenarios, both logical and inane, petting Lexie as she lay beneath my desk, and trying to tune out the creepy cries that Gigi continued to make in the not-so-distant kitchen.

At ten o'clock, I told Lexie to stay and shut her again inside my office. My feet started sidling toward the kitchen.

Polly Bright was already there. So was Elaine. And Gigi, too. Instead of moaning, she was once again issuing ear-splitting shrills.

"Should we go someplace else to talk?" suggested Elaine.

"For a few minutes," Polly agreed. Pale, plump, and poised, she was clad once again in bright, flowing colors—turquoise slacks and a loose blue-and-magenta blouse, with a long yellow scarf wound around her artificially red hair and trailing down her back. "And then, if you want me to try to help Gigi, I'd like to spend time alone with her. She needs an application of parrot psychology, but I may need to startle her first to get her attention." The brilliant smile she sent my way seemed to double her double chin. "Something like your singing the other day." Smiling back, I shepherded her toward the former bar. Elaine joined us, and we all sat at a booth, each nursing a cup of coffee, though Polly had brought her own black mug wrapped in plastic that she extracted from her tote and jammed full of our java. Since it was Saturday, Elaine was dressed somewhat casually for her: dark brown slacks and a beige sweater with small green and pink flowers forming a pattern across her chest. A lacy blouse collar peeked out at her neck.

I had to ask. "Can you describe macaw psychology for the layperson in twenty-five words or less, Polly? I mean, Gigi was screaming even before she saw Ezra killed. Is there something wrong with her?"

Sadness seemed to shadow Polly's face, and she fastidiously folded the napkin that she had wrapped about her cup. "Only that Ezra bought her for all the wrong reasons."

"Like?" I prompted, not even attempting to hide my impatience.

"Well, I met Ezra briefly a few weeks ago because I'm a friend of Bella Quevedo's, a lawyer with the firm Ezra used to work for, Jambison & Jetts. I helped Bella train her wonderful Amazon parrot, Pinocchio. Bella told me she'd dated Ezra for a while when she joined the firm a couple of years ago—but she wound up marrying a partner, Jonathon Jetts." Polly's frown forced the ridges of her pudgy eyebrows nearly together. "There was bad blood between them, you know—Jonathon and Bella on the one side, and Ezra on the other." She shook her head. "When I heard about what happened to Ezra, well . . ." Her words wound down, and she took a serious sip of coffee.

"Well what?" I had to ask, confused as to how this related to Ezra's purportedly ill-conceived acquisition of Gigi.

"Well, I shouldn't have said anything. As I mentioned, I'm a friend of Bella's. But . . ."

She wouldn't meet my eye or Elaine's, though Elaine and I stared at each other.

"Are you trying to not say that you think Bella or Jonathon might have been Ezra's murderer?" I blurted.

"I didn't say that!" Polly exclaimed indignantly. And then she wilted a little, while still studying her coffee cup. "But . . ."

Though she didn't finish the thought, her "but" spoke tomes.

Chapter Ten

SNAIL-SLOW, I PRIED from semireluctant Polly the little that she knew, with Elaine uttering encouragement as we bided our time in the booth.

Polly proclaimed that Pinocchio was the epitome of Amazon parrots, and his owner, Bella, adored him. A noted corporate lawyer in her late fifties, Bella had joined the Jambison law firm a year ago, which was when she'd met both Jonathon Jetts and Ezra.

Why she'd decided to date Ezra, Polly hadn't a clue. She herself hadn't met Ezra till near the end of the saga. By then, Bella had broken up with the irascible older guy and taken up with Jonathon . . . enough of a take-up to wind up marrying, a month ago, the stable, somber lawyer who was five years her junior.

Which I found interesting in itself. Jonathon Jetts had been here hollering at Ezra the day before he died—allegedly for stealing firm clients but I'd bet good ol' ordinary male jealousy skulked behind it. Jetts, a murder suspect? Sure. I'd make sure he was high on the investigating detectives' list, though from my previous dealings with Ned Noralles, I imagined Jetts was already there. But above or below Jeff?

I definitely questioned Bella Quevedo's taste. She'd taken up with irritable and irritating Ezra, then dumped him for the dumpy Jonathon. Maybe Jetts had a heart of gold when he wasn't picking apart a former law partner, though the way Polly spoke of him suggested he pinched pennies till they fused together.

I posited that Ezra had remained angry over losing Bella. Perhaps his rage was a major reason for his being forced into retirement. He obviously didn't depart easily.

Plus, from what Polly proclaimed, he'd made it clear he would outdo both Jonathon and Bella. That was when he'd sought out a bird of his own, not long after their nuptials. And not just any old pet of the parrot family. No, if Bella had a nice but relatively common Amazon, then he would acquire something even bigger and better: a macaw.

Aha! Here at last was Polly's elucidation of why she considered Ezra's purchase of Gigi inappropriate.

Ezra had started with scant research, though, and ended up begging Bella to introduce him to her bird expert for help after already adopting Gigi. Polly had pretty much disliked the guy on first sight and hated being in the middle of the mixed-up relationships involving her friend Bella.

"But I felt sorry for poor Gigi," Polly said with a sigh. That was why she agreed to provide a lesson for the mature and partly trained Blue and Gold Macaw. She snorted. "Ezra didn't know the first thing about macaws. He was angry that poor Gigi didn't talk as much as Pinocchio and what she did say wasn't an imitation of his grumpy old voice."

From what Polly said, although macaws could be loving and learned lots of tricks, they weren't the speech

mavens of the parrot family. With patience, some could be
taught to speak, and they even occasionally sang. "But
they're simply not Amazons or African Greys when it
comes to skills in speaking or repeating things they hear,"
she finished.

"Not even when they hear it in an emotional situation?"
I had to inquire.

"Well, like people, every bird is different. Certainly
some macaws might pick something up in a crisis. But
Ezra wanted a bird who'd outdo Bella's in everything, including speech. He might have been happier with a bird
more similar to Bella's—smaller, too, like Pinocchio. It is
simply too bad that he did not seek expert advice first. Had
he asked, Bella might have introduced us sooner, and I
have studied the parrot family for so many years that I am
known absolutely everywhere as . . . well, no matter. At
least he did one thing right: choosing a Blue and Gold over,
say, a Hyacinth Macaw."

"Why is that better?" I asked in follow-up, as I figured
she wanted me to.

"Hyacinths are even larger and noisier," she responded.
"And many have worse dispositions. Of course, they're as
individualistic as humans, but on the whole Blue and Golds
are fairly even tempered. Some people even refer to them
as the golden retrievers of the macaw family."

"How do you propose to help Gigi calm down?" Elaine
asked.

"I have techniques to try," Polly said. "Trade secrets."
She smiled. "As I said, I'll startle her if I have to, but I'll
use a kinder and calmer approach first, talking to her, and
even bribing her. I've brought some veggies along to tempt
her with. Of course, I washed and sliced them myself."
Still seated in the booth, she reached into her large tote bag
and extracted plastic containers that held green peppers,
carrots, and celery.

She stood. "Gigi, here I come."

And a good thing, since the macaw's moans still resounded through the office, a lot more audibly once we exited the bar.

I HIED MYSELF back to my office, where Lexie seemed pleased to see me. I sat again at my computer and started tossing my proposed T.O. strategy onto it. I virtually vomited my ideas out first, intending to refine them later before passing them along to my client in memo form.

My cell phone sang, and I opened a drawer and reached into my purse for it. The readout told me it was Jeff.

"Hello," I said stiffly.

"We need to talk, Kendra," he said. Before I could tell him to chew on whatever he wanted to say and choke on it, he continued, "But not now. Ned Noralles has been asking a lot of questions of people who know me—neighbors, my employees . . . Althea was so incensed that she used our usual legitimate resources and a few that aren't to run a search on Noralles." His tone contained a grin, but it vanished with his next words. "I'll show it to you sometime, but right now I need to really dig in and try to find the SOB detective a better suspect than I am. Can I come talk to you about it?"

I wasn't eager to see Jeff, not even to discuss my own home security issue, but after having been the subject of a Noralles top-suspect list, I couldn't help feeling sorry for him. "Sure," I said. "I'm at my office, and a few other people are here today. Some knew Ezra better than I did— Borden, for one, and Elaine Aames. Maybe you can chat with them and get ideas. Oh, and there's always his pet macaw and her trainer to talk to."

"The bird. Right. Well, I'll be right over to speak with anyone with information."

I still hadn't told him Darryl's talking bird theory of murder investigations. Maybe it was just as well.

Being interrogated by a P.I. with an important agenda of his own might rob Gigi of any progress Polly might make in calming the macaw down.

JEFF ARRIVED HALF an hour later. I knew that because Lexie told me, leaping around frenetically and digging at my closed office door. I opened it, and she ran out, circling Jeff and clearly searching for his Akita.

He must have thought so, too, since he bent down, patted Lexie, and said, "Sorry, girl, but I left Odin at home."

As if she understood, Lexie sat and glared, though she wasn't too miffed to pull away from his petting. Or to snub the biscuit he picked from the pocket of his navy sport jacket.

When Jeff stood up again, elevating to his full six-foot height, my irrational lower body began buzzing as if wishing for some petting, too.

Until I reminded it about Amanda's visit last night.

Coolly, I said, "Come with me. You've already met Borden and Elaine, and I'll introduce you to the other attorneys who are here today. And to Corrie Montez. She was a paralegal with Ezra's old firm. You've met Gigi, too, haven't you?"

"The bird? We haven't been formally introduced, but I've seen her and been privy to her screeching."

As I led Jeff down the hall, my most senior partner appeared from his office. "Hi, Borden," Jeff said. "I'm assisting with the investigation into Ezra's death." I noted that he naturally sidestepped on whose behalf he was helping— not the cops', of course, but his own. "Can I talk to you for a few minutes?"

The older attorney looked a bit suspicious, but he nodded. "Sure. Come in."

I had work to do before departing to meet Darryl's referral, so I left Jeff to his own investigative devices. About forty-five minutes later, when I was getting set to go, I decided first to check on his progress. With Lexie strolling beside me, I peered into each office door as I passed. No Jeff.

Corrie Montez appeared from the room containing the firm's photocopier with—surprise—an assortment of files in her arms.

"Have you seen Jeff Hubbard?" I asked.

"The detective? He sure asks a lot of questions. But I don't know where he is now."

That was when I noticed him exiting the now-quiet kitchen with a cup of coffee in his hands.

"So you did speak with Gigi?" I teased, happy that whatever technique Polly was using must be at least somewhat successful. No screams filled the office air.

"Her teacher wouldn't let me," he responded with a shrug. "But at least she answered—" A song suddenly rang out, and Jeff reached into his pocket. "Hello," he said to his cell phone.

Okay, I had no reason to immediately assume it was Amanda, but I did. I started to stalk away, but Jeff met my gaze and mouthed a different name that started with an "A": Althea.

"No kidding?" Jeff's grin was deliciously devilish. "How long ago?" He paused, then said, "I'll definitely look into that. Not that it'll change things, but . . . Right." He flipped his phone shut. "Wait'll I tell you what she found out about—"

He suddenly stopped speaking, and his cute smile segued to a cold frown as he faced someone over my shoulder.

"What brings you here, Mr. Hubbard?" asked a familiar silky voice from behind me.

"Just doing your job, Detective," Jeff replied to Ned Noralles. "About time someone did it right."

I pivoted so I could plant myself between them, my

arms out to ensure they didn't draw too close. "Chill out, gentlemen," I cautioned.

Fortunately, Jeff's cell phone chose an excellent time to sing its rhythmic ringtone again. He glanced down, flipped it open, and intoned, "I'll call you back later, Althea."

"Gee, she must have thought of something else to tell you," I said unnecessarily, keeping my tone totally light. I turned toward Noralles. "Is there something else we can help you with, Detective?"

"Sure thing. Is Ms. Aames here? I have a few more matters to discuss with her." When I assured him that Elaine had indeed reported for work on this Saturday, he seemed pleased. "Oh, and the macaw? How is she getting along?"

"Better, I think," I told him. "We've brought back our bird specialist to assist her over the trauma."

"Good," he said. "I'll want to talk to her again, too."

Gigi or the specialist? I had a fleeting suspicion, as I considered the question, that Detective Noralles might read the same mystery novels Darryl did. Only, from what Polly had said, other birds would be better than a macaw at conveying clues.

At this opportune instant, Polly Bright popped her head out of the kitchen. She glared at the group of milling people just as Elaine and Corrie joined us. "Too much noise out here," she complained. "Elaine, please come in here. I want to show you how I'd like you to work with Gigi for the next day or so."

The hesitant expression on Elaine's aging face emphasized her wrinkles and belied her prompt response. "Of course," she said, then added with hope, "I don't hear her complaining."

"Of course not," Polly said. "We've made some progress." She beamed—brightly, of course—with apparent professional pride. "But she's still going to need some TLC."

"Definitely," Elaine agreed.

"When you're done working with the bird, I'd like a word with you, ma'am," said Noralles. He flicked open his cop credentials. "Police business."

Polly backed up, as if taken aback. Then, after examining the badge, she nodded. "Give us about ten minutes, Officer, and then we'll talk."

WHEN NORALLES MADE it clear he intended to question Jeff alone during his wait, I swallowed my sympathy for Jeff and used the opportunity to pick up my purse, leash Lexie, and leave the office. I headed my Beamer toward Darryl's.

Doggy Indulgence was now open every day but major holidays. Since it existed in Studio City and catered to a showbiz crowd, it had a decent clientele even on weekends.

When Lexie and I entered, Darryl rushed over to us. "You're right on time. Good. Irma Etherton is waiting for you in the kitchen." His kitchen was the pet resort area where Darryl introduced me to his referrals, previously for pet-sitting and now, in addition, for lawyering. It was the best location for potential privacy in this place.

Darryl unleashed my Cavalier, who today chose the canine area filled with human accoutrements. She sailed up onto one of the several sofas and curled into a ball beside a much bigger mixed breed who seemed mostly black Lab. Her companion opened an eye then shut it again, obviously okay with letting the cute little intruder join him.

Satisfied she'd be occupied—snoozing usually enthused her when she wasn't insisting on attention—I followed Darryl to the kitchen.

The lady who sat at the staff lunch table seemed to be in her sixties, with a bouffant of black hair. Her bone structure suggested classic beauty, but the skin around her eyes and mouth sagged sufficiently to show her age.

"I'm glad to meet you, Kendra," she said in a soft alto

after Darryl introduced us. Her handshake was cool and quick. "Darryl's told me so much about you."

"Let's see," I said, sitting across from her. "I've been keeping score." I raised my hand as if to tick stuff off on my fingers. "Best I can figure, you can believe about fifty percent of what he says."

"And you can put even more stock in the other half," said the man I'd just maligned. He stood behind me so I couldn't see his face, but I knew he'd take my teasing in stride.

He always did.

"Well, let's hope that what he told me is in the second half," Irma said. "I really need to rely on it . . . and you." My banter didn't make her back away. In fact, she'd begun to smile, a good thing since my first impression of her serious expression was of a woman who'd lost her laugh.

"So tell me your problem," I prompted. "Darryl said it's a legal issue?"

"Absolutely," Irma replied. "A stolen inheritance. I need for you to get it back for my dead lover's dog."

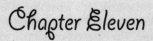

A PASSEL OF legal principles immediately started circling in my head. The most important was that pups *were* property. They couldn't *own* property. Ergo, hounds were forbidden by law from inheriting fortunes from deceased owners.

I didn't blurt that out, though. Not with the way Irma Etherton's gray eyes had puckered, and tears puddled in them.

"I'm sorry to get emotional on you," she said, "but it's just that my dear love Walt recently died. He left everything to Glenfiddich."

I blinked, but instantly made an obvious assumption. "Glenfiddich is the name of his dog?" I doubted that Walt had attempted to make a Scotch liquor manufacturer his heir.

Still, I had a sudden image of some guy named Walt giving a final toast with Glenfiddich before keeling over.

"That's right. We call him Ditch. He's Walt's Scottish terrier, and Walt's kids have kept him away from me, which is the worst part of this mess. I'm supposed to have custody of dear little Ditch . . . as well as the million dollars Walt left to him."

Dear little Ditch indeed!

"Please tell me what to do to save Ditch's fortune, Kendra," Irma entreated. "It's what Walt wanted."

Okay, I'd learned lots of tact as a litigator. And as I've mentioned before, I'd been a law school scholar and had learned to think like a lawyer. Every side to a legal issue had arguments that could be asserted to promote a client's position.

But I believed this was black letter law. No inheritance rights for pets . . . Still, without seeing the will and how it phrased the purported inheritance, and without doing legal research on the current state of case law, I couldn't completely burst Irma's inheritance bubble. Or Ditch's, either.

"I'll be honest with you, Irma." I leaned toward her, hoping my expression suggested earnestness, not hopelessness. "This doesn't sound like a case we're likely to win. But I'll be glad to look into it for you. I'll need for you to obtain a copy of Walt's will for me. In the meantime, I'll have a paralegal start some research."

"Really? You'll look into it?" Her careworn demeanor seemed to turn instantly optimistic. The age lines on her face grew shallow. She smiled. And my insides sank. Especially when she continued speaking. "I don't know whether Darryl told you, but I've spoken with several other attorneys, and none thought the matter was worth fighting. But I have to, for the sake of Walt's memory."

"I understand," I said in my most solemn lawyerlike tone. "But you need to recognize that all those other lawyers could have been right. I can't make any promises."

"Except to look into it, right?" Anxiety started again divoting wrinkles into her face.

"Absolutely, I'll at least look into it. And another thing I can promise is to charge you no more than a fixed amount

if what I find out makes it imprudent to continue fighting."
I named an amount that I thought would be fair, a couple of
hours' worth of time at the rate Borden charged for my current work.

"Oh, that's too low," she said. "I'll be glad to pay your
standard fee."

Interesting, I thought as I said a temporary farewell to
Irma. If money wasn't the object, then she must desperately
want to give effect to her dear, departed Walt's wishes.

And if that was the case. I'd make every effort to help
Irma gain what she wanted.

IT WAS TIME for my eagerly anticipated pet-sitting tour of
duty. I rounded up my sleeping pup, then Lexie and I said
goodbye to Darryl.

"Do you think you'll be able to help Irma?" my thin
friend asked anxiously.

He stood at the large reception desk holding a container
of beef-flavored biscuits. He'd been studying the box from
over his wire-rims till I approached. Treats for his favorite
patrons, I surmised and reached out my hand. He deposited
a biscuit in it, and I broke off a piece for a bouncingly eager Lexie.

"She's a neighbor of mine," he continued, "and she's really bummed out about this situation. Did she mention that
a lot of lawyers already turned her down?"

"You could have let me know that before I talked with
her," I chided him cantankerously.

"If I did, you might not have agreed to see her. Although
I'd have enticed you by mentioning it was a juicy pet law
matter."

"Which it is, though from the way she described it, I'm
afraid her buddy Ditch and she are out of luck. Terriers
can't inherit in this state." Of course, my mind had been
mulling over this matter for . . . oh, five minutes by now.

"Then again, as I told her, I need to see the will. If her departed friend was handed incompetent legal advice by the attorney who drafted the document, that's one avenue to explore. And maybe, as a layperson and not a lawyer, she's not fully describing what the will attempts to do. Maybe—"

"I knew you'd throw yourself into the case." Darryl's triumphant grin elicited a return one from me, though I attempted to obfuscate it by gnawing on my lips.

"Don't count Ditch's inherited millions before they're in his little Scotty paws," I grumped.

Darryl's lanky arms enveloped me in a bear hug that enticed Lexie to leap on both of us. He bent and gave her a hug as well, and then we were off.

I TOOK MY time during my gamut of pet-sitting rounds that evening. It was still Saturday, a sloppy day in January since the skies had decided to sprinkle a fine mist around L.A. That meant making sure my canine charges had dry feet after their constitutionals and before being let loose in their owners' homes.

My feline friends Abra and Cadabra took the opportunity to unnerve me. When I reached Harold Reddingham's home, left Lexie in the car, and let myself in, I saw no sign of cats anywhere. They hadn't eaten the food I'd left yesterday, and not even their litter box appeared used. I sniffed the air for an indication of kitty accidents elsewhere but sensed none. Harold had warned me once that I'd never see his kids, but I always had . . . before.

"Hey, guys," I called out. "Don't do this to me. You're here, aren't you?" Just in case, I examined all the windows in Harold's one-story abode, along with exits to the outside and the garage. No indication of a way the cats could escape. That was a relief, yet my psyche grew even more macabre, and I imagined deceased felines lying around somewhere, dying alone with no one to care for them. "Please come out," I cried.

I doubt it was because they deigned to feel sorry for me, but I discerned a faint mew from the direction of Harold's den. I hurried down the hall and slung open the door.

I'd hunted in here before and would swear the room was catless. But wherever they'd been, Abra and Cadabra now lolled on opposite sides of Harold's desktop. They both barely opened their eyes as I entered, as if my fear for their well-being was of no concern to them whatsoever.

Which was probably the case. But I was so happy to see them that I picked up Cadabra first and hugged him, then did the same with an affronted Abra.

"Don't do that to me again," I pleaded.

Both cats closed their eyes.

And me? I checked their food, water, and litter again before I left. After all, they were still my charges, even if my attention filled them with ennui.

AS ALWAYS, I left my own home as my final stop, to take care of Beggar for my temporary tenant, Russ Preesinger. Unless his wayward daughter had decided to see to the Irish setter herself.

Which, it turned out, she had. Not only that, Russ himself had come home to deal with the situation of Rachel's presence in California. I learned that when I knocked on the door of my main house and Russ responded. He looked really harried.

He waved me outside, where he tugged the door shut and proceeded to vent his frustrations to me.

"Rachel wants to stay here, with me," he said with what sounded like utter frustration. Russ's red hair was as dark a shade as his Irish setter's. He was of moderate height, muscular build, and masculine looks that undoubtedly made a lot of female heads turn. He'd certainly caught my attention when my tenant Charlotte LaVerne had introduced us.

Of course, I considered myself in a kind of committed relationship—then. Maybe. Jeff and I were trying to deal with Amanda back in his life. That wasn't long after we'd decided just to let whatever happened between him and me happen.

Besides, Russ hadn't handed me any indication he'd found me appealing. He probably hadn't, if the description Rachel had given of the kind of woman her dad liked was correct: a skinny, show-biz-type blonde. The guy struck me as less shallow, but hey, what did I know? I'd developed a distinctive knack for getting myself attracted to the wrong guy, commencing with the senior partner of my old law firm, up to and including Jeff.

In any event, like Jeff, Russ traveled a lot. He had only recently moved here from Arizona—where his daughter, Rachel, had fled from—because he'd left his job promoting industry for the City of Phoenix to join a local company as a Hollywood location scout.

I knew all this because it had been on his application to sublease my house. But there'd been no place on the form for him to fill in info on his former marriage and wayward daughter.

"How do you feel about her wanting to stay here?" I asked, realizing my question sounded as if it had come from a shrink. I wasn't sure myself whether I'd like having that difficult young adult occupy my house, especially when her dad was on the road.

Russ surprised me by laughing. He had a pleasant laugh that sounded as if it emanated from deep down in his diaphragm.

"Can you guess why she said she came?" he asked.

I suspected his question was essentially rhetorical. Sure

enough, he gave me no time to respond before he continued, "She's nineteen, and she's made it clear she doesn't need a custodian—just a meal ticket. Mostly, she wants me to introduce her to movie people since she wants to become a star. In fact, she seems damned sure that's the main reason I moved here to Hollywood—to help with her intended career. Not that she'd ever expressed an interest in acting before."

"How do you feel about her becoming an actress?" I asked, unsure what else to say—and again sounding like a shrink.

"At least it would have the potential of giving a direction to her life." He expelled air in a huge sigh. "But I'm just getting started in this business myself. I don't have contacts to get her into the industry, even if I wanted to. And then I'm traveling so much I can't be around to keep an eye on her—which I suspect is another reason she decided to come here. I know she's not getting along well with her mother, so I hate to send her back without a job or direction. But keeping her here . . ."

"Is a temporary solution," I supplied. "Put her on probation. Lay down some rules and say she can stay only if she sticks to them."

He peered at me peculiarly. "I had the impression you'd never been married and don't have kids," he said.

"That's right," I acknowledged.

"Then how do you know so much about how to handle them?"

My turn to laugh. "I was a kid once myself," I said lightly. I didn't intend to go into my own background, though—how my parents had divorced a couple of decades ago, and my dad was now happily remarried with a new, young family in Chicago. My mom was happily unmarried and a lawyer in D.C. My brother and I were as close as two very different people could be. He'd become a wealthy hotel mogul in Dallas.

I guess I saw a little of myself in Rachel Preesinger, though I hated admitting that even to me. The difference was that I doubted, when I was her age, that either of my parents would have been even marginally pleased to see me show up on their doorsteps.

Enough nasty nostalgia for one night. "Good luck with your decision," I told Russ, bent to pat Beggar, who'd joined us outside, then headed for my apartment over the garage, where Lexie waited.

I checked my answering machine.

Jeff hadn't called.

I sought out my cell phone display.

Nothing.

I sighed. It wasn't that I missed him exactly. But I was miserably curious about what happened at my office after I'd left Jeff and Noralles together. Not alone, of course, but Noralles had hinted he had a whole lot more questions for Jeff about Ezra's murder. No surprise, if he genuinely considered Jeff a real suspect.

As impossible as that was . . .

Oops. Somehow my fingers had slipped and my cell phone was dialing Jeff from its recall list of last numbers dialed. Might as well make the best of it.

"Hello," said a familiar voice in an unfamiliar tone. Shaky.

"Jeff, are you all right?" I demanded immediately.

"Not really," he said softly. "Why didn't you tell me how hellish it is to be considered a murder suspect?"

This wasn't a good time to tell him I had. He and I had just been getting to know each other back then, and I'd relied on him to help investigate who actually could have committed the killings I was accused of. With his travel schedule, though, I'd managed most of the legwork myself. But we'd talked often on the phone, and seen a lot of each other when he was in town.

And though I'd tried to put on a brave front, I'd never tried to hide my misery at being Noralles's main target.

Well . . . I hadn't tried too hard. In fact, I guess I'd attempted to put on a big, brave front, daring diva that I am.

I wasn't used to Jeff not being Mr. Macho. Which worried me a lot.

"Hey," I said. "Lexie just told me how much she misses Odin. Would he and you mind a little company tonight?"

"No," he said, sounding a teensy bit more cheerful. Which boosted my ego about a hundred notches. "Come on over. And while you're at it, could you stop for some dinner? Make it Thai."

Chapter Twelve

THE INITIAL PART of our evening together almost seemed like the edgy, exciting early days of our semirelationship, when we'd occasionally let our attraction overrule our common sense.

Had it been only a few months ago when pad thai and mee krob had seemed like the sexiest of aphrodisiacs? Heck, they still did—especially considering the way Jeff's blue eyes bored into mine with a heated expression that had nothing to do with the spiciness of our Thai food.

By the time we'd finished, I felt ready to grab Jeff's hand, hurry down the hall, and leap into bed with him.

Lexie and Odin reminded me of realities, though. Of course, both begged for leftovers before we left the table. And after we'd stood and started to bus our dishes, they determinedly herded us toward Jeff's back door for their evening outing.

We leashed them up and both put on water-resistant jackets with hoods. Once again, the January weather was less than Southern California perfect, and we were pelted with rain.

Which doused the fire that had ignited inside me at the dinner table. At least for now.

We walked along the sidewalks of the pleasant residential Sherman Oaks street. Illumination from houses and streetlights sparkled in the myriad of lakelike puddles along the avenue's shallow curbs. I'd always suspected that city engineers had scrimped when it came to installing adequate storm drain systems. Sure, L.A.'s rainy seasons tended to be short, but often strong storms turned streets into rivers.

At least the sky wept slowly tonight.

I told Jeff my Rachel tale, and he scolded me for forgetting to lock the house and gate when I left—especially after all that had happened previously in my ferret situation. He promised, though, to review my security situation again soon.

"Okay," I said next. "Spill it. And I don't mean empty the rain from your shoes. Tell me what went on at my office after I left this afternoon."

"Things were probably just as you'd assume, with Ned Noralles looking at me as his primary murder suspect." Jeff's disgusted sigh resounded beneath his rain hood. "I can't remember ever seeing the ass so happy before."

Jeff had known Noralles for ages, and the gallons of bad blood between them when they'd both been beginner cops with the L.A.P.D. obviously hadn't, even now, begun to evaporate. Jeff had told me the story before. The end of the tale had been when they'd resorted to raw and macho physicality. Ned Noralles had considered himself a lean, mean, fighting machine, but Jeff had nevertheless decked him. That incident led to Jeff's resignation from the department and the instigation of his new career as a private investigator. He'd claimed it had been worth it.

In the years since, they'd apparently tangled now and then even before my foray into the nightmare of being a murder suspect. Jeff had been ever so eager to help me trounce his former nemesis Noralles.

And now, it seemed, Ned Noralles was enjoying his revenge for all past problems between them. He'd hinted to Jeff that he had first volunteered as second-chair, out-of-jurisdiction detective on this case simply because I was connected with the crime scene, and had felt as if he'd struck gold when he found supposedly legitimate reason to look at Jeff as chief suspect.

"He claims that my bad temper is enough to constitute motive," Jeff grumbled now as he yanked on pokey Odin's leash to get his Akita strolling. "A lot of people heard my arguments with Ezra. As to opportunity, there was a crowd around your offices that night after the VORPO meeting. Doors probably weren't locked. Anyone could have come back. Even an activist or two from Vancino could have followed us there. But Ned seems sure that the one to return was me."

"Pretty flimsy," I fumed. "But in my admittedly limited experience, Ned loves to seek the easiest answer. He'll bird-dog it relentlessly till someone else pops probative evidence implicating a genuine suspect smack in his face. In your situation, he has the added benefit that his false but simple solution reaps revenge on you."

"Amen." Jeff's response resounded like a heartfelt growl.

I carelessly kicked at a few wet leaves on the sidewalk in front of me. It wasn't as if Los Angeles had a genuine fall season, but leaves from some of its trees briefly changed colors, died, and dropped to the ground over the rainy season's several months. Lexie stopped to sniff the end of a hedge, suggesting to me that a male dog had recently left his scent. She squatted on the spot, as if to show him she had equally territorial instincts, even in a territory that wasn't her home.

"So how else does Ned think he has you?" I asked Jeff. "I heard the alleged murder weapon was found on the floor—an unregistered gun." That's what I'd reaped from the law firm grapevine, no thanks to notification by Noralles.

"That's what I gathered," Jeff agreed.

"Your fingerprints aren't on it, of course. Nor anyone else's to clear you?"

"Nope." Jeff stopped walking, and the expression he turned on me seemed sharp in the shadows of the street-light. "You know if you weren't so pissy about my helping Amanda with her problem, we'd have been together that night. We could have supplied each other with verifiable alibis."

"Each other?" My voice was as shrill as Gigi's. "Are you suggesting that I should be considered a suspect in this one, too? That might make it easier on you, sure, but—"

I didn't finish. And not by choice . . . exactly. Jeff shut me up with a kiss.

One I didn't want to end.

When it did—it had to, after all, since we stood there along a residential street with the dogs straining at their leashes—Jeff stepped back and shrugged with what I took to be contrition. "I'm sorry, Kendra," he said softly.

"For the kiss?" I teased while realizing what he really meant.

"No, for not dealing with this whole thing very well. And for not understanding what you were going through when Ned was on *your* case."

"Tell you what," I told him. "Let's go back to your place, and I'll show you my suspect list. Maybe we can divide up which one of us speaks to whom. But we'll need to share notes and impressions."

"So you're going to play detective again and solve another murder?" There was a snap to his tone and a glint in his eye, neither especially appealing to me.

I stood up to my full five-five, glared right back into his

baby blues, and said, "As a matter of fact, Mr. Hubbard, I am. I intend to clear you of this crime, whether you want me to or not."

I anticipated an argument. Instead, I received a deep, genuine-sounding laugh. And another kiss.

"Something tells me it's time to head home," Jeff soon said hoarsely, still staring down at me—but smiling now.

This time, even the dogs agreed.

WE DIDN'T GO over my list until the next morning, and we had to hurry then since we'd overslept. Well, overstayed in bed. "Slept" was a major misnomer for what we'd been doing.

It was Sunday, but my pet clients were unlikely to sympathize with their sitter's sensual proclivities, let alone the idea that at least some lawyers forbore from working—much—on what was supposed to be the last day of the week.

So, after I rose, I left Lexie in Jeff's and Odin's company once more and prepared to visit my charges.

"If you wind up at your office, would you do me a favor?" Jeff asked before I departed.

"How did you guess I'd be going there?" I queried querulously. Was I becoming that much a creature of habit?

Maybe so.

"Well, stick it on your list for the next time you're there, but could you check to see if I left my navy sports jacket in your office? I can't find it, and I seem to recall taking it off yesterday when I was there."

He'd probably doffed it to free his fists in case he and Ned Noralles engaged in a free-for-all.

"Sure," I told him. "I'll look for it."

I spent the middle of the day in the Yurick offices—with only Gigi as company. Of sorts. At least, for the moment, she wasn't shrieking. I considered shoving her huge cage back to Ezra's office so she'd have more privacy, but decided against it. She seemed somewhat at home now in the kitchen.

"Gorgeous girl," I prompted her after making myself half a pot of coffee. She didn't respond. "Bottles of beer," I sang. Still no attempt at a tune.

I did some online research on whether hounds could inherit and, with Jeff's okay, spoke with his techy guru Althea over the phone. She promised to have dirt on everyone I named sometime the next day.

Eventually, it was time to do the day's second petsitting. Since I'd resumed my legal career, I'd had to give up my midday mutt-walking clients, since most were weekday customers. I stopped in briefly to pick up some stuff at my place and saw that no one, including Beggar, was at home in the main house. Did that mean Russ was bonding with daughter Rachel—or that he'd driven her to LAX to send her home?

Eventually, the Beamer headed its well-constructed metal nose back toward Jeff's. No Thai tonight. He and I went out, to a local diner, where we stared at each other over overdone fried chicken and tough pot roast.

That night was much like the prior one: fun. Once again we overslept, so to speak, the next morning.

"After I do my pet-sitting," I told Jeff over coffee and a buttered English muffin at his kitchen table, "I'll be at my office most of the day. I have legal matters to work on." Which included my dog bite case, the VORPO affair, and my new doggy-as-heir dilemma. "And I need to get the skinny from Althea about the suspects on my list. But this afternoon, I think I'll go see a lawyer about a former client."

So THERE I was in Century City on this dreary Monday afternoon. The law firm of Jambison & Jetts was in a high-rise on the Avenue of the Stars, so I parked in the lot for the Shoppingtown at Century City and strolled over.

I hadn't warned Jonathon Jetts I was coming. I figured that, even if he wasn't there, he wasn't the only person I wanted to see.

I got off the elevator and pushed open the door marked with the firm name. Behind it was a tall, forbidding desk. Behind the desk sat a tall and forbidding receptionist. Her dark hair was pulled straight back from her frosty face, and her eyes peered haughtily over a nose sufficiently pug for a prig of a person.

"May I help you?" she intoned as if by deigning to ask she was doing me a humongous favor.

I could help you, I thought. Or rather Mignon could. Maybe a few lessons from our friendly greeter would help earn this place the return of some clients.

I doubted that donning a friendly demeanor would get me through the door. Instead, I straightened my shoulders and intoned with a litigator's hauteur, "I am Kendra Ballantyne, here to see Jonathon Jetts."

"Mr. Jetts is with a client right now." She sounded pleased to put a roadblock in my path. "Do you have an appointment?" Was this how she'd been trained to take care of the front desk? She'd not last an instant in any firm where I had something to say about it.

"I'm early," I equivocated. "If he's not available immediately, I'd like to see Bella Quevedo." Had she taken Jonathon Jetts's last name when they'd wed? Uncertain, but unwilling to allow a little detail like that to deter me, I blustered on, "You may tell her I'm with the lawfirm of Yurick & Associates, and I'm here to discuss some clients that Ezra Cossner brought to us to handle."

This got a reaction from the repugnant receptionist. Her eyes widened and her lips curled. "I'll let Ms. Quevedo-Jetts know you are here," she said. Barely removing her gaze from me, as if she thought I'd purloin one of the potted plants if she looked away, she lifted a phone and punched in an extension. She murmured something too low for me to hear, then paused while someone on the other end replied.

"Ms. Quevedo-Jetts will be out in a moment," she eventually said. Her tone had lightened up by light-years. Had she been cautioned to treat me civilly?

A minute later, a lovely Latina who appeared to be in her early fifties came through the door. She was short but strode with self-confidence, her mid-calf skirt swishing about her legs. Her black hair, smooth around her face, was ornamented with a streak of white along one side. The shallow brackets about her mouth gave an impression that she smiled often—unlike her firm's drip of a dour receptionist.

"Ms. Ballantyne?" the attorney said in a tone denoting welcome.

"I'm Kendra, Ms. Quevedo-Jetts," I said with a smile.

"Then I'm Bella. Please come with me."

I wondered what this woman could have seen in a cranky codger like Ezra Cossner—or even in the chunky character she'd married, Jonathon Jetts.

Even more, I wondered whether she might have come to dislike something about Ezra enough to have ended his life.

And how I'd finesse the question without giving away that its answer was the real quest that had led me here. Or maybe I'd simply shed any subtlety.

I'd soon see.

Chapter Thirteen

OKAY, SO I'D gotten used to the informal aura pervading the Yurick office suite. I liked it. A lot.

As a result, my nose nearly lifted as snobbishly in the air as the receptionist's as I followed Bella. She led me down one hall and around a close-by corner. The hushed inner sanctum of the Jambison offices seemed even snootier than the reception area, and each wall harbored a piece of artwork that appeared authentic. Assuming I'd know authentic from fine faux.

I spotted a Picasso and a couple of Mirós. Prints? Perhaps. But if so, why the ornate frames, or the security cameras trained on them from the corners of the room?

I made mental note of the logos on the cameras so I could discuss their pedigrees with Jeff.

No one in this uppercrust firm seemed relegated to something as shameful as an open-air cubicle. Everyone apparently had an office, including support staff. Ponderous and private closed doors lined the long hallway on either side.

All this told me a lot. For one thing, Century City rent

wasn't cheap, though L.A.'s downtown was this year's winner in the perpetual prestige challenge between the two locales. And even that gorgon of a greeter probably took home a hefty salary. This firm's overhead was probably out of sight.

But its presence reeked. The scent sliming the air suggested that no one enforced L.A.'s ubiquitous smoking ban here—a result of working in a high-stress occupation in an even higher-stressed law firm.

I wasn't here to ogle the environment, though. I needed to instigate a conversation. "Your offices are very nice," I exaggerated to Bella.

"Thank you," she said. "Here we are."

She flung open one of those forbidding doors, revealing a sizable office lined with lots of wooden file cabinets and filled with sleek modern furniture: a large desk, naturally, faced by two tall chairs. Then there was the prim sitting area containing a white overstuffed sofa and matching seats that sat there and stared at one another.

Bella beckoned me to her side and sat gracefully on one of the chairs across from the couch.

I'd prescribed my opening line: a request for info about T.O., once her firm's client and now mine. But Bella spoke first. "So you knew Ezra?" she said with a sad sigh.

"Yes, though not for long. But he'd asked me to help him on some of the legal matters he brought to my firm." *And away from yours,* suggested my unspoken gibe. But prodding this seemingly kind and grieving person no longer seemed as appealing.

"You're representing T.O. in that difficult situation out in the Valley?"

"That's right," I agreed.

"And what about—" She rattled off a large list of companies, many I'd heard of, though I didn't realize Ezra had usurped their legal work and towed them along to the Yurick firm.

"Some," I acknowledged. "I haven't looked through the files, but a paralegal is indexing them for us. She's organizing the T.O. materials first, since it's the most pressing issue."

"Corrie Montez?" Bella asked.

"That's right. Ezra brought her with him, too, didn't he?"

"Ezra took a lot from us," Bella agreed, appearing not at all pleased about it.

"You knew him personally," I prompted.

The crinkles edging her dark eyes crumpled further as she glared at me. "Did Corrie tell you that?"

Revealing my initial source as her prize parrot trainer did not seem politic, so I ignored the question. I intended to quiz Corrie more anyway. "I gathered that you and he were an item for a while, but that you chose another partner here over Ezra."

She rose as the office door opened. I half expected to see her law partner–husband, Jonathon, stalk in to stand at her side. Instead, a young woman trod in bearing a tray with two steaming coffee mugs. She set them on the low, round table between us and hurriedly left after casting me an uncertain smile.

I wondered what the buzz was about me around this office. I hadn't hidden my name, but neither had I broadcast my background or reasons for being here. And only one of them was likely to be discernable to this circle of snooty strangers: my need to learn what I could about Ezra's clients.

No one would know what else was on my mind: scouting suspects in Ezra's murder.

Bella hadn't bothered to ask if I wanted a refreshment, but I was happy enough to indulge. The brew was strong, not necessarily a good thing. I didn't need a caffeine high to keep on my toes. My nerves were on edge already.

Inside, I stewed a bit about the bad timing of having

this stuff brought in. I'd hoped to delve more into Bella's background with Ezra. Now I'd have to introduce the topic again.

But the next interruption that occurred seconds later saved me from that situation. This time, Jonathon Jetts burst in. The burly brute of a height-challenged lawyer stood in the doorway for only a second, scowling. "What are you doing here, Ms. Ballantyne?" he barked.

"Hello, Mr. Jetts," I said sweetly as I stood and offered my hand. As angry as he looked, I hoped he wouldn't use it as a lever to tug my arm out of its socket. "I was hoping to get background information on some of the cases Ezra brought to the Yurick firm. We're going through his files, of course, but any additional insight would be greatly appreciated."

"No need to tell you anything," he snarled, though he shook my proffered hand professionally. "All those clients will come back to us now."

My smile broadened. "If I didn't know better," I said, "I'd think that gave you a motive to kill Ezra. *Another* motive," I added tellingly, taking a quick, hard look at his wife's now-pasty face. "Although I'm not sure whether you were both in on it. What about it, Bella?"

"I think you'd better leave," she said. Or at least that's how I interpreted the garbled words that came out as she ran to grab her husband's flailing fists. He'd moved away after our handshake, but now took several strides back toward me, and it was all I could do not to recoil.

"Of course," I said with contrived cheerfulness. "If necessary, I'll ask our new clients to insist that you talk to us about their cases. Oh, by the way—care to explain the allegations you made against Ezra when you met with him in our offices? Something about his advising clients to act illegally."

"No," Jetts growled.

"Then I'll have to assume it was an exaggeration, that

he acted like any good lawyer and advised his clients to approach legal limitations, if practical, without breaching them."

Jetts didn't deny it.

I couldn't help adding as I stood at the door, "Wish we'd had more time, Bella. I'll look forward to chatting again. I knew Ezra long enough to understand why you dumped him, but why you took up with this guy instead"—I gestured toward Jonathon—"is infinitely beyond my understanding. Maybe next time you can introduce me to Pinocchio. I'd love to meet your parrot."

And then I was alone in the big, pretentious hall, hearing an ear-battering argument from the office I'd just evacuated. Not very nice, for near-newlyweds.

Mentally, I conducted a twisted tally. I could hang Jonathon Jetts and his wife, Bella Quevedo-Jetts, high on my handy suspect list.

But I hadn't obtained a shred of evidence and had only useful, yet unreliable, instinct to prove that one or both were involved in Ezra's murder.

CENTURY CITY IS on the left side of L.A., if you're studying a local map. Not near the ocean, and decidedly east of nearby Westwood. Which was where I headed now.

To Jeff's office.

Would he be there? Not if my demanding druthers came true.

I found a metered space on Westwood Boulevard and walked some blocks to the four-story structure that housed Jeff's private investigation agency. The elevator to the third floor was slow—or maybe my impatience was immediate.

His office sat beside the elevator lobby. The plaque by the closed door proclaimed: HUBBARD SECURITY, LLC, followed by, JEFF HUBBARD, LICENSED PRIVATE INVESTIGATOR.

I opened the door and ambled in. No receptionist greeted me. In the waiting room, a couple of straight-backed chairs settled around a table containing a phone and magazines. The place reminded me of the end of an airline terminal, with spokes radiating from a central source. Several doors opened onto this room, and each gaped wide.

I wondered which was Jeff's.

I also wondered why, after knowing the guy several months and being close to him for much of the time, I'd never before ventured here. Had I subconsciously considered it his personal sanctuary?

If so, I'd probably have beelined here long before this.

"Who's there?" called a female voice that was definitely familiar. I'd heard the direct, no-nonsense tone numerous times over the phone.

It was Althea, Jeff's indispensable techy guru, the middle-aged maven whose Internet research skills—legitimate and more than slightly shady—were incredible. And invaluable.

"Hi, Althea. It's Kendra Ballantyne." I headed toward the voice's source, walking the long way around the offices.

I figured out which was Jeff's. It was the largest. It contained crates labeled with names and logos of security equipment suppliers that even I recognized. And it just happened to have his name on the door.

Fortunately, he wasn't there.

The next office was occupied by a young guy with hair shaved close to his head. His mouth spouted invectives into a phone. "You swore yesterday we'd have everything to-day. Damn it, that's not good enough. We promised to in-stall the rest of the system tomorrow. You effing well better get it to us fast." Obviously a security honcho, though maybe he engaged in investigations, too. The plaque next to his door proclaimed he was Buzz Dulear.

A woman walked out of the next door down and stood

watching me, with arms crossed and a suspicious stare. "You're Kendra Ballantyne?" Her tone tendered disbelief. She was pretty in a *Playboy* kind of way—curvaceous in her jeans and U.C.L.A. T-shirt, with blond hair that barely skimmed her shoulders.

This was the woman Jeff spoke of glowingly as his middle-aged computer geek, his aging techy wonder—mousy single mother of five grown kids, who was now in her fifties?

"You're Althea?" I sounded equally incredulous.

"The way Jeff described you, I knew you were one pretty lady, and smart, too," she said, still studying me. "He thinks so highly of you I expected a cross between Cameron Diaz, Hillary Clinton, and Maria Shriver. Oh, and also, since you manage pets, I threw in that pretty, outspoken wife of the Crocodile Hunter."

I shrugged as I smiled. "Well, here I am in reality."

"The reality's pretty good," Althea countered as I squirmed under her unyielding assessment. "A little self-conscious," she continued. "Attractive enough without being a bombshell. Blue eyes—a little chilly, but I'll bet they warm up now and then. And nice hair."

That, at least, was a lie. My unhighlighted mop was mousy.

She'd stopped speaking. Payback time. "And you're supposed to be some frumpy middle-aged marvel, not flippin' gorgeous!"

"Well preserved," Althea admitted with an unabashed grin. "I *am* fifty-four. And one of my kids is about to make me a grandma."

The guy Buzz, who'd exited his office, grinned gleefully at us. I hadn't realized when he was seated that he was a tall dude, a few inches over six feet. "Care to assess me?" he asked.

"No," Althea and I responded in unison.

"Come into my office," she said to me. "We'll talk."

"Jeff 's in *big* trouble," said Buzz.

IN MERE MINUTES, we were old friends.

We *were* old friends, from a few months back. I'd commenced holding helpful conversations with her when Jeff assigned her to reward me with research on anyone I needed dope on, back when I was accused of murder. We'd chatted often over the phone.

Her office was piled with paper, surprising since its inevitable pièce de résistance consisted of a state-of-the-art computer. It was connected to all means of ultramodern electronic gadgetry, including a printer that appeared as if it could talk. It probably *did* talk.

She'd known Jeff for a lot longer than I had, so after I'd removed a stack of paper from her single extra chair, I regarded her earnestly over her desk and asked, "Do you think Jeff could have killed Ezra Cossner?"

She snorted. She might be beautiful, but she obviously eschewed airs, unlike the snobs at the law firm I'd just left. "What do you think, Kendra? You've known him for a while."

"Ned Noralles has known him longer and considers him a suspect."

"Ned Noralles considered *you* a suspect a few months back, and we all know how that turned out."

I laughed. "Got it. So neither of us believes Jeff's a killer."

"I didn't say that," Althea riposted.

Which stopped me cold. "You *do* think he's a killer?"

"I didn't say that either." But she'd sounded serious. "I just don't see him killing Ezra Cossner in cold blood. And as far as I know, he hasn't killed anyone lately."

"He did as a cop?"

"Could be. Now, I've got printouts of info on everyone you said could be a suspect in Ezra's murder. Anyone else whose past you want me to pry into?"

A quick change of subject. It made me curious, but she obviously wouldn't fill me in further.

Jeff had already shown me the fruits of Althea's search on Ned Noralles. He'd had an interesting background that included minor transgressions as a teen, but nothing we could turn against him to twist him away from Jeff as a suspect.

"Yes, there is," I responded to Althea. I hadn't previously inserted Bella Quevedo-Jetts onto the part of my suspect list I'd imparted to Althea. I explained the lady's prior relationship to Ezra. "You know," I finished, "it wouldn't hurt to add the other attorneys at the Jambison firm to your search. It's not large, maybe ten lawyers. Any one could have resented Ezra's alleged client conversion."

"Okay. Oh, and I'll add Borden Yurick, too, and not just Elaine Aames from your current firm. Jeff told me to hold off on him, but Borden obviously had a history with Ezra or he wouldn't have hired him."

"Bordon couldn't kill anyone," I contradicted indignantly. "But it won't hurt to rule him out." My tone had deflated. "I can't think why he might have had it in for Ezra, so motive would be a mystery to me, but Ezra obviously had a talent for rubbing everyone the wrong way."

"Okay." Althea had been making notes, and now she looked up again. "What about anyone else Ezra might have known?"

"I only met him last week. I've no way of knowing about other acquaintances who despised him, but I can't help assuming there were many. He'd at least been greeted by others around our firm—attorneys, secretaries, our receptionist. And I've spoken with his parrot psychologist, though he was introduced to her only after he got Gigi, a few weeks ago. But the people I'm asking you to check are those I'm aware he was openly feuding with, and I'll feed you more names as I find out about them."

"Fine. Anything else?"

"Well . . . yes." The main reason I'd come here hadn't yet been broached, mostly because I'd obscured it from myself. "What can you tell me about Jeff's ex, Amanda?"

Althea's brown eyes grew agog. "You think she's a suspect?"

"No, but . . ." I stopped. "I didn't think so," I said slowly, "but with Jeff in the hot seat, if she resented him and thought the murder would be pinned on him . . ."

"Far-fetched, but worth exploring," Althea agreed. "What you were asking, though, was more about what made their relationship go south—and then come north again?"

"Exactly."

"Gossiping about one's boss isn't good form," she replied primly.

"Neither is researching the dirtiest little secrets of total strangers, and even resorting to hacking to do it," I retorted.

She grinned. "Who's hacking?" she asked innocently.

I laughed, and she responded by regaling me with the tale of how Jeff and Amanda met four years ago, when Jeff's security and investigation business finally started to take off. Amanda, in commercial real estate, met Jeff when her employer hired him to add a security system to a moderate-sized office building. Something clicked between them, and they were married a few months later.

Whatever it was had unclicked soon thereafter, though Jeff tried to keep things together for a year before giving up. But like the proverbial cobbler whose own kids go unshod, it was only at the end that Jeff considered checking Amanda's credit rating and love life. There *was* no credit rating—not any longer. She was way overextended, which definitely cast a pall on Jeff's finances.

And there was a love life that was unrestricted to Jeff.

He divorced her. End of story.

Only it wasn't. She was back.

I had to ask. "I know she's got him convinced she's being stalked."

"She *is* being stalked. I've checked. After Jeff and she broke up, she went wild on the dating scene. Hooked up with some real losers—and that one, Leon, has a record of abuse, stalking, you name it, short of murder. I can understand why the bitch sought out the best source to help her—her beloved ex, Jeff."

"Oh," I sad softly. "Then maybe I've read things wrong."

"No, you haven't. Amanda is genuinely and justifiably afraid for her life. But she's also using Leon to weasel her way back into Jeff's good graces. She probably realized she blew the best part of her life and wants it back."

"And him?" I had to ask. "What does he want?"

"He's a man, honey." Althea's beautiful full lips sucked in sympathetically. "He thinks with body parts beyond his brain. I love the guy like a brother more than a boss, but there are times I'd like to kick those brains right out his butt."

"Then—"

"Then if you want him, Kendra, you'll have to work at it. Good luck. Oh, and I'll have the skinny on these additional murder suspects for you tomorrow."

Chapter Fourteen

THOUGH—OR BECAUSE—Althea assured me that Jeff was expected back any minute, I said my farewells to Buzz and her, then buzzed back to my office.

A mistake, maybe. Gigi was at her loudest all over again. "Did something upset her?" I asked Mignon the moment I walked in.

"Sure," Mignon replied with a pained expression beneath the sharp crimson nails on the hands she'd slapped over her ears. "But no one knows what it is."

I resisted the urge to place my own, less dangerously tipped hands atop my own rebelling noise receptacles, and strode straight for the kitchen.

Elaine stood there looking frustrated and forlorn. "I don't know what to do with her," she shouted. "I've tried all the techniques Polly Bright suggested."

I knew the parrot professional had proposed that we distract Gigi often—as I'd inadvertently but instinctively assayed before. "I've got an idea," I called back. "Wait here."

I headed out to make sure the path was clear and the

prospective perch prepared. I also enlisted Borden, who'd secluded himself behind his shut office door.

Together, the three of us awkwardly propelled Gigi's cage down the hall and into Ezra's office. Maybe one person could have accomplished it less clumsily. But the kitchen clearly failed to provide a suitably soothing environment now. Hopefully, someplace slightly more familiar would do the trick. Of course, this particular place also held miserable memories for the confused macaw. But perhaps drastic measures trumped none.

To my amazement, my ploy succeeded—after, of course, an initial five minutes of screeches and flaps. Or maybe it was simply the act of accomplishing the unforeseen—relocating her. But suddenly Gigi grew so quiet that my ears started ringing.

"Great idea!" Borden told me. I hardly heard his soft words for the imaginary sounds in my head.

"Good thinking," echoed Elaine, her grin huge. It faded fast, though. "I don't know if I'll be able to adopt her," she said with a sigh. "I may not be creative enough to come up with things to surprise her, and so far I'm still in my condo. No more house hunting, at least for now."

"Aren't macaws supposed to be tame enough to perch on their owners' shoulders?" I asked.

Elaine shrugged her own. "You're the pet expert. But I'll ask Polly one of these days."

I watched while Elaine and Borden exited the office, leaving me standing there with the alert bird.

"What are we going to do with you?" I remarked rhetorically. I really liked this gorgeous girl, despite the quantity of personality quirks she exhibited. I wished I could come up with a way to keep her content.

Gigi's response to my query was to make a sound I hadn't heard from her before. It was songlike. Oh, yeah. I'd been informed that birds of the parrot class knew how to croon. Though this sound seemed vaguely familiar, I couldn't put my finger on what it was.

Oh, well. I had a few loose legal ends to work on before this day ended, so I couldn't stay here playing "Name That Tune."

"Glad you're feeling better, Gigi," I said. "I'll let Elaine know it's okay to feed you dinner whenever she's ready."

As if she understood what I'd said, Gigi stopped singing and started swaying on her perch, squawking quietly but rhythmically.

"I know she's fed you regularly," I told the macaw. "So don't try to convince me you're about to keel over from hunger."

She stopped swaying and squawking, and I used that opportunity to make my exit.

AFTER REVIEWING FILES and planning follow-up legal efforts, I headed off for my delightful pet-sitting duties of the evening.

I fortunately found Abra and Cadabra without any effort. Apparently their practical joke the other day had been enough. Both cats condescended to turn up in Harold Reddingam's kitchen, the tips of their tails curved in regal question marks—like, why hadn't I arrived earlier to feed them faster, as was their due?

"My apologies, your majesties," I said in pseudo-abjection as I poured kitty kibble into their dishes.

I expected Harold home in another few days. I'd miss visiting his personable pussycats.

Same went for Alexander the pit bull. His owner would be back in town at the nether end of this week. I hadn't many other pet-sitting clients lined up after lessening my availability.

Should I give up pet-sitting in favor of spending all my

time as an attorney again? The thought made me sigh as I sat in my car after tending Alexander. I liked the soothing routine of tending to generally grateful nonhumans.

I aimed my Beamer for my own home—ostensibly to check on Beggar, since Russ Preesinger had called to say he was back on the road scouting locations. He'd left Rachel in charge, but wasn't convinced he could count on her to care for his setter the way she should.

If Lexie had been parked at our apartment, I wouldn't have had to go anywhere else that evening. But she'd been left at Jeff's to keep Odin company. Kind of.

In some ways, it had been a conscious decision to convey to the private investigator of my dreams—who often kept me from sleeping at all—to assure him of my belief in his innocence.

It meant I'd have to go there tonight to at least retrieve Lexie . . . and after this weekend I figured it would be hard to head home. A good thing? Was I really putting the whole scenario about his ex-wife at the back of my mind?

If so, then why did it keep coming to the forefront to torment me?

I reached my home in the hills and pressed the button to open the gate. I drove inside and parked the Beamer in its regular spot, then headed for the house.

The door opened before I even got there. I anticipated I'd see Rachel.

Instead, I saw Russ. His sheepish grin seemed sweet and boyish, and I'd an impulse to ruffle his red hair.

Now, where had that come from?

"I thought you were out of town," I said somewhat snappishly.

His grin was replaced by a sigh and an embarrassed shrug. "Running late," he explained.

"Dad, I've given Beggar his dinner, but what does he get for dessert?" Rachel had slipped up behind Russ, and so had Beggar, who pushed his long red muzzle out the door and into my hand.

"Doggy dessert?" I asked.

"Of course," Rachel replied, her brown eyes landing incredulously on me. "All good dogs should get special treats. You're a pet-sitter. You should know that."

"Dessert's a people term," I pointed out.

"For dogs, it means extra treats like biscuits or stuff like rawhide that they can eat, or anything that's special but good for them." Her superior air would have irritated me under other circumstances, but I kind of liked her comment.

"I do give my charges treats," I told her, "but I've never called it dessert. Till now."

That earned me a smile from my house's subtenant and his pet-loving offspring. Enjoying their presence and attitude, I smiled back.

"Time for me to join Lexie," I told them. "I left her at a pet-sitting assignment where I usually spend the night." I didn't explain that the pet owner was sometimes home on those same nights. I wasn't sure I wanted Russ and Rachel Preesinger to know I had a kind-of relationship with Jeff.

And that made me extremely uneasy as I retrieved my Beamer and drove it toward Jeff's Sherman Oaks abode.

ON THE WAY, I recalled I'd scheduled a meeting first thing in the morning with Michael Kleer, the VORPO attorney. But I'd neglected to tote a necessary part of the file along to review when I'd departed my office.

An excellent excuse not to go to Jeff's till I'd cleared my mind a little more. If I couldn't understand what was going on in my addled brain, I didn't want to subject anyone else to my misguided mood.

I called Jeff. "I'll be there a little late," I said. "Have you taken care of the dogs?"

"They've been fed and walked, but they've been edgy. Guess they're missing you." A pause. "Me, too."

"I'll get there as soon as I can," I said in a surly tone, then, much nicer, I finished, "They deserve dessert, you know. So do we." I hung up before he could extract an explanation.

This time, when I saw lights on in the Yurick firm office, I was surprised. I soon discovered that the person present was Corrie Montez. "Surely Borden didn't exclude the support staff from his promise that we'd have fun practicing law," I told her when I found her inundated with work at her cubicle, files mounded all around her.

She smiled. Her big brown eyes drooped drowsily, and even her inevitable bright red lipstick looked as if it could stand refreshing. At least she was dressed down enough for late-night work, in faded jeans and a violet T-shirt. "I ought to get a life," she acknowledged. "But I wanted to finish indexing this file so I can get to that research I promised you—on how animals can inherit from their deceased owner."

"I appreciate it." I perched my butt on the border of her desk. "But don't kill yourself to do my work. I've assumed Borden's attitude about practicing law." Sort of. Old litigation habits lingered despite all excellent intentions. "We take cases we find interesting," I continued, as if convincing myself, "and enjoy working on them without billing humongous numbers of hours like our big-firm counterparts."

"I get it. Just a few more minutes, and I'll log off."

"Since it's my stuff you're working on, log on as long as you'd like." I laughed.

She laughed, too. "I don't need much sleep, but I promise to stop when I get too tired to take in what I'm reading. I can always come back early in the morning."

"Bet your former firm loved that attitude," I said. I had a sudden thought. Well, maybe not so sudden, considering where I'd been before, that day. "Speaking of megafirms and slave drivers, I visited your old employer earlier today."

"Jambison & Jetts?" At my nod, she inquired, "Why?"

How disclosing should I decide to be with her? After all, she'd known Ezra Cossner well, which landed her on my suspect list—even though I couldn't see Corrie offing her boss.

But to extract her reaction, I said, "Ostensibly, I was there to obtain whatever information I could on clients Ezra brought here, assuming they'd hang out with us. I didn't succeed in getting a lot of low-down from the lawyers there."

"But you had another reason to visit them?" She looked a little livelier now, and a lot more interested.

I nodded. "After learning that the feud between Jonathon Jetts and Ezra was somewhat fueled by a fight over a female, I wanted to meet that apparent vamp and assess Jonathon and her as possible murder suspects."

Corrie blinked, then brought the edges of her mouth up into a sad-seeming grin. "Poor Ezra. I heard of your reputation of solving murders, but . . . Well, a lot of people didn't like him. I don't suppose you've figured out yet which of them killed him?"

"No, but I'm working on it," I said. "What about you, Corrie?"

Her fingers rose defensively. "I honestly liked the guy. I wouldn't have killed him."

I'd purposely made my question ambiguous to see what her reaction would be—and I found it indubitably interesting. I hastened to act as if I'd erred in my phraseology. "I meant, do you know who killed him? I certainly don't think you did it." I punctuated my partly false statement with a laugh.

Her slim shoulders relaxed back into her desk chair. "That's a relief," she said. "And no, I don't know who killed Ezra. I wish I did."

So why did I have the sense that she was lying?

Chapter Fifteen

MY MIND WAS spinning around my conversation with Corrie when I edged into Ezra's office to see how Gigi was getting along.

The moment the macaw saw me, she started squawking, but at least it wasn't the worst of her shrieks with which she bombarded my eardrums this time.

Putting my purse down beside the open door, I let my mind lope down the list of suggestions Polly had made to calm and tame the ever-edgy bird. I squawked back at her as a distraction, but she kept chiming right in. I whistled, then sang several choruses about bottles of beer, but that only inspired her to grow even noisier. I even spoke soothingly, to no avail.

More drastic measures were required. I unlatched her cage door and shoved in my arm. "Step up, gorgeous girl," I told her. This was the typical parrot command that Polly taught and included in her books—some of which she'd left here, so I'd scanned them.

I was wearing a long-sleeved shirt, in a shade of blue

that complemented the macaw's colorfulness. To my surprise, Gigi did as I'd instructed. She soon sat on my shoulder, clamping her claws down, but not painfully. Did her squawks suddenly sound like purrs, or was that solely my optimistic imagination?

"You're very welcome," I said to her, assuming her sounds asserted thanks. "If you're really good, I'll let you come along with me, as long as I'm here."

I walked around Ezra's office, hoping that if Gigi got the urge to soar away, it'd be now, in this confined area. Since she made no indication of intending to ascend, I cracked open the office door.

Thankfully, she stayed on my shoulder as I gingerly edged down the hall toward my own Yurick digs. Once in my office, I closed the door. That way, Gigi would stay somewhat restrained should she change her mind and decide to fly. She scooted along my arm, and I wondered whether she'd maintain her bird balance when I bent to retrieve the files I'd come after.

No problem, for this nimble macaw.

Her weight on my arm and body was more substantial than I'd suspected, but heck, I shouldn't have been surprised. She was far from a sissy-sized bird.

"How would you handle the VORPO matter?" I asked aloud as I thumbed through the pages of notes I'd jotted, copies of the client's continuously changing site plans, and purchase and sale agreements for the properties already owned by T.O. I could see the per-square-foot price increase only slightly by agreement date, showing that T.O.'s strategy had succeeded in pulling the fleece over the property owners' eyes . . . till now.

From what I gathered, the only two unsold lots left on the subject block of Vancino Boulevard were the home of Millie Franzel's Pamperville Pet Place, and one owned by a company I hadn't heard of: SkinFlint Associates. Sounded rather risqué for such an upscale area, assuming the emphasis was on "skin" and not the usual meaning of "skinflint." I'd have to find out.

Perhaps it was time for a bloody field trip to the battle-ground the moment I had some extra time, which wouldn't be before tomorrow's VORPO-T.O. summit meeting.

I hadn't intended to boot up my computer, but decided to anyway when my thoughts started thrusting out an as-sortment of strategies on how to handle VORPO—some feasible and some largely ludicrous. But even the wildest could lead to tamer, more tangible possibilities, given time and reflection.

With Gigi's weight still perched steadily on my back and my subconscious smartly on the job, I opened a new file on my computer and let my fingers run free on all pos-sibilities. I saved it and sent the pages to print.

And yawned.

Which was when I heard a cry from down the hall. I stood quickly, wondering what was going on. The last time I'd heard a scream in the night, it had emanated from the pretty blue being who still stood on my shoulder.

My office door burst open. Corrie flew in, and stopped, staring at me, her hands at her throat, her young, face pale. "Oh, there she is. Thank heavens! I went into Ezra's office to see about Gigi, and she was gone."

"We're spending a little quality time together while I dig into some client files," I told Corrie. Her grand en-trance had excited Gigi, though, and the macaw let go of me and flew toward the door. "Close it!" I shouted.

Corrie complied, just in time.

"Okay," I said with a relieved sigh. "Enough fun for one night. I'm too tired to read anyway. Gigi, it's time for you to crawl back into your cage."

I let Corrie take Gigi, but we all walked down the hall in unison to Ezra's office.

"Here you are," Corrie said to Gigi when we reached her cage. She put out her hand, and Gigi fluttered her wing feathers. "Step up," said Corrie when her hand brought Gigi to her in-cage perch. Gigi complied without comment, and Corrie closed and latched the cage door.

"G'night, Gigi," I said, realizing I sounded sleepy. "Are you calling it a day . . . er, night, too?" I asked Corrie.

"Pretty soon, but I've worked up momentum briefing some of Ezra's client files and want to finish the one I'm working on so I can focus on your research tomorrow."

"Thanks, but like I said—"

"I won't overdo it on your account, I promise." She grinned. "Even if I can't finish your assignment."

"I didn't say *that*," I admonished and smiled back.

We headed toward the office door. I said good night to Corrie and Gigi, picked up my purse, and retrieved the files from my office that I'd determined to scan once more. When I got outside to the Beamer, I pulled my cell phone from my purse, wondering if I should warn Jeff that I was on my way to his place.

In case Amanda was there . . .

No. If I caught them *in flagrante delicto,* that would make up my mind where my relationship with Jeff was going. Fast.

With the light on inside my Beamer, I noted I'd missed a call. I checked the message. It was Jeff.

"Okay," I murmured to myself. "Now I've got an excuse to call him back."

Which I did. Only this time *he* didn't answer.

Heck.

I left a message on his machine and prepared to peel out of the parking lot toward his place. At least Lexie would be glad to see me. Odin, too. And, I hoped, Jeff.

Jeff. Oh, yeah. I remembered what he might have been calling about besides how much he missed me.

He'd requested that I search for his navy sport jacket, which he'd accidentally abandoned here the other day.

I could search for it tomorrow, of course. But since I

was still here, why not take a final foray around the office to see if I could spot it?

I stepped from the Beamer and used my key to unlock the office door once more.

In time to hear a highly human voice scream: "No!"

Followed by a massive, ugly, explosive sound that could only be a gunshot.

Gigi's now utterly recognizable avian shriek started, too.

My heart thudded so hard that I feared it made as much commotion as the bird and the gun. I backed quickly out of the door, closing it behind me. With quivering fingers, I yanked my cell phone from my purse and pressed in 911.

And was put on hold again.

Déjà vu all over again? Not quite. Last time, an unanticipated bird had precipitated my panic.

This time that same bird was involved, but I'd distinctly heard a human voice screaming "No!" And that gunshot . . .

Okay. I admit it. I'm not the boldest lawyer in the world. Not even the pluckiest layperson. What I wanted to do was run. Continue to hold for 911. Keep my own ordinary-sized nose out of trouble.

Only . . .

I'd feared before that someone had been hurt, when I'd first heard Gigi's screams, and I'd forced myself to investigate.

This time, I could assume with assurance that someone really had been hurt. Perhaps Corrie Montez, the only human inhabitant of the Yurick office that evening whom I knew about.

I had to find out if she was all right.

But someone who might still be inside there decidedly had a gun.

I tried 911 again. Hooray! This time I got an actual operator.

"I heard someone scream, then what sounded like a

gunshot," I exclaimed softly, not wanting anyone else who might be hanging around here to hear.

At the operator's urging, I identified the address and myself.

She told me to stay outside and await the police officers she was preparing to send.

Fine with me.

Except . . .

Sure, call me stupid. Foolish, at least. But what if Corrie had been shot and was still alive?

How would I feel if I learned later that I could have helped her but didn't?

If I didn't go back inside, I would surely survive to know exactly how I'd feel, one way or the other. That was the smartest, safest course of action.

But . . .

The *buts* were beating me over the head. I had a can of pepper spray in my purse, the result of prior danger and of my pet-sitting, which often got me out alone in the dark. I reached down into my bag, felt around till I identified the familiar tube-shaped container, and pulled it out. Aimed it ahead of me. Prepared to push the button, just in case.

As if it would outblast a gun . . .

I slowly opened the office door and peered around its edge.

Saw no one.

I slipped inside, wishing Gigi wasn't still screaming. Her shrieks could mask the sound of someone sneaking the other direction. Toward *me*.

I made my way slowly through the reception area and down the hall toward Ezra's office.

Was that where this latest shot had been discharged— like the one that had ended Ezra's life? Or had just the sound, and not the sight, been what had set Gigi shrieking?

I had to look in if I could, to make sure my friends the

macaw and the paralegal were okay. How could I do that without getting myself killed?

As I may have mentioned before, I occasionally watch cop shows and take in violent movies. An idea struck me.

But I didn't want any bullets to do the same.

I ducked while duck-walking a few feet backward from the door. And then I screamed, "This is the police. Come out with your hands up."

I half hoped I'd hear nothing but Gigi so I'd feel somewhat okay about bursting in.

Instead, what I heard sounded like shattering glass. A window breaking?

Damn my sense of self-preservation and any unchained torpedos! Full speed ahead.

I stood and shoved the door open.

And then it was my turn to scream in accompaniment with Gigi, who remained flapping and shrieking, inside her cage.

On the floor lay Corrie Montez, her formerly pretty violet T-shirt covered in blood. Her brown eyes were open and glazed.

Frantic, I scanned the room to ensure I wasn't about to be attacked, too, but saw nothing else that hadn't been there before.

Except said shattered window.

My eyes darting everywhere, I knelt and felt Corrie's neck for a pulse.

Nothing.

I grabbed her wrist and sensed the same.

Nothing.

It was my turn to scream, "No!" Stupidly I stood and rushed toward what had once been a window.

I glanced outside and saw a dark shape dashing through the parking lot.

Unfortunately, the shape saw me, too. It didn't stop, but

I saw what looked like a hand raise—one holding a gun that glinted in the faint outside lighting.

I ducked, even as I heard another detonation of gunfire.

The little bit of glass left in the window exploded and rained down where I crouched.

I didn't move for several long seconds.

At least.

I recognized then that I'd unconsciously picked up the sound of sirens in the distance, drawing nearer.

In a minute, I heard, though I couldn't say from where, what sounded like a long-delayed echo.

"This is the police."

Chapter Sixteen

I SAT IN a booth in what was once the restaurant's bar, wishing the place was still stocked with Chivas instead of cops. Officers popped in and out as often as lounge patrons. Only two people stayed without stirring.

One was me.

I was, in fact, stirring somewhat, though I hadn't shifted positions in probably fifteen minutes. My body still shook, although the temblors had slowed from Level 6 on the Richter Scale to spasmodic shudders every minute or so.

"No," I said slowly and distinctly to Detective Candace Schwinglan, the supposed top cop on this case, though I anticipated Ned Noralles's "assistance" on this one as well. For now, Schwinglan barraged me with questions. "I didn't see anyone sneak in," I continued. "I was sitting in my car in the parking lot, and I couldn't see the office's front door from there, even if I'd been sure it required an attorney's observation. My space was too far along the side of the building."

I kept my hands clenched on the table in front of me.

My legs, in their dark blue slacks, also wedged together to still their shaking—somewhat.

"Mmm-hmm," Schwinglan said, sounding somewhat affirmative, but I figured she just made a noise to keep the conversation going. Though she seemed smart, Candace Schwinglan wasn't as astute an interrogator as her putative partner Ned. She seemed awfully wide awake for so late at night, but of course her thinness, emphasized by her black pantsuit, suggested that she stayed perpetually active. Or maybe she had great genes to assist in the weight department. "And you're sure no one was in the building besides Ms. Montez and yourself?"

"No." I sighed. "I'm not sure. I didn't see or hear anyone, but someone could have sneaked in and hidden somewhere."

Schwinglan leaned forward in the booth, clutching her notebook in one hand and stretching out the other, as if she had an urge to shake something more useful from me. Maybe impatience kept her thin.

A sound from the doorway startled me. I looked up to see—who else?—Detective Ned Noralles standing there. The handsome detective approached our booth and motioned the scowling Schwinglan to scoot farther into her seat. "I'm here to help again," he said, and to her credit she didn't tell him what to do with his help. Instead, she did as he asked and slid in.

Noralles's suit was a lighter shade than usual, medium brown, and it was rumpled, as if he'd donned it fast to dash into the night to play assistant detective.

"I don't suppose the cops outside nabbed the killer," I said sorrowfully. I couldn't tell a thing from the guy's steadfast expression, but figured he'd be grinning if he had good news.

"No," Noralles admitted. "But they did find the gun."

"Really?" I perked up a bit. "I don't suppose it was registered, and you've already run down the shooter's I.D. Or that it was covered in the killer's good, strong fingerprints."

"You suppose right, Kendra, though the lab will check

for prints anyhow. Doesn't look likely they'll find anything, though."

Ah, we were on a first-name basis today, probably a good thing. He always referred to me as "Ms. Ballantyne" when we were at odds against one another—the usual state of our acquaintance.

But Ned sounded stymied, which wasn't what I was hoping for. "Any idea who it was?" I asked, looking at Schwinglan, again at least nominally in the top cop spot on this investigation.

"Why don't you tell me?" she countered, arching her already curved brown brows. "You were the one who was shot at."

"Corrie, too," I reminded her.

"Corrie, too," she acknowledged. "But she for certain isn't talking."

My shuddering started all over again. "Wh-what about any other witnesses?" I queried them both quietly. "Did any neighbors happen to hear something and peer out their windows?"

"This is mostly a commercial area," Schwinglan refreshed my emotion-ravaged recollection. "There's a gas station with a convenience store at the end of the block and a coffee shop across from it, but the closest buildings to your offices are stores that were closed."

"Someone driving by on Ventura Boulevard?" I proposed hopefully.

Ned's turn to take over. "The office where Ms. Montez— and Ezra Cossner, of course—were killed is at the side of the building, which isn't easily in view of the street."

I nodded knowingly. "Plus," I added, "I saw the killer head the opposite direction after shooting at me. Did any people living in the apartments behind our offices see anything?"

"We've got people canvassing them," Ned said, "but so far I haven't heard of anything useful."

I sighed. So did both Ned and Candace—which was how I currently thought of Schwinglan, since Ned and I were now first-name chums.

And then Ned said, "I'm sure you've gone over this with Detective Schwinglan, but was there anything in particular you noticed about the suspect when you saw him running away?"

Almost involuntarily, I replayed the bloodcurdling occurrence in my mind: the dark, indistinct fleeing form, the burst of light ricocheting off the gun, the ear-splitting blast, the shower of exploding glass.

"Not especially," I responded, then described aloud all the shudder-inducing details I'd seen.

"Did you notice the suspect's clothing?" Ned asked, his voice soft yet insistent.

I pondered for a second before saying, "Not really."

"Any facial features?"

"It was too dark to see," I responded.

"How about the way he ran—anything special? Anything familiar?"

And then I got it. Talk about staying obtuse. "No," I countered curtly. "What is it you're driving at?"

"I'm not driving at anything," Noralles prevaricated in a particularly innocent tone. I noticed him share a short glance with Schwinglan and grew certain my suspicions were true.

"I've told you all I know," I said. "Now share something with me."

"Like?"

"Like, who's at the top of your suspect list?"

Only for an instant did Ned's studiously blank expression suggest triumph. "Oh, we're still working on that."

"But you think it's Jeff," I blurted baldly, having an urge to reach across the table and start torturing this tormenting detective, tearing out his hair strand by dark strand.

Not that his temporary detective-in-charge, Candace, would let me get too far in fulfilling that fantasy.

"Hubbard?" Ned said snidely. "Why do you say that? Did the suspect remind you of him?"

I stood. "Don't turn it on me, Detective. I'm just guessing here. Why do you think it could be Jeff?"

"Did I mention him?" he goaded with a grin.

"You thought he might have killed Ezra, but at least you had a teensy chance of making a case there, since Ezra and he had been arguing. But what possible motive would Jeff have had to murder Corrie?"

"You tell me," Ned said. "But if what you come up with involves the possibility that Ms. Montez saw Jeff around your offices at the time Mr. Cossner was killed—or even witnessed the murder—well, you just might be reading my mind."

That bright, baiting grin again. My fury intensified, and I grabbed my purse from the booth. "If you have questions I haven't already answered, you know where to find me, Detectives."

"Your home or Mr. Hubbard's?" Ned asked, obviously still passionate about provoking me. He shared another knowing glance with stone-faced Candace.

"Good night," I shouted over my shoulder.

I'd have stalked out of the offices, but I couldn't help staying concerned about Gigi. Her screams had stopped, but I still heard a loud squawk now and then. I forced my feet to take me to the hall outside Ezra's office. But Gigi's voice didn't emanate from there.

"Where's Gigi?" I asked a guy in a shirt that identified him as a Scientific Investigation Division sort.

"Who?"

"The bird."

The guy's grimace told me that Gigi hadn't scored any positive points with him. "The kitchen. I think."

Sure enough, that's where she was. Her large cage had

been wheeled in, and she stood on her perch staring at me as I entered the room. "Hi, girl," I said softly. "I know it's a silly question, but are you okay?"

She shrieked and flapped her wings. I noticed a few blue feathers at the base of her cage. Too many feathers for her simply to have shed them.

"Don't pluck yourself," I pleaded sympathetically. When I'd thumbed through some of Polly's bird books, I'd scanned slowly through particularly poignant parrot details. For one thing, I'd learned that emotional parrot-types sometimes pulled out their own plumes. "No more than you already have, Gigi. Please."

Her response was another sorrowful squawk. I wanted so badly to soothe her that I started singing what had become our anthem. "Ninety-nine bottles of beer—"

She interrupted me with a song of her own, of sorts. It was a tune she'd tried out on me before, one that sounded vaguely familiar without my being able to place it. She ceased after a few croaky notes.

"Hang in there," I told her, glancing at her talons, which held tightly to her perch. "And if you happen to be able to tell me—"

"I thought you left, Kendra," said Ned Noralles's voice from the doorway.

Gigi started screaming once more.

"I'm going now," I told him. "It's your turn to calm this poor bird down."

"She's our only eyewitness to both murders," Ned Noralles said. "And I understand that she's a talking macaw." He approached Gigi's cage. "Hiya, bird," he crooned. "How 'bout telling us who you saw shoot Mr. Cossner and Ms. Montez."

Gigi's demeanor didn't change.

I wondered again whether Detective Noralles read the same mysteries or engrossed himself in the same TV fiction that Darryl Nestler favored.

And whether there was a semblance of truth in those stories—that a bird actually could assist in identifying a murderer.

If so, the noisy, nervous Gigi clearly wasn't about to do so. Not now.

Ignoring Ned, I again neared the cage. "Good night, gorgeous girl," I said softly. "See you tomorrow."

Just as I reached the door to exit, it was yanked open and Borden Yurick rushed in.

I'd called him earlier to let him know what had happened. I didn't exactly remember when. I'd called Elaine, too. Both had answered immediately and sounded as if I'd awakened them. Maybe. That didn't necessarily eliminate them from my elongating suspect list.

"Kendra, are you all right?" Borden demanded, grabbing my shoulders in his skinny hands and examining me with eyes that were magnified and full of concern beneath his bifocals.

"More or less," I said sadly.

"Hello, Mr. Yurick," said a female voice from behind me. I left Borden with Detective Schwinglan.

And then, finally, I dragged my dog-tired body to my Beamer.

I DIDN'T CONSIDER Jeff a genuine murder suspect.

But on the short drive to his Sherman Oaks home, I couldn't help contemplating that I'd missed his call earlier . . . and that he not only hadn't answered when I'd attempted to return it, but also hadn't rung me back.

He'd have realized I'd tried to reach him. Why hadn't he phoned to at least find out where I was? It was now nearly 2 A.M. I could have had an accident somewhere and been lying injured and alone on the perilous shoulder of some far-off freeway.

I could have been shot and laid out in the County Coroner's Office . . . like Corrie Montez.

As my stupid shaking started again, my cell phone finally sang "It's My Life."

Better than wailing, "It's My Death . . ."

I'd taken surface streets so, stopped at a light, I retrieved my receiver from my purse and looked at the display while under a streetlight.

Jeff's number.

Had I somehow reached him through extrasensory perception instead of our respective cellular networks?

"Hi, Jeff," I answered, simulating cheerfulness.

"Where the hell are you, Kendra? Are you all right?"

"Just fine. And you?"

"I'll be a lot better when I know you're here safely. Where've you been?"

"I'll be pulling into your driveway in about"—I glanced at the digital readout on my dashboard—"four minutes. Did you get my message before, when I tried to return your call?"

"No. I . . . fell asleep."

Damn, but I'd always assumed a professional private investigator would have nailed seamless lying as a special skill of the profession.

Where had he been?

In the same neighborhood as I was, shooting a paralegal to death and scaring me shitless with the same gun?

I didn't really believe that . . . did I?

No, more likely he'd had a torrid tryst with his ex, Amanda. She'd have called him, sobbing that her lurid stalker Leon was after her yet again, and couldn't big, brave Jeff come and protect her?

He'd have responded heroically to that request, and while he reassured her that she was safe, she might have sniffled and sighed and changed into something sexy, and seduced him.

Now that I could absolutely believe.

I knew from experience that Jeff buried himself uninhibitedly into his infinitely sexy lovemaking. So much that he inevitably became exhausted.

And fell asleep.

"Damn!" I exclaimed inside the Beamer as I made the final turn onto Jeff's block.

I parked in his driveway and trudged up the walk past his big black Escalade to his front door. At least there was no cherry red Camry asserting Amanda's presence, too.

Might Amanda be the murderer? The thought had crossed my mind once in Ezra's case, but her connection was far too tenuous to be taken seriously.

I didn't have to use the key. Jeff was waiting right there for me, along with Odin and Lexie.

The two pups greeted me with such adoration and enthusiasm that I burst into tears.

"What's wrong, Kendra?" Jeff demanded, dragging me into his arms.

Okay, I'm human. I needed a hug right about then, even from one basis for my blasted misery. I let him hold me, even as Lexie and Odin rubbed against my legs.

"What's wrong?" Jeff asked again as he gently guided me in the direction of his bedroom.

"Corrie Montez was murdered tonight," I rasped, then regaled him with the *Reader's Digest* version of what happened, including the fact I'd been shot at, too.

His resulting anger, outrage, and fear couldn't have been faked.

At least I didn't think so.

But as I'd reached his Escalade on my way into the house, I'd let my hand caress its hood.

The car hadn't been home long, for it clearly hadn't had time to cool down.

Its engine remained revealingly hot.

Chapter Seventeen

No, I DIDN'T confront Jeff with the confusing suspicions invading my brain. Maybe my exhaustion inserted them there.

Or maybe not.

I did ask again where he'd been. I said I'd stumbled against the Escalade on my way into his house and had noticed its engine was warm. Wasn't that an indication it had been driven recently?

"Sure," he replied breezily as we completed our procession to his bedroom. "I took the dogs for a ride when I got home. We stopped for a treat: ice cream for me, the cone for them."

I glanced at the adorable beggars by our feet. If they knew that wasn't the truth, they weren't barking about it.

We all went to bed—together in the same room. In the same bed, even. And without Jeff and I indulging in hanky-panky that awfully early hour of the morning, we slept.

Sort of.

Even as tired as I was, I couldn't quite turn off my brain.

Maybe someday someone would invent a remote control for the mind, like the kind you can just point at your TV and, pop, off it goes, into suspended animation.

I needed one that night.

Too much mischief kept teasing my thoughts, and now it was all underscored by Jeff's soft, rhythmic snores. The sleep of the innocent?

Ice cream, my eye! But I still preferred assuming he was sleeping with Amanda to considering him a killer.

HEY, I THOUGHT as I awakened to the sound of a news reporter on the clock radio a few hours later, *I'd actually dozed off!*

Jeff, pups, and I got moving immediately and did our regular breakfast-and-romp routine.

I needed to move my mind off the horrifying murders in the Yurick offices. And the lesser yet fearsome fact that I'd been shot at.

And the increasingly sorry situation between Jeff Hubbard and me.

When I left a short while later, I brought Lexie along as I performed pet-sitting rounds, then headed back to our Hollywood Hills home. Both Russ Preesinger and his daughter, Rachel, were in town, so pet-tending Beggar wasn't necessary. I didn't see people or pup anywhere, so Lexie and I headed to our apartment over the garage.

There, I sat at my small desk in the corner of my bedroom and aimed a quick call at my client Brian O'Barlen. *Where were you last night around eleven?* I demanded in my head. "Have you heard what happened at our offices last night?" was what I asked aloud.

Of course he'd heard of the most current Yurick firm murder. L.A.'s reporters were nothing if not omnipresent. They'd jumped on this new twist and started twirling it, so the whole world now knew that poor paralegal Corrie

Montez was blown away in the very same office that her former boss, Ezra Cossner, had been.

Oh, yes, and an attorney who'd happened to be around was also shot at. Fortunately, none mentioned me by name.

"Should we cancel our meeting with the VORPO folks?" O'Barlen asked.

"Let's reschedule for this afternoon instead of this morning," I suggested. "We'll change the location, too. I'll call their attorney, Michael Kleer, and say we'll be at his office around three this afternoon."

Maybe, out of respect for Corrie, I should have canceled altogether, but I didn't think she'd mind—especially since my intent was to surreptitiously interview the attendees as to their activities last night. I had an urge to see all the players in this situation as promptly as possible. I wanted to examine the looks on their faces. Maybe their expressions would expose which of them could be a double murderer.

Next, I booted up my own computer and tapped remotely into the Yurick firm's access to the best research databases in the legal world. I needed to escape my reality for a while, and lose myself in research about deceased dog owners and what could happen if they tried to make their surviving pets their heirs.

I spent a couple of hours on this, wondering woefully if I was replicating research Corrie had already accomplished. I might never know, if her files were confiscated by the cops as Ezra's were, although his were sealed at least for now, thanks to our assertion of attorney-client privilege. And I wanted to get started on this case since Darryl's nice neighbor, Irma Etherton, had seemed extremely concerned when I'd conversed with her a couple of days ago.

When I'd spent all the time I had available for now, I hadn't yet devised a strategy to set things right for the heir-triggered pup. I doubted Irma's four-footed friend would have a legal leg to stand on. Somehow, though, I'd have to find a way for her to win.

Next, I spent some quality time on my dog-bite case. Poor Lester the basset hound. I just didn't see him as a nasty neighbor-nibbler.

I'd done a good job so far in presenting my client's case to the court via pleadings and arguments supporting them. I didn't anticipate success in my summary judgment motion, so I wouldn't feel dejected to lose. I'd warned my client Cal Orlando, Lester's owner, to expect a possible loss, and let him know I'd keep my costs low but wanted to argue the motion as a legal maneuver. It would harass the plaintiff, Sheldon Siltridge, and cost him beaucoup bucks, since his attorney, Jerry Ralphson, had a reputation of taking his good old time in handling each case, and charging clients for every split second.

Okay, so I'm not the nicest person in the cosmos. I'm a litigator . . . again. And this type of tactic isn't unfamiliar in the lawsuit world. If nothing else, seeing dollars sail out the window sometimes gets a plaintiff to consider acting reasonable across a settlement table.

Speaking of Cal Orlando, I decided to give him a call. Not to find out where he'd been late last night, as I'd wondered with everyone else I wanted to talk to that day, but just to give him a few client strokes over the phone. Let him know what I anticipated next.

"Hi, Cal," I said when he answered on the first ring. "This is Kendra—"

"I was just going to call you. He's at it again."

"Who's at what?" I responded, sounding stupidly like the old Abbott and Costello "Who's on first" routine.

"Sheldon. Next door. He must have been mad about that motion you filed. I saw him throw some of his mail into my yard this morning. I'm sure he's just waiting for me to let Lester out so he can sneak behind my fence and start beating my poor dog with a rolled newspaper again. If he did that to me, *I'd* bite him."

"Too bad it's not a federal offense to tamper with one's

own mail," I mused. "At least I don't think it is. Tell you
what. Just pick the stuff up and toss it back into his
yard . . . this time. I have an idea."

After we hung up, I made another call—to one of those
very people whose whereabouts last night I'd pondered.
All night, in fact.

"Jeff, hi," I said, noting that he answered his cell phone
immediately this time. "I'd like you to do me a favor, for
one of my clients."

"Sure, darlin'," he replied with a little of his old confidence coming through. I told him what I needed. "I'll get
on it right away," he agreed immediately.

"Thanks."

"See you tonight?"

In your dreams, I thought. "Sure," I said, not quickly
coming up with a suitable excuse . . . like, I kick the *cojones*
of guys who lie to me. I don't sleep with 'em. "I'll call you
later and we'll make plans." By then, I'd have come up
with something as false as what he'd been feeding me.

When I hung up, I didn't have a hell of a lot of time to
hang around home moping. "Come on, Lexie," I said. "My
meeting starts in an hour."

When we reached the Beamer, though, it wasn't alone.
A small green sports jobby blocked it in the driveway—
shades of when my tenant Charlotte was around, tossing
parties right and left. Only then I was more often blocked
out than in.

Pissed, I stomped up to the front door of the main
house. It opened nearly as fast as I rang the bell. Rachel
stood there, more dressed up than I'd ever seen her, in a
very unteenage low and satiny black tank top, and a short,
flowered skirt. Or at least it all appeared more adult than I
would allow a teen of mine to toss on her body if I were
that old and encumbered.

Beggar barked somewhere inside the house, from the
direction of the kitchen.

"Whose car . . ." I began to ask, and then saw Russ behind Rachel. He wore what looked like an Armani suit, charcoal over a paler gray shirt, no necktie.

It all went well with his deep red hair. He looked damned good. And apparently he hadn't vetoed his daughter's display.

"Sorry, Kendra," he said. "We just popped back here to get dressed for an audition I'm taking Rachel to, so she can see what they're really like. I thought we'd leave faster than this, so I parked any old way."

"Your car?" I asked.

"Rented for the day. It's part of the show biz ambiance—the false front. You know. I'm trying to demonstrate the frivolity to Rachel. How shallow it all is."

"And you think that'll keep her from wanting more?" Especially when every guy on the set started ogling her . . .

We were talking right in front of the subject of our discussion, who stood there smirking at the silliness of the older generation. Not that I considered myself part of that portion of the population.

"It's just a game, Kendra," she said. "And if I can get my dad to play it with me for a while, why not?"

Okay, so tact wasn't always uppermost in my litigator's mental library. "Your outfit's a little risqué, Rachel, isn't it?"

"Part of the game," she tossed out airily as if daring me to play.

I didn't. "As long as you understand . . ." I started, instantly realizing I came across as an old fogy . . . even worse than her permissive papa. "Hell," I finished. "Break a leg. Better yet, break both. Your arms, too. And land a really meaty role."

"Whose side are you on?" Russ's ambivalence steamed over me.

I hissed it right back. "I'm on the side of enjoying life while you can." And realized I meant it. These days, my life had taken a turn for the better, after the awfulness of a few months back. But even at that, I was all too aware of its transitory nature, after seeing first Ezra's, then Corrie's, corpse and being shot at myself.

Hell, where had all this philosophical musing emanated from? I thrust it all way back into whatever lobe of my brain had shaped it.

"I've got to run," I said, "so if you wouldn't mind letting me out of the driveway . . ."

"Right away," Russ said, and he and his daughter per-ambulated past me and slid into that cool car.

Maybe I'd be able to talk him into a ride, if he didn't have to turn it in too quickly . . .

I USED LEXIE as my excuse to visit Darryl before dashing off to my meeting. I mean, I couldn't exactly have her act as my escort for a conference at a major law firm. And so, I accompanied her inside the Doggy Indulgence Day Re-sort for a short visit. Mine, not hers. She was going to linger for a nice, long while.

Darryl was in his office, and after releasing Lexie to the care of one of the resort's enthusiastic caretakers, I dashed inside to say hello.

"You're all right." The sentence contained both a ques-tion and an observation from my dear friend Darryl, who stood up at his desk the instant I entered. He stared search-ingly at me through his wire-rims.

"Physically, fine." With Darryl, dissembling was unnec-essary.

"You've gone through an awful lot," he observed. "Want to talk about it?"

"I sure do, but I don't have time now. I'm already running late for a big meeting. Keep a close eye on Lexie for me?"

"You know I'll take good care of her. And you take bet-ter care of *you* or I'll tie you down here like one of my nas-tier charges."

"Sounds kinky," I said.

"The kinkiest." He grinned goodbye, and I left.

VORPO'S LAWYER, MICHAEL Kleer, might have looked as if he was barely older than a survivor of the frenzied first year of law school, but he had the backing of a major firm behind him. Martin, Martin & Mays had offices in all major California cities, including San Francisco, Sacramento, San Diego, and L.A.'s San Fernando Valley—Woodland Hills, to be exact. I wondered if they'd ever considered opening an office in a place that didn't begin with the letter *S*.

Their offices took up the better part of an elegant three-story building in the upscale commercial area known as Warner Center. I met Brian O'Barlen and his convoy of sycophants in the parking lot, and we stalked inside together.

Brian was clad in a cable-knit sweater over nice slacks. His toadies were similarly attired. We were all told to take seats in the reception area by a professional-looking older woman, who spoke to someone on the phone and then ushered us into an adjoining conference room.

In a few minutes, Michael Kleer sidled in, accompanied by his clients, including Millie Franzel and the VORPO pres, Flint Daniels. What, no broker? Bobby Lawrence was missing once more.

Kleer looked like a kid playing dress-up in his button-down shirt and crisply pleated trousers. Daniels's scowl didn't disguise that he hadn't thought this meeting worthy of wearing anything better than sweats and jeans. Millie wore one of her doggy-decorator blouses, of course.

After serving ourselves coffee from a waiting carafe, we all took our places around a vast table.

Let the glaring begin!

Which it did. I decided to take charge of the meeting first off. But not exactly the way I'd planned it.

"I don't suppose any of you would admit to being on Ventura Boulevard in Encino at about eleven o'clock last night, would you? Oh, and carrying a gun?"

"I would," Millie said.

Chapter Eighteen

MICHAEL KLEER WAS immediately on his Ferragamo-clad feet, pushing his upholstered chair far from his firm's vast conference table. "I'm counseling you to keep quiet, Millie," he exclaimed.

"I've nothing to hide." She waved him back down with hands that were, surprisingly, unmanicured, in contrast to her otherwise pampered appearance.

I leaned forward, anticipating one heck of a confession to spew out—even though, of my suspects, Millie sagged way down on my list of those I'd like to be guilty.

I was soon deflated on the confession front, but not by the not-guilty part. Millie's proclaimed motive for hanging out in the neighborhood last night wasn't the most innocent, but neither did it equate with a shooting spree.

"I worked till all hours at my shop doing inventory and sending out online orders," she said. Her shadowed, lined, and mascaraed brown eyes batted a couple of times as if in recollection of how exhausted they'd been. "I lost track of time, so it was late by the time I headed home. I live way out in Thousand Oaks, so I still had a ways to go. I dropped down toward the 101 Freeway and decided to drive by your offices, Kendra, since I was kind of in the area. I hadn't been by there since Mr. Cossner was killed, so I was curious."

I peered around the table to eyeball how everyone else appeared to react to this far-out tale. All the men in this meeting acted engrossed by the prima pet-boutique proprietor.

"Uh-huh," I encouraged. "And what time was this?"

"I couldn't say for sure, but probably around ten-thirty."

"So you saw some lights on?"

"Yes, which intrigued me. I mean, I know lawyers work hard, but that late?" She glanced at Kleer as if assessing how diligently the young lawyer engaged in efforts for his clients. He lifted his tight chin as if considering a positive nod.

I aimed another inquiry at Millie. "But you didn't decide just to drop in and shoot at whoever was there? You did mention, didn't you, that you happened to drive by in the company of a gun?"

Millie sat straighter and said, "This isn't the first time I've forgotten how late I'm working. It happens a lot, so I've taken shooting lessons and keep a licensed handgun locked in the glove compartment of my car. And no, I didn't shoot anyone last night or anytime. I only drove by. After I heard of the murder this morning, I called the police and told them what I saw."

My turn to throw back my chair and stand. "You saw something? Someone? Do you know who shot at us?"

Her long nose wrinkled as if she'd suddenly grown disgusted with my denseness. "No, the point was that I didn't see anything important, though I was there near the critical time. Not that I hung around long, but I was able to describe a couple of cars in the parking lot—which I now think were yours and poor Ms. Montez's. There wasn't much traffic, so I slowed down but didn't see anyone lurking in shadows or waving a pistol or anything."

Which meant that, as a witness, she wasn't worth a criminal's conviction. Her timing had to have been off.

Or was her apparently innocent admission a means of explaining herself out of an arrest in case anyone saw *her* in the area at the critical time?

Mentally reviewing my malleable suspect list, I forbore from X-ing Millie from it. In fact, though I liked the lady and loved her shop, I elevated her above a few others in the order of possible perpetrators.

"Okay, Millie," I finally said. "Thanks for being so up front about your whereabouts last night. Now, I think we'd better get our meeting started."

"Good idea." Kleer straightened his shoulders as if he saw himself taking charge.

That wasn't my intent. Instead, I looked at Brian O'Barlen. "Mr. O'Barlen, please show Mr. Kleer and the others T.O.'s proposed development plans for the block on Vancino Boulevard."

Michael Kleer lifted a hand as if to stave off something nasty that would offend his clients' sensitive ears.

I, in turn, lifted my hand to stave off his anticipated protest. "I understand that VORPO has concerns about this development, Mr. Kleer. But please let Mr. O'Barlen describe what he'd like to do, and then you and your clients can explain your objections."

While one T.O. employee unrolled a giant cylinder of blueprints and another held an end to stop the stack from curling, Brian explained each sheet and all it represented.

As innovative megadevelopments went, this one was something. It included upscale retail shops along the street, topped by luxury office suites above. Behind those would be a separately entranced building containing an assortment of elegant apartments. Parking would be plentiful for the whole shebang, on several underground levels. Traffic patterns and security concerns had all been anticipated. Perfection!

But it drew pouts from the naysayers sitting across the table.

"It's so ostentatious," opined a grumbling Flint Daniels. He was about my age, which worried me since his face was already falling into flab. His extra weight wasn't as obvious when he smiled, but that wasn't an expression he wore now. "Our area is a nice, settled community. Like everywhere in the Valley, we've had some owners come and go thanks to rising property values, but most people who move into Vancino to live or do business stay for a long time. This development is likely to bring more transients."

"It'll also increase your property tax base, so you can command more services and amenities from the City of L.A.," O'Barlen pointed out.

"Assuming they pay attention to where the increase comes from and don't just use it where politicians direct it," Kleer said.

"I'm not selling my property," Millie Franzel asserted stubbornly, her arms crossed and her face puckered in a frown. "You can keep your property taxes and stop spending money on your pretty pictures. No deal."

"But, Ms. Franzel," O'Barlen said in the sweetest and most syrupy tone I'd ever heard from the acerbic businessman, "with the money we'll offer you—generous, you can be sure of that—you'll be able to move your shop anywhere you want and have funds left over besides. You'll be able to—"

"No deal." Millie pumped her crossed arms up and down in emphasis.

"Let's talk a little about this in private," said Flint Daniels, with a look at Michael Kleer that I interpreted as meaning that the two of *them* needed to talk, without

Millie's obstinate interjections. "There are some things about your plans that would need to be modified substantially if VORPO decided to voice no objections to the city planning department," he said to O'Barlen. "Now that we've gotten a better idea of what you'd like to do, we'll come up with our own suggestions." Delete that last word and replace with "demands," edited my brain.

"Go ahead and waste your time," steamed Millie. "I'm not selling."

With that, the meeting deteriorated even further. We adjourned a few minutes later.

BY THEN, IT was late afternoon. I met with O'Barlen and crew for a few peeved minutes outside in the parking lot.

"What can we do about that Franzel woman?" O'Barlen spat.

"We'll think of something," I said, hoping I was right. And not just for my client's sake. Millie needed a satisfactory solution, too, since it was clear T.O. wasn't simply going to shred its plans and tiptoe silently away.

Back in my Beamer, I called Borden, and he told me that the police hadn't yet released the offices as a crime scene under investigation.

"They said they'd try to let us return tomorrow but the next day's more likely," he said. "I wonder if they think that letting us come back so soon the last time made them miss something that led to Corrie's murder."

"I doubt it's that calculated," I told him, watching out the window to make sure the people getting into the car next door didn't ding my beloved Beamer. "Do you know if Elaine has been able to tend to Gigi?"

"I talked to her a little while ago. She said they wouldn't let her take the bird away, which was fine with her, and they've supervised her every step when she's fed Gigi."

"That should work. Well, hopefully I'll see you tomorrow, Borden."

"And you're really okay, Kendra?"

"As okay as someone can be when she was target practice." Before he could spout some comforting platitude, I said placatingly, "Don't worry about me, Borden. Honest. My nerves are much more of a mess now thanks to the meeting we just had with VORPO."

"Do you have any idea whether the solution you suggested will work?" Borden inquired when I was done describing the unsettling nonsettlement session.

"Not yet," I said. It truly needed some teeth. "Let me sleep on it."

OF COURSE, IT was a long while until bedtime, and I had lots to do before then.

Next step was to retrieve Lexie from Darryl's so she could come pet-nurturing with me that night.

When I arrived at Doggy Indulgence, I was immediately leaped upon by my lovable pup, and at the same time confronted by a clearly concerned Darryl. "Irma Etherton is here. She called to see if you'd left Lexie here, and when I told her yes, she dropped by."

Once more, with Lexie sticking Cavalier-close by my side, I met with Irma in the doggy resort's semiquiet kitchen. She looked even more depressed than the last time I'd seen her only a few days earlier. Her bouffant black hair sagged as much as the skin on her sixtyish face, and her gray eyes were ringed in red.

"I'm so glad you're here, Kendra," she said, sounding surprisingly upbeat. "The timing will work fine."

"What timing?" I inquired in confusion.

"Walt's kids said I could have a supervised visitation with Ditch if I was there before six this evening."

I glanced at my watch. It was four-thirty in the afternoon. "Ditch is the beneficiary dog?"

She nodded. "I need for you to accompany me to see for yourself how he's being treated."

"You can leave Lexie here," Darryl said from the doorway. He was leaning his skinny shoulder on the jamb, obviously eavesdropping.

There wasn't much more I'd intended to do that day, plus I'd still have plenty of time for my pet-sitting chores. "Okay," I said. "Let's go."

IRMA DROVE US in her powder blue seventies Cadillac sedan. It was certainly roomy, although I was suspicious of the lap-snapping seat belts.

"Walt's daughter, Myra, lives in Glendale," Irma said. "She's taking care of Ditch. If you can call it that."

We soon pulled into the driveway of a petite but pleasant house not far north of the 134 Freeway. The front yard was postage-stamp size but boasted a couple of mature fruit trees, laden this January morning with lemons and oranges.

We walked up to the front door and rang the bell. No barking sounded. Strange.

The door opened after a minute. A woman who managed to look pretty and harassed at the same time stood there, glaring at us. Clad in jeans and a short T-shirt, she held the hand of a little girl who looked about four. "Come in," the woman said, sounding not at all pleased about the prospect.

"Hi," I said to the child, who remained where she was, inhibiting our entry. "I'm Kendra. What's your name?"

Before she could respond, the woman said, "Are you the lawyer? I'm Walt's daughter, Myra, and that's Ellie. My brother Moe's on his way."

"Fine," I said. "Where's Ditch?"

"This way."

I noticed that Irma hadn't said a word, not even of introduction. When I glanced at her, she pursed her lips, as if it was an effort not to use them to blurt something offensive.

So far I'd seen nothing to merit a nasty-gram. But there'd obviously been time and unpleasant circumstances enough for the two women to construct a huge wall of antipathy toward one another.

We followed Myra, who now held Ellie in her arms, down a hallway and through a tiny kitchen. She opened a door at the far end, which led into a storeroom.

Inside was an adorable Scottish terrier, who tore out and headed straight for Irma, who elevated him high, with a hug. "Hi, Ditchy," she crooned. "I'm so glad to see you."

The black dog wagged its erect tail, obviously excited to see her, too. He licked her face and nuzzled her, and she did the same in exchange, substituting kisses for licks.

"Everything okay here?" demanded a male voice behind us. I turned to see a guy stride through the small kitchen. His facial features suggested Myra's, in a more masculine way. Little Ellie yanked away from her mom and hurled herself at the man. "Uncle Moe!" she exclaimed. Since it was the first thing I'd heard her say, I had to figure she was fond of her uncle.

"We're fine," Myra said. "They've been here . . ." She looked at her watch. "Five minutes. They're allowed ten more."

"We're being timed?" I inquired.

"Of course," Myra said. Her brother, holding his niece, drew up to her side, and the two of them, shoulder-to-shoulder, stared similar sharp daggers at us. "We're just being nice to let her"—she nodded brusquely toward Irma—"come at all."

Irma whirled, obviously intending to counter with something equally nasty. I hastily interjected, "I guess you both know I'm an attorney. Are you represented by counsel?"

"Yes," Moe said with a sneer.

"Fine. Then give me that attorney's contact information, please. Now that I know"—though I'd of course suspected before—"I'll need to ask permission before coming here again." I was skating on ethical thin ice—which, after my earlier ills, I usually eschewed at all conceivable costs. And yet, in this instance, I'd leapt at a visitation with the subject pup without having another attorney around counseling these people to be humane to their charge as long as, and only when, they were under observation. I was definitely dismayed by what I'd seen here. Poor Ditch, confined to a closet.

Poor *rich* Ditch, if he'd been allowed to inherit . . .

I accepted a sheet of paper on which Moe had written the name, Hollywood address, and phone number of a lawyer. All the while I watched from the corner of my eye how Irma and Ditch reacted to one another in this obviously fond reunion.

I knew what the law said, though I hadn't finished my research. And I still hadn't seen Walt Shorbel's will.

One way or another, I would find a way to get this poor persecuted pup and his generous inheritance into Irma's hands.

STILL, ON THE drive back to Darryl's, I couldn't hold out false hopes to Irma. "I didn't like what I saw there," I said.

"Of course not," she sputtered, stopped at a light. "Those terrible people. They're treating Ditch like a . . . dog!"

"I can't make any promises, but I'll do all I can to fix things for the poor pup."

"Thank you, Kendra," Irma said, her words sounding so hopeful and heartfelt that I felt like a heel and a liar. Litigator or not, how could I create a winning case in this loser of a situation?

Back at Darryl's, I lifted Lexie into my arms and gave

my wriggling pup as big a hug as the one Irma and Ditch had indulged in.

I realized I was starting to miss the days when I'd spent more time pet-sitting, when law wasn't so much on my mind. But to help Irma and Ditch, law *had* to stay centered in my stressed-out thoughts.

I was pleased, though, when on the drive toward my first dog client of the evening my cell phone sang out a call from a number familiar yet seldom heard from lately. It was Avvie Milton. She was an associate at the law firm where I'd once worked, and my onetime protégé. I'd long since forgiven her for her bad judgment in taking up with my former lover there, senior partner Bill "Drill Sergeant" Sergement. After all, I'd forgiven myself for the same bad judgment.

Kind of. I still had dire doubts about my terrible taste in men . . .

"Hi, Kendra," Avvie said. "Are you okay? I mean, I've seen a lot in the news about the murders at Borden Yurick's new law firm." She was one of the many people at Marden & Sergement, formerly Marden, Sergement & Yurick, who hadn't forgiven Borden's defection with a substantial segment of the firm's client base. As a result, I figured everyone who remained was ecstatic about Borden's execrable publicity—the more lurid the better.

"I'm fine, though I'd love to have a little less excitement in my life."

"I'll bet. You weren't the lawyer who was shot at, were you?"

"Not exactly," I dissembled. "How are things at the old firm?"

"Great! In fact, Bill and I are going on a business trip to New York next week, and I'd love for you to watch Pansy for me. You are still pet-sitting, aren't you?"

Partial translation: Bill and she were going on a

trumped-up business trip–slash–tryst, which excluded Bill's wife. Well, that was their business, not mine.

My business, though, did concern her last question. And I enjoyed Avvie's pot-bellied pig a whole lot. "Yes, I'm still pet-sitting, though taking on fewer clients. But I'd be glad to watch Pansy for you."

"Excellent! I'll be in touch next week to make arrangements."

We hung up, and Lexie insinuated herself onto my lap from the passenger's seat. At least we were on surface streets, so she wasn't too distracting.

In a while, I took my time walking and caring for my clients, letting Lexie accompany me inside every place I could. I hugged every pet possible, even the haughty kitties. "Just remember how good you have it, even with me in charge," I told them, and described poor Ditch's life.

When I was done, I realized I had a decision to make: to Jeff's, or not to Jeff's. I figured I'd call him first to assess our respective attitudes.

He answered his cell phone first thing. "Hello, Kendra," he said in a tone most formal. Which made me figure I'd sleep alone that night.

I was ready to say something silly and ring off when he said, "Kendra, do you suppose you could call your friend Esther Ickes on my behalf?"

Esther was a simply superb attorney who specialized in criminal law. I'd considered referring Elaine to her after Ezra's murder but fortunately hadn't had to.

I drew in my breath now so sharply I felt it sting. "Why? Are you under arrest?"

"Imminently," he admitted, and I heard a touch of trepidation in his tone. "It seems that my missing sport coat wasn't gone after all. It was found on the ground near your office. And some of Corrie Montez's blood was on it."

Chapter Nineteen

"THANKS SO MUCH, Kendra," said Esther Ickes over the phone.

I settled back onto my own apartment sofa. I'd called Esther the second I'd hung up with Jeff, notwithstanding the late hour. She hadn't answered, but I left a sufficiently detailed message and she'd just phoned me back.

As an attorney specializing in such intense areas as bankruptcy and criminal defense, Esther was used to having clients call at all hours to weep on her sweet-little-old-lady shoulders—which weren't far from her go-for-the-jugular fangs. I'd certainly done so when I'd been on the top of Noralles's suspect list for two murders a few months ago.

"I really appreciate your referral of so many nice murder suspects to me," she finished.

"You're welcome," I said, then paused. "Is there such a thing as a murder magnet?" I blurted. "I mean, there've been so many in my life lately. Even when I'm not an alleged killer, people I know keep dying violently, and others—friends and acquaintances—are the topmost suspects. Am I doing something wrong?"

"From the perspective of my firm's pocketbook, dear, you're doing something *right*."

I laughed, and we chatted about what pleasantries I could manage for a few more minutes, and then I hung up.

Jeff was the primary suspect in the murders of Ezra Cossner and Corrie Montez. Partly because of his lost sports jacket. The one he'd asked me to locate in my office.

"What do you think, Lexie?" I asked my Cavalier, who'd curled up against me on the comfy cushions on the beige sectional couch. Her soulful brown eyes popped open immediately, and she gazed seriously up at me, her black-and-white tail hazarding a halfhearted wag. "I mean, let's assume he did leave it there after wearing it at a meeting that included the top honchos on my suspect list. I figure that the person most likely to want Ezra dead would have been one of the VORPO folks—although I've partially written off Millie Franzel."

Lexie gave a Cavalier snort, which told me she disagreed.

"I know. Her admission of driving innocently around the area when Corrie was killed, and just happening to have a gun along for the ride, should make her a key suspect, at least in that murder, but I've given her some credit for honesty. And I don't know her alibi for when Ezra was assassinated . . . yet. Anyway, let's assume the killer noticed Jeff's jacket in our offices and knew whose it was. He or she might have leapt at the chance to enlist it to drag Jeff into deeper shit, since he was already soiled with suspicion in Ezra's murder."

The allusion to poop got Lexie's attention. She leapt down to the floor and woofed.

"Is that a request to go out?"

Judging by her fervent circles, it was.

"Okay, let's take a little walk. Maybe it'll help me clear my head while you clear your innards."

I clipped on her leash and we clomped down the stairs beside the garage. The evening was already late. The only overhead illumination was artificial, from my security lights and my neighbors'. It was sufficient to impart some sense of safety as we took a short walk up and down our slender, serpentine street in the Valley side of the Hollywood Hills.

While Lexie sniffed and squatted in the chilly evening air, I mused about the matters on my mind. I had to assume Corrie's killing was related to Ezra's. Had Corrie witnessed her boss's murder? That was certainly a possible scenario.

But what if it had worked the other way? What if the paralegal was the projected prey in the first place, and Ezra was snuffed for being in the wrong place at a Corrie-less time?

By force of long-standing habit, I'd stuffed my cell phone in my slacks pocket. Impulsively, I pulled out my phone and pressed in a now-familiar number. Unlikely my target would be there so late, but—

"Hubbard Security," responded the voice I'd been hoping for.

"Althea? It's Kendra. Have you heard from Jeff?"

"Sure did. Damn that single-minded freak Noralles anyway. Just because Jeff bested him—how many years ago was it?"

"We'll have to ask him," I replied. "Did Jeff request that you do any digging for him?"

"Not specifically," Althea said with a sigh.

I had to hang on, both to leash and phone, when Lexie spied a cat speeding across the street. "Just a second," I said to Althea via the bouncing cellular apparatus. "I need to convince my dog her evening constitutional is complete." Which I soon did. Lexie stayed at my side as we entered the wide front gate to my home. "Sorry," I said to Althea. "Anyway, I've been considering who might be the most compelling suspects in both murders but I need some more background info. Can you help?"

"In a heartbeat. What do you want, and on whom?"

I'd come to really revere this woman as well as like her as a friend. Computer geek and consummate hacker? Middle-aged marvel? Heck, she was simply Althea.

"I'm still mulling over what I need," I said. "But first thing, could you do a search on Corrie Montez? I want to know everything you can find about her. Could be she was killed only because of what she knew about Ezra's death, but just in case . . ."

"Got it," Althea said as I juggled the phone between shoulder and ear so I could insert the key into the lock on my apartment door. Yes, I was consciously staying more cautious about securing my stuff while dog-walking these days, thanks to the way Rachel had apparently maneuvered into my main house.

"Anything else?"

Yeah, there was. It was something I knew I needed to ask. Probably an angle Jeff was already pursuing, assuming he was able to do anything while under interrogation. But it was something I needed to know myself. Even if it might not provide him with the alibi he needed.

"Yes," I said. "Could you give me Amanda Hubbard's phone number?"

I HAD TO prepare myself for this phone call. Lexie bounced at my feet, begging for a biscuit, as I headed for the kitchen.

"Treat for you, bigger treat for me," I told her. I dropped a doggie cookie and she caught it in her eager mouth.

I poured myself a glass of chardonnay. A small one, since I figured my driving might not be done for the day.

If it was, that would be the time to double my dose—for medicinal purposes, of course.

I glanced around to decide where I wanted to sit while I spoke on the phone. Over the bathroom commode, in case I needed to toss my chardonnay?

Courage, Kendra, I ordered myself.

I went back to the living room sofa and dug around in my pocket for Amanda's number.

And stared at it for a second as I boosted my bravado. *Now!* I pushed in the numbers and pressed the "Send" button.

It rang only once before a breathy and all-too-familiar female voice responded, "Hello?"

"Hi, Amanda. This is Kendra Ballantyne."

Silence. What did I expect? A wonderful welcome from my lover's ex?

"Have you spoken to Jeff lately?" I asked swiftly to end the mounting silence. "I mean, within the last few hours?"

"No . . ." she said suspiciously. "Why?"

I thought the number Althea had supplied me was probably for Amanda's cell phone. As a result, I couldn't picture where she might be located, but I could definitely envision what she looked like in my mind's envious eye. I'd still not gotten a wide-ranging report on the woman's background, but my imagination had penciled in a few possibilities: a fading fashion model; a genuine Hollywood insider instead of a panting wannabe; a gorgeous heiress who'd enjoyed all the cosmetic surgery money could buy . . . I was feeling so catty that I might as well have meowed an answer to her.

Instead, I said calmly, "He called me before to ask me to line up a criminal attorney for him. He's apparently being held as a suspect in Corrie Montez's murder."

"I heard about that woman on the news. She worked at your office, too, like that man who was killed the other day, right?"

"Yes," I said shortly. "I wanted to find out from you whether you would be of any help to Jeff." I took a deep breath, swallowed a bunch of bile, and belted out, "Were you with him last night?"

"Why, yes," she replied without hesitation in a voice so sweet that it suggested she relished rubbing my face in its saccharine. "I was all upset after hearing again from that awful Leon. I called, and Jeff came right over."

"And what time was that?"

"He was with me from, oh, about ten P.M. to after one-thirty in the morning."

So much for Jeff's alleged outing for early-morning ice cream. I wasn't sure where he'd claim to have found a cone at that hour anyway. Or maybe it had been Amanda who'd supplied it . . . along with whatever other treats she'd given him.

"What time do they think that woman was killed, Kendra?" Amanda asked.

"They've pinpointed the time, thanks to me," I said. "I was shot at, too." That was something I could suspect Amanda of doing, but she'd have had no reason to get rid of Ezra and Corrie first. Besides, just as she was supplying Jeff with an alibi, he would be able to do the same for her. "It was around eleven o'clock."

"No problem, then," Amanda all but cooed, and I wanted to kick her for it. "Jeff was definitely still at my place then. Shall I call the police and tell them?"

"I'll let them know," I told her. "But I'm sure they'll get in touch with you."

I didn't bother to mention that she was hardly more credible a witness than I'd have been, had I elected to fake a false alibi for Jeff. We both had reasons to endeavor to exonerate Jeff.

Amanda would wish to keep her momentum moving to get him back.

And I would adore the enjoyment of telling him exactly where to take his sexy bod and shove it.

I'D BEEN RIGHT to limit my wine imbibing, since a short while later I found myself in my Beamer. Lexie accompanying me, we were on our way to Jeff's.

I'd called Detective Noralles and notified him as to what I understood Amanda would testify. He didn't sound surprised. Jeff had probably slipped him that absolving item of information before, and he'd elected to consider the source and discredit it, as I'd anticipated. He'd thanked me nevertheless and promised to look into it.

I likewise took the opportunity to tell him I'd been hunting for Jeff's lost jacket earlier that evening, and my theory that the murderer bathed it in Corrie's blood to implicate Jeff. Noralles seemed as unimpressed as he'd been with my proffering of Amanda as a witness. His single-mindedness had doubtless decreed that both women in Jeff's life might lie to exonerate him.

As if I, an officer of the court, would do such a dire deed.

He hadn't let me speak to Jeff—who now had his cell phone either off or confiscated, I couldn't tell which. But I'd gathered that I shouldn't expect his appearance anytime soon.

Odin shouldn't have to suffer for his master's mistakes or misfortunes, so Lexie and I headed there to administer comfort and company.

The Akita was perceptibly pleased about our presence. His breed isn't always prone to gratuitous shows of emotion, but he engaged in a bout of doggy one-upmanship with Lexie and seemed utterly grateful when we joined him on a long jaunt to take care of his final concerns of the night.

Sitting on Jeff's sofa, we tuned into the TV for a while—while I watched my watch. I tried one more useless time to reach Jeff on his cell, but only reached his voice mail again.

I was convinced of his innocence of murder, whether or not Amanda fabricated their assignation. As a lawyer—and one who'd once been a murder suspect herself—I was more than familiar with the basis of this country's laudable legal system: a person is deemed innocent until proven guilty.

That was intended to apply in all instances, both for accusations of murder, and for lesser offenses.

But I acknowledged to myself that I was prepared to convict Jeff of a less-than-innocent assignation with Amanda without further evidence otherwise.

Instead of all of us piling into Jeff's bed, I herded the dogs to the guest room, where I'd resided when all I'd been was simply Jeff's pet-sitter.

I lay in that cramped bed long into the night, listening in vain for Jeff to come home and attempt to persuade me against his presumed perfidy.

Chapter Twenty

STILL NO SIGN of Jeff the next morning, so I tended the two pups and departed, bringing Lexie along. Poor Odin. But I wasn't sure whether I'd want to return if Jeff came home tonight. If I left Lexie and had to come back for her, I'd have to convince myself to converse calmly with Jeff and I wasn't sure I could do that just yet.

We headed home so I could change clothes before facing the day. Outside the gate, I saw Rachel walking Beggar—or rather, the eager Irish setter towing his slower-striding owner.

"Hi," I called, driving my Beamer up beside them. Then, recalling Rachel's glam outing with her dad the day before, I asked, "How did you enjoy the audition?"

The waiflike teen, clad today in mundane jeans and a sweatshirt, seemed almost ready to cry. "So many people trying out for one part! I thought moving to Hollywood would make it easier to get into films, but—"

I'd no doubt her "but" was the battle cry of thousands of frustrated actors. It undoubtedly energized some to try all the harder. But others, forced to face reality, watched their designer-clad dreams of fame and fortune slip instead into the uniforms of underpaid restaurant servers and other unsung positions.

"Hey," I said. "I have an idea. Lexie and I could use a little help this morning before I go to my law office. How would you like to be a pet-sitter's assistant for the day?"

To MY ASTONISHMENT and amusement, Rachel parlayed herself into a pet-sitter extraordinaire. Perhaps she was just acting but she appeared to enjoy it. She threw herself into ensuring that Alexander the pit bull had a bully time on his walk, plus plenty to eat and drink. She laughed over the snooty antics of Abra and Cadabra, the disappearing non–Cheshire cats. While we were in the car driving from client to client, she talked lots to Lexie, who lapped it up.

When I received a panicked phone call from Avvie Milton saying her trip was unexpectedly commencing that very afternoon, we headed for her home—where Rachel also seemed ecstatic about interacting with Pansy, the pot-bellied pig—an adorable, fuzzy black-and-white porker with a protracted snout and cloven feet.

"Do you mind if I have Rachel help while you're gone?" I asked Avvie. Even now, frazzled about her impending trip, my former legal associate still looked professional in a pantsuit and neatly trimmed and highlighted hair. Thanks to me, I thought as usual. I'd insisted that she lose the short skirts and silly demeanor she'd started out with when she'd first joined the Marden firm—which now seemed eons ago—when I'd been the firm's foremost litigator.

"Not at all," she said. "As long as we add her to your pet-sitting contract." I'd faxed her what I was using now, since I'd lately determined to approach my pet-sitting as professionally—almost—as my legal career.

"Good idea," I agreed.

A little while later, we were back at my rented-out home so I could drop off Rachel. Her dad was still in town but would be leaving on a location-scouting mission later that day, so I was unlikely to see him for a while. A good thing? Probably. I was annoyed by the idea that I found him attractive. Especially now, while I was so confused about the other man who I thought was in my life.

"Thanks a lot, Kendra," Rachel said, and I noted that the pout I'd first seen on her pretty, young face had been replaced by a more permanent smile. "Will you come by for me later, before you take care of your pet clients this afternoon?"

"Sure thing," I said. I didn't necessarily need an assistant. On the other hand, if things worked out well, it would allow me to take on more pet-sitting clients while my law practice continued to grow.

Before Lexie and I had driven fully down the hill, my cell phone played its song. Jeff? Was he free and focused on talking?

No, it was Darryl. "Hi, Kendra," he said. "Can you come by here today? Irma Etherton dropped off an envelope for you. She said it was important, and that you were expecting it."

Walt's will, I figured. "Lexie and I will come by in a little bit," I said. "And since we'll be there anyway . . ." I glanced over at my alert canine companion. "How would you like to stay at Darryl's today?" I inquired.

Her fuzzy tail wagged ferociously.

"You've got another customer today, if that's okay," I said into the phone.

"Lexie's always welcome," Darryl responded, as I'd been certain he would.

As BORDEN HAD hoped yet hadn't expected, we were permitted to practice law in our own offices that day. The atmosphere felt even gloomier than after Ezra's exit. Because we'd now experienced two murders here, or because Corrie was even more the sort of person who'd be sorely missed? I couldn't say.

I tracked down Gigi before starting anything else. She was again in the kitchen, clutching her perch and looking listlessly through the slats in her cage. She seemed miserably sad today as she regarded me somberly with one of her beady black eyes, her blue head bent and her wings tucked to her sides.

"Gorgeous girl?" I prompted without eliciting any response. "Gigi?"

"She didn't eat much breakfast this morning," said Elaine from behind me. She as usual wore a neat suit, but she looked as downcast as her avian almost-adoptee.

"Have you talked to Polly Bright about poor Gigi apparently witnessing a second murder—and how she now seems so dispirited?"

"I intend to call her later today."

"Will you let me know what she says?" I pleaded.

"Positively."

I'D WAITED UNTIL the privacy of my own office—now unkempt and untidy after so much chaos and crime-scene investigation inside, outside, and around it—before opening the envelope Irma Etherton had left for me with Darryl. The will was substantially as Irma had described: a document dated two years earlier that appeared properly executed and witnessed, effectively making Walt's adored Scottish terrier Glenfiddich his heir. He had named his two children in it so it would not appear he'd forgotten them. Each inherited a thousand dollars from his estate. Along with the formal will was a wholly handwritten codicil dated about eight months ago naming Irma as Glenfiddich's caretaker and heir.

I stared at the stuff, then, still ignoring the abnormal disheveled disarray of my environment, I picked up the phone and poked in some numbers. I got through first try to the fellow I sought. "Hello, this is Dennis Kamura."

"Mr. Kamura, this is Kendra Ballantyne. I'm an attorney representing Irma Etherton regarding the estate of Walter Shorbel—"

"I've been expecting a call on this. Would you like to come to my office to discuss it?"

"Absolutely," I said.

THE LAW OFFICE of Kamura & Dunn, P.C., was in downtown L.A., not far from my old Marden, Sergement & Yurick digs.

I enjoy walking in the bustling downtown area, especially these days when people even live here, mostly in chic lofts constructed within lovely antique structures—at least antique for L.A., which is far from the oldest metropolis in this youngish nation. The Kamura office was just off Figueroa near Ninth Street, not in the mainstream of major office buildings, but no longer in a panhandler's paradise.

I was shown in immediately to see Dennis Kamura. He had a vast corner office, with all the trappings of a successful and lucrative law practice. Did he earn rent money by rooking his clients? *Keep your mind and ears open, Ballantyne. And not necessarily your argumentative mouth.*

Dennis Kamura was fortyish and Asian-featured, with a thin face and even thinner black hair.

"Please sit down, Kendra." He motioned to a stiff-backed chair facing his glass-topped desk.

I complied. The instant I opened my mouth to inform him of my errand, he interrupted.

"I know what you're going to say, and you're wrong. Partly. I've practiced estate law for fifteen years, and I did not commit legal malpractice with the will I drafted for Walt Shorbel."

That blasted the wind out of my steaming sails. Not that I'd have overtly accused the guy of malpractice. What I'd been about to say would have been substantially more subtle.

He continued, "It's elementary that personal property cannot inherit under the law of the State of California, and a pet is considered personalty. I advised Walt against his silly estate plan. If he wanted his dog taken care of, I told him we'd set up a trust. But he asked me what would happen if he just left everything to . . . Ditch. That's the dog's name, isn't it?"

I nodded but stayed silent. Maybe it was self-serving hindsight guiding him, but this attorney appeared agitated, as if amazed at the stupidity of a client who'd shunned competent legal advice.

"I told Walt that a court would probably toss out his will. Heck, a judge worth his gavel would probably question the testator's competency at the time of entering into such an absurd estate plan. I said that, if the will was disregarded, Walt would be held to have died intestate, so the statutes governing people who died without making any will at all would apply. He sounded pleased when I explained that, since he was a widower, his two surviving children would probably inherit everything. He said that if his kids inherited that way, it would show them he felt more loved by his dog when he was alive."

Poor Walt. And Ditch. And maybe even Walt's kids, though since they were Irma's opposition, I'd never let on that I thought they might have been wronged as well. "What about the codicil?" I asked. "The handwritten one, written afterward, designating Irma Etherton as Ditch's guardian."

Dennis shook his head. "He didn't consult me before doing that, though I heard about it when Irma called me after Walt's death. I told her I was sorry, but I couldn't represent her to fight Walt's legitimate heirs over this travesty of a will. By the way, I had him sign an acknowledgment that the terms of the will were written against my advice." He thrust a piece of paper over his desk toward me. "Here's a copy. I wanted to go on record as having counseled him competently, in case this wound up in court, which I assume, since you're here, it will."

"Probably," I admitted. Although now, Irma's case seemed even flimsier. If the Shorbel kids got hold of the disclosure Dennis wrote and Walt executed, they'd have even more likelihood of having the will virtually shredded by the court and tossed in the trash. Why hadn't the guy agreed to a trust? He could have arranged for Ditch to be nurtured and cared for, for the rest of his canine days. I didn't ask Dennis. He claimed he'd advised Walt that a trust was the way to go.

"Thanks for your time," I told the agitated attorney, holding out my hand as I prepared to depart.

He shook his head. "I know better than to wish you luck, Kendra, but for Walt's sake—and his dog's, of course—I do."

I'd study the acknowledgment he'd handed me later, I thought as I left. But unless I could prove Walt's signature was forged, it would effectively eliminate any chance I'd have had to get Dennis's malpractice insurance to cough up the amount of Walt's estate on Ditch's—and Irma's—behalf.

Poor Ditch's case was likely to be as much of a goner as Walt.

But I'd learned well how to think like a lawyer. Every client had an argument, one that might withstand all evidence to the contrary.

I wasn't about to give up.

Chapter Twenty-one

DESPITE MY DETERMINEDLY optimistic outlook on the Glenfiddich situation, I felt a bit bummed as I aimed my Beamer north on the 101. I decided to do something even worse to spoil the rest of my day—as if inevitably heavy Hollywood Freeway traffic wasn't enough.

I would go to the vital block of Vancino Boulevard for a visit. There, I could see for myself what a new and uplifting mixed-use development by T.O. might do for—and to—the place.

T.O. Ezra had explained that the initials stood for "Tomorrow's Opportunities," but I had figured out the actual significance of those two letters in tandem: "Taking Over."

Not inevitably a bad thing. Hey, I wasn't against responsible development.

And when a client's interests were involved, well, like I've often said, I was damned good in the "think like a lawyer" department.

So, while I was there, I'd consider how best to represent T.O.'s interests in acquiring the remainder of the property, and then in obtaining the requisite permits to build their project. Maybe even seek a solution that would garner support from the locals who now objected so obstreperously.

And if I happened to find some additional information about how much antipathy any VORPO sorts might have had against Ezra—enough, perhaps, that I'd form a more educated opinion on who killed him, and Corrie—well, why the hell not?

Better yet, I'd discover evidence to free Jeff from further inquisition by Detective Ned Noralles and his supposed superior in these investigations, Detective Candace Schwinglan.

And then I could break off whatever I didn't have with Jeff without residual feelings of guilt that I'd abandoned him at a time he needed assistance.

I eased into the merge with the 134 Freeway and continued west. After passing the interchange with the San Diego Freeway, I took an exit and turned onto a northbound street. Soon, I found myself on Vancino Boulevard. I meandered till I located a vacant metered space and shoehorned the Beamer into it. And then I looked around.

This block was unquestionably commercial. On the north side, all storefronts seemed occupied, including a greeting card and gift store, a dry cleaner, a mortgage lender, and the inevitable chain coffee shop.

On the south side sat Pamperville Pet Boutique among a couple of vacant shops and one that showcased a people boutique. Another was a cellular phone store.

Nothing out of the ordinary. But it still elicited a question from me.

Wishing Corrie were available to call—she would absolutely have had the answer—I sat back down in the Beamer after paying the parking meter and called Brian O'Barlen. He wasn't available, but I was connected with one of his assistants. "What's the address of the site on Vancino Boulevard that's still owned by SkinFlint Associates?"

I asked. Besides Millie Franzel, SkinFlint was the other property owner on the critical block.

The address was congruent with the clothing boutique on the corner. I called Althea.

"Could you please find out for me who's behind SkinFlint Associates? They own property on Vancino Boulevard."

She promised a detailed response as soon as possible. "Oh, and Kendra?" she said. "As you requested, I've been checking into everything on Corrie Montez. I haven't found anything unusual in her background. She was born in El Paso to a Mexican immigrant family, moved to L.A. a few years ago, and attended college at night, became a paralegal, and worked for the firm of Jambison & Jetts, and recently left there to start working for Yurick & Associates. She rented an apartment in North Hollywood, owned a four-year-old Nissan but no real property, and was overextended on one credit card but up to date on three others. Shall I keep looking?"

Nothing there mentioned how she'd made mortal enemies. "Only if something exciting comes to mind."

When we hung up, I walked the block. I strolled the street behind it, too—full of nice enough houses that in the local real estate market likely cost a mint. If plopped down by a tornado in, say, Kansas instead of popular and overpopulated L.A., they'd be moderately priced.

I popped in and said hi to Millie Franzel. Her store was full of shoppers, so I couldn't casually ask if she'd decided yet to confess to the murders after admitting that she was in the area of Corrie's demise while toting a gun.

As I exited her shop, my cell phone rang. Althea. "Here's the scoop on SkinFlint," she said.

This time I had to extract a notebook from the big purse I always carried. Stopping close to the shop window so as not to disrupt the sidewalk's ample foot traffic, I said, "Go ahead."

Well, hell. I should have figured that out at first, all by

myself. One of the biggest investors in SkinFlint was the outspoken president of VORPO: *Flint* Daniels.

He was already high on my suspect list as one of those angry after Ezra's outburst at the big VORPO meeting. I was certain Daniels held property around here, since all VORPO members did, although many owned homes, not commercial sites.

"Thanks, Althea," I said, and hung up.

I needed to speak with Flint Daniels. I also needed to converse with broker Bobby Lawrence. But both were VORPO members and hence represented by counsel—at least on development issues.

Had either of them, or anyone else in their association, hired criminal counsel yet, just in case?

An interesting question. Maybe Ned Noralles would know.

But would he tell me? I assumed he'd rather pour hot pepper on his notes and eat them than disgorge anything to this nosy attorney.

So what next, I asked myself. Well, first I sat back in the Beamer. I still had time on my parking meter, although I received some irritated honks and insulting finger gestures when I didn't exit my prized Vancino Boulevard space pronto.

Forbearing from gesturing back, I used my talented fingers instead to punch in the number Althea had given me for SkinFlint Associates. "I'm Kathy Barnes," I prevaricated when someone answered. "I'm with the *Daily News.* Could you tell me whether SkinFlint Associates is a member of VORPO?" If Flint Daniels himself was the member and not his company, then I might be able, ethically, to discuss his activities with someone else on staff.

But the organization itself maintained membership in the property owners' association. As a result, obtaining answers to my questions for Daniels was delayed.

Not so with Bobby Lawrence. His real estate firm,

Nessix, held no VORPO membership. No one at his office knew if *he* did—although of course everyone was quite interested in what the organization did, since its actions could have an effect on area property purchases.

That's what the person who answered the line informed me when I again suggested I was with the press. And no, Bobby wasn't there currently. He was out showing a client some property. But his secretary was there.

"What's her name?" I balanced my notebook on my knees behind the steering wheel—not exactly comfy, but sufficiently efficient for now.

The answer to my inquiry was Jessie. Of course I asked to speak with her.

"Hi, Jessie," I said so cheerily I nearly made myself cough up my sugar hype. "My name is Kathy Barnes." Same name, different needs, ergo another backstory. "I'm with T.O. Development. I understand one of our guys has been talking to Bobby Lawrence about representing us for some property purchases in the Vancino area. Would you know anything about that?"

Silence. "Who did you say you are?"

"Kathy Barnes. I'm an administrator here, and I was told to follow up on the proposal to hire your firm, specifically Bobby Lawrence."

"I think you've gotten false information, Ms. Barnes. Are you sure you wanted this office?"

"Yes, that's what I was told. May I speak to Mr. Lawrence?"

"He's not here now."

Whew. "Well, we were referred to him as being an expert in property in the Vancino area, and—"

"There has to be some mistake. I know he recently approached T.O. and was told they wouldn't hire him. He has listings in the Vancino area, and knows the area well, but . . ."

Very interesting. I decided to make a giant assumption

from this little innuendo. "Do you happen to know if it was T.O.'s attorney who decided we wouldn't hire Mr. Lawrence?"

"T.O.'s attorney?" Her hesitation made it clear she hedged.

"Ezra Cossner," I said, poising my pen to write her response. The Beamer was becoming stiflingly stuffy, but I didn't want to take time to crack open the windows or crank up the engine and air-conditioning.

"The guy who was killed?"

"Yes," I said. "I—"

"Who is this?" yelled an angry male voice that clearly wasn't Jessie's.

"Identify yourself, please," I responded, "and I'll do the same." It wasn't simply the stuffiness in my sedan that caused my face to feel so hot.

"This is Bobby Lawrence." Shit. But who else was I expecting—Governor Schwarzenegger? The only accent on the other end suggested the deep South. "And you are . . . ?"

I doubted my temporary alias would engender cooperation, so I decided to come clean. "Kendra Ballantyne."

"The lawyer who's now representing that slimy outfit T.O.?"

"Except for the slime, yes."

I heard some muffled conversation and cursing, suggesting Bobby held his hand over the phone as he chewed out poor Jessie.

"Mr. Lawrence," I called without a heck of a lot of hope that I'd capture his attention. Should I drive to his office and try to talk to him there, now that the proverbial cat—in this instance, my not-so-secret identity—was out of the bag?

In a moment he was back. "My secretary said you asked if T.O. wanted to hire me to act as their broker in scooping up the Vancino property. Like I told the cops, that's exactly what happened when O'Barlen contacted me before the

VORPO meeting the other night. I told him I'd think about it, but then I got another call, this one from that Cossner guy, who told me to go pound sand. He said O'Barlen's call was a mistake, and I told him where to go. So, not that it's any of your business, but I did argue with Ezra Cossner before he was killed."

Wow . . . Mining for minor information, I'd struck gold!

"So why am I telling you this? Well, I've done my homework like always and I know you snoop into matters that aren't your business, Ms. Ballantyne. The Internet has lots on how you solved the case when *you* were accused of murder, and how you helped some friends when *they* were. I've told the police everything, and admitted I was mad at Cossner but I didn't kill him. I'm telling you so you'll stay off my back, assuming you're looking into this murder, too. Which, since you knew the guy, I'd imagine you are. Are the cops checking into you, by the way? If they have any smarts, they should be. You know an awful lot of people who get murdered."

He was right, of course, but my only response to his finger-pointing over the phone was to flinch—and I was thankful he couldn't see that.

"So you're saying you didn't kill Ezra, Mr. Lawrence?"

"That's right. And before you ask, yes, I knew Corrie Montez, too. I represented her last year when she tried to buy a condo in the area, but the deal fell through. And no, I didn't kill her, but I told this to the detective who questioned me, too. I have nothing more to say to you, Ms. Ballantyne. If you call me or my office again, I'll call the cops."

The slam of his phone seemed so loud that I'd have sworn it rocked the Beamer. The whole conversation certainly rocked me.

Now I knew two people—Bobby Lawrence and Millie Franzel—who'd disliked Ezra, perhaps enough to slay him, and they'd both confessed their antipathy and sworn their innocence to the police.

The hell of it was, I was afraid I believed them both.

My suspect list was shrinking.

So who killed Ezra and Corrie?

Chapter Twenty-two

I FINALLY PULLED the Beamer from its parking space—an occurrence that made the day of one approaching driver. I headed for my office, the lair of a couple of my least likely murder suspects: Borden Yurick and Elaine Aames. They each knew Ezra and Corrie. Perhaps they'd had reason to hold one or both in temporary disfavor. But shoot them?

Shoot! I just couldn't see either of them as killers.

When I reached the office, Mignon sat at her regular greeting spot. "Hi, Kendra," she chirped. "Elaine's been looking for you."

"I'll stop in and see her." And ask her, just in case, if she'd decided finally to confess to the two murders.

Not.

I headed down the hallway. To reach Elaine's office, I had to pass the one that had been Ezra's—and was now, in addition to the kitchen, Gigi's domain.

The yellow crime-scene tape had been removed—again. Impulsively, I opened the door and slipped inside.

Gigi was there, in her large golden cage. "Hi, gorgeous girl," I said.

She looked at me with her nearest dark eye, then started nodding her whole body in a rhythmic dance.

"Does that mean you're happy to see me?" I asked. She didn't really respond, but she ceased her bobbing.

Talk about impulsive behavior, I was on a roll that afternoon. I unlatched Gigi's cage and reached my arm in. "Step up," I said. She didn't seem upset or aggressive, but who knew what odd mood this bird could bring on without warning? Would she peck holes into my flesh with her pointed black beak?

No, instead she slipped off her perch and onto my arm. I lifted her out of the cage, and she continued to climb my sleeve. She still weighed several noticeable pounds, but that didn't bother me. "So, Gigi," I told her, once she'd settled mostly on my shoulder. "Any chance Darryl was right and that you could explain exactly what you saw on those two terrible nights when you witnessed those murders?"

She didn't answer. Nor did she move.

"You've been through a lot," I said. "How about coming along with me for now? You'll have to be back in here soon, but we'll see about that later."

She stayed perched on my shoulder as we exited Ezra's office. Elaine's was next door, and I knocked.

"Come in," she called, and we did. Elaine's suit today was pale peach. So was her complexion beneath her neat gray hair. She gasped at her unexpected guest. "She seems so calm now." She smiled at Gigi. "Do you think she'll stay that way? If so, maybe I could take her home with me, start getting her used to her new owner."

"Ezra's heirs are okay with that?"

"Couldn't be happier. They made it clear they were interested in his money, but not his macaw."

"That's good for Gigi. You, too."

"They're not holding a funeral for him once his body's

released by the coroner, by the way," Elaine said with a sigh. "They're following his wishes to be cremated and have his remains returned to Seattle, where he's originally from."

"Any memorial service planned for him in L.A.?" I asked.

"No, but I may put one together when things are more normal around here."

If they ever are, I didn't add. Instead, I said, "Did you want to see me about something?"

"Just curiosity. Since you have a reputation for knowing what's going on about crimes around you, I wondered if you knew whether they had any suspects in Ezra's and Corrie's deaths."

Jeff Hubbard, but I was reluctant to reveal that. "I'd hoped you called me in here so you could confess." I regaled her with a roguish grin, even if I was only half joking. But in all honesty, even if I wanted Jeff off the hook, I hoped it wouldn't leave someone else I liked on it. Like Elaine or Borden. Or even Millie Franzel. Better that it be a stranger, one I hoped would stay that way, like Bobby Lawrence. Or Jonathon Jetts. I'd found little to like about either the real estate broker or Ezra's former law partner.

Neither had I found any kind of evidence pointing directly to either of them as the most probable murderer.

But my comment had made Elaine pale, and she suddenly was straightening some piles of paper on her desk. "You're not serious, are you, Kendra?"

"Of course not," I responded, a bit too boisterously.

Her office door suddenly burst open, quick enough that it startled Gigi, who began to squawk and flap her large blue and gold wings. I reached up a hand to reassure the bird, especially when I saw that the intruder was Borden.

He stood still in the doorway, obviously taken aback by seeing both the bird on my back and Gigi's reaction to his appearance. He crossed his skinny arms quickly over his chartreuse sweater, cleared his throat, and stumbled, "Er, Kendra, Mignon mentioned you might be in here. I wanted to talk to Elaine and you about shifting around some of our caseload with Ezra gone. I've already discussed it with some of the others, and Geraldine and William have each agreed to assume three of Ezra's cases."

But Geraldine Glass and William Fortier, though both great litigators in their day, were even older than Borden, Elaine, and Ezra. Or at least they looked to be in their eighties. "Are you sure they can handle that much extra work?" I asked him.

"It'll be on a trial basis, so to speak," Borden acknowledged. "And I suggested that you could help out. At least until we hire another paralegal or two to assist in research and pleading preparation."

"I'll do all I can," I assured him.

"Including taking on another three matters yourself? And you, too, Elaine?"

The abundant wrinkles radiating from her eyes seemed to disappear as her arched eyebrows rose. "You're not serious."

But he was. And despite seeing any free time I might have had evanesce, I assured them, "I'll help out. I think I have someone to help with pet-sitting sometimes, so I should be fine."

"You're not going to give up pet-sitting now that you're practicing law again?" Elaine asked.

Partly to explain to her and partly as a reminder to our boss, I replied, "That was part of my deal coming to work for Borden. I can continue to take on my own cases, including low-paying pet-law matters, plus I can still pet-sit. Right now, though, I need to follow up on my T.O. matter, so, Elaine, if you will . . . ?" I didn't give her a glimmer of choice. I drew near, told her to hold out her arm, and ordered Gigi, "Step up!"

To my pleased surprise, the bird again obeyed without a hassle. She even seemed happy about it. In fact, out of the blue she started singing a song—if you could liken that awfully raspy noise to genuine music. It sounded kind of like a familiar tune, although I couldn't place it other than the fact I'd heard Gigi whistle it before.

"Gorgeous girl," I encouraged her. "Bottles of beer."

"Oh, one more thing before you leave, Kendra. That Detective Noralles called and said he's coming over again in about an hour. He wants to ask us some more questions."

"Thanks for letting me know," I said. With luck, I'd be long gone before he arrived.

I left Elaine and Borden with the bird.

I'D NO SOONER taken a seat at my own desk than Mignon gave me a call. "Jeff Hubbard is here to see you, Kendra," she sang.

"Send him in," I said, wishing I could instead say I wasn't really here.

Was I ready to face Jeff? I hadn't spoken to him since I got an earful from Amanda that might absolve Jeff from remaining Noralles's prime suspect in Corrie's murder. Had she also claimed she'd been with him all night when Ezra had been killed? Since she had called Jeff that night and I had gone home alone, I wouldn't know whether she lied about either or both assignations.

My office door opened, and Jeff stepped in. His face appeared as faded as his jeans, and his blue eyes stared instead of twinkled.

Poor guy. I knew exactly how agonizing it felt to be the number one suspect in a murder investigation. Interrogations. Angst. Concern about the future—and whether there'd ever be one beyond this horrible present.

I had a nearly uncontrollable urge to approach and envelop him in a huge hug. The *nearly,* fortunately, prevailed, since the urge was trumped by my knowledge of his alibi. I might be busting my buns trying to detect who really committed the killings. But Amanda was the one whose supposed eyewitness testimony might save Jeff.

Instead, I simply said, "Hi, Jeff. Come in and sit down. I doubt you'll want to stay long, though. I just learned Ned Noralles will be here to question us all some more."

Jeff flinched. "I'll leave in a minute," he agreed. His usual proud stride absent, he slunk around the front of my desk and planted the butt I liked to admire down on the bright blue upholstery of one of my wooden chairs. "It's a nightmare, Kendra," he began hoarsely. "Noralles is so pleased to be able to treat me like a common felon. He let me go so he could check out some . . . some eyewitness testimony."

Only then did Jeff's eyes meet mine, and they immediately tugged away again. As if he had something to hide.

"I spoke with Amanda earlier," I admitted to him. "I know she's providing you with an alibi." *Is it true?* I ached to ask.

"It's true," he replied without prompting, as if he was reading my mind. This time his haggard gaze didn't flee from mine. "Enough to prove I couldn't have harmed Corrie. Or Ezra, for that matter. I was with Amanda on both nights."

"That's wonderful," I chirped as cheerfully as Mignon ever did. "I'm so happy for you. But I need to leave now. I have a meeting." One as imaginary as my earlier assumption that my lifelong inability to choose anything but a louse as a lover had finally slunk away. "I'll be gone by the time Ned gets here."

"She wants me back, Kendra." He was taking big gobs of sea salt from his crocodile tears and rubbing them relentlessly into my wounds. Maybe my eyes, too, since they stung.

"Of course. Now if you'll excuse me . . ." I stood and approached my office door. "I need to prepare for my meeting."

He rose then. I thought with relief that he was going to leave with no further scene.

Instead, he came close and drew me into his arms.

Some perverse part of me wanted to melt into them, but my blood froze icily inside my veins. I stood stiffly, feeling his body heat and ordering myself not to thaw.

"She's willing to lie for me, she said, but it's not a lie. I was with her, Kendra. That part's true. I went to help her with her stalker problem. She showed me proof that Leon was hanging around, calling her, threatening her. She was scared, and I only wanted to help get rid of the guy for her." His laugh held the humor of a sobbing disaster survivor. "Not that I would kill him or anyone else."

"I understand that you did kill someone once," I blurted out, immediately regretting it when he blanched an even paler shade.

"Yeah, as a cop," he said softly. "It was a legitimate use of lethal force, to save myself and a fellow officer. It's why I know I'd do almost anything to avoid doing it again. How did you know?"

I didn't aim to point fingers toward my amiable and expressive friend Althea. Instead, I asked, "So how are things going with Amanda?"

He glared at me. "I swear to you, Kendra, I didn't sleep with her. Either that night, or any other time since I've met you."

"There've been some enjoyable nights when you haven't *slept* with me, either," I riposted in a juvenile attempt at a joke.

"I didn't make love with her." His teeth were gritted beside my ear, or so it sounded as he didn't let me leave his arms. "I didn't have sex with her. I didn't—"

Saved by the bell. Or rather, by the tone of his cell phone. A song, one I'd heard often before.

He pulled away and answered it.

I looked him in the eye. He didn't extract his steady gaze.

"Hi, Althea," he said. "No, I'm not in custody. I've been released, although I may have to cancel that business trip I have scheduled starting tomorrow. Yeah, yeah, it sounds like a trite cop comedy, but I'm not supposed to leave town. Right. I'll be at the office soon." He snapped his cell phone shut. "That was Althea," he said unnecessarily.

"So I gathered."

"And I'm sure you heard that I'm not leaving town. Will Lexie and you come to my place tonight?"

"I don't think so. That meeting I mentioned—"

"Won't last all night. You'll need to think of a better excuse." The expression on the face I'd once considered damnably dear became bleak.

"I don't need an excuse, Jeff," I reminded him gently.

"No, you don't."

"But I'll be there. For dinner. And then we'll see."

As I opened the door as a signal for him to exit, I saw Elaine strutting proudly down the hall, Gigi on her arm. At the same time, Jeff's cell phone chimed again. The macaw looked at us and spread her wings wide. She let out a huge squawk, then started to sing.

I felt my eyes pop open in astonishment. And recognition. And a certain amount of shock.

The mostly unrecognizable tune she was tearing into?

A hoarse, unrhythmic and inharmonious rendition of the four initial notes of the catchy song on Jeff's cell phone.

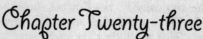

Chapter Twenty-three

MY REACTION MUST have been readily ascertainable, since Elaine said, "Kendra, is something wrong?"

At the same time Jeff inquired, "Are you okay, Kendra?"

"Kendra's just ducky," I responded, sticking a stupid smile on my face. "Glad Gigi's doing so well, Elaine."

Which she wasn't. Not then. The macaw seemed eager to lift off from Elaine's arm. The older woman kept her fastened down by some fingers on her back. Elaine turned and ducked into Ezra's office, apparently ready to relinquish the bird to her cage.

"See you later, Jeff. Right now, I really need to get ready for my meeting." The one with the ghoulies and ghosties playing ugly little games in my overimaginative mind. I fluttered my fingers in a wave goodbye, then shut my office door behind me.

I dove for the bookcase, where I'd left not only my favorite law tomes, but also a copy of one of Polly Bright's parrot books. I looked in the index but wasn't sure what I wanted to look up. Sounds? Repetition? Emotions?

Eventually I gave up on a rational approach and pulled open pages of the chapter on how members of the parrot family learn to talk.

Ah, there it was—pretty much as Polly had pointed out. Some parrot-types picked up not only people-type words, but also sounds . . . immediately when in an emotional situation.

Like murder.

Only . . . this book suggested that African Grey parrots and Amazons were the ones that repeated stuff precisely as they heard it. Macaws might learn to sing, and certainly could speak words, but they weren't as apt to duplicate something heard during a disturbing state of affairs.

So why was Gigi using Jeff's ring tone as her off-key aria? And was her squawking and flapping a reaction to running into the man with that phone?

She'd picked up the phrase "bottles of beer" fast.

Could Gigi, the only witness to both killings, have heard Jeff's cell phone ring during one or both of the horrible happenings and picked up on the sound? Maybe macaws didn't usually do that, but murder wasn't a usual situation.

Jeff had admitted Amanda would lie for him. Maybe she already had. Maybe he hadn't actually been in her company on either night. Maybe—

Hold on. Did I really believe Jeff was a killer?

He might be a louse as a lover, and absolutely abominable as a prospect for a permanent monogamous relationship, but a killer?

I just couldn't buy it.

But I also couldn't buy that this particular birdbrain of a witness could lie.

Worst of all, I'd already wondered if Ned Noralles read the same books and watched the same movies that Darryl did. I might convince myself to slough off the obvious answer regarding Gigi's new song, but Noralles might not.

He was on his way here. He might want Gigi around, just in case she emitted some avian revelation.

Would Gigi's terrible tune be used as incontrovertible evidence against Jeff?

I WAS STILL musing over all this when that same man slung his dejected body back into my office. "I almost forgot to show you," he said.

"Show me what?"

"This." He gestured for me to get up from my desk chair so he could plant his own trim behind in it. He turned to my computer. I didn't have anything confidential sitting on the screen, so I let him commence kanoodling with my keyboard.

In less than a minute, he logged on to a website, and what looked like a black-and-white video came up on my computer.

"Here you go," he said.

"*Where* I go?" I replied, then took a position at his shoulder overlooking the view.

And quickly chortled with glee. Until I gasped and growled, "Is that who I think it is, doing what I think he's doing?"

"Yes, and yes," Jeff responded, apparently able to interpret my imprecise inquiries. "It's a video filmclip from the security camera my company installed at your request. I had my employee Buzz set it up as soon as you asked, doing it after dark so no one would see it."

"Thank Buzz for me," I said, recalling the tall dude with a shaved head I'd seen at Jeff's office when I'd visited there. "He did a great job!"

"He sure did, and at a timely moment, too."

"I'll second that."

The film showed Sheldon Siltridge, neighbor to my client Cal Orlando, tossing his own mail into Cal's yard.

Poor old Lester the basset hound must have seen the trespass, as he was intended to. He soon appeared, barreling across the footage, in time for Siltridge to whip a rolled-up newspaper from behind his back and start bopping the pup with it. Lester cowered at first, then got mad and started snapping.

"A sequence just like this must have led to Sheldon's getting a bite taken out of him by Lester," I crowed. "The bite he's suing Cal about, the bastard. Oh, this is great. Willful misconduct, assumption of the risk . . . I'll need a couple of copies and access to this website so I can send it on to Sheldon's shyster lawyer, Jerry Ralphson."

"I thought lawyers avoided calling each other shysters out of professional courtesy," Jeff said.

"I do it only when the shoe fits damned snugly," I told him.

"Like now?"

"Like now." I couldn't help it. I leaned over his substantial shoulder and gave him one heck of a kiss. Which he gave as good back. And that started me thinking that I just might decide to stay at his place for the night.

Only . . . even if I could ignore Amanda, there was a little matter to be reconciled between Jeff and Gigi. And Jeff's cell phone.

"May I see your phone?" I asked him.

He gave me an odd look. "Sure, if you tell me why."

"I just want to see whose numbers you have programmed in." And listen to its unique, Althea-generated ring tone. And—"

"You're in it. So is Amanda. Is that what you wanted to know?"

"Well . . ." I didn't want to go into my whole unwinding thought process yet, till I made sure my suspicions weren't just planted by my unraveling mind. "Yeah, that's it. Would you please bookmark that site for me on my computer and e-mail me the web address? Right now?"

"Okay." He spoke slowly, as if he sensed I had something entirely separate in my brain. But he did as I asked . . . even as I slipped over to the side of my desk and lifted the phone receiver.

And called Jeff's number.

And heard the *Magnum, P.I.* theme song ring tone. Gigi's version consisted of a repetition of the first four notes, raspy and off-key, and without the catchy rhythm.

"It's only me," I said. "Checking to see where you keep your phone. Do all men stick it in their back pockets like that?"

He finished fiddling with my keyboard and stood. His dusty blond brows were knitted into one scorcher of a scowl. "I don't know what you're really up to, Kendra, but I know it has something to do with the murders—and whether you think I committed them." He apparently either hadn't heard Gigi's rendition of his cell phone song or hadn't a clue about the supposed significance. "Obviously you haven't yet exonerated me, based on what Amanda's said or otherwise."

"I thought I had," I said softly, my eyes staring at the light Berber carpet on my office floor.

"You know what? I think we should skip your visit tonight. I'm feeling a bit sick."

I glanced up to meet his stony gaze.

"Good idea," I said. "You ought to rest. I hope you feel better."

Me, too, I thought this time as I watched him walk out my office door.

Now I REALLY did have a meeting to prepare for. After Jeff left, my anguish segued into anger, and I made a few phone calls. The first was to my client Cal Orlando, who didn't know the Internet from a basketball net, but had a brother who successfully surfed all day. I told him where to find the case-finishing film, then called opposition counsel, Jerry Ralphson. I likewise reeled off the web address to him and suggested a time that afternoon for all parties to meet and confer. And if all went as spiffily as I anticipated, settle.

I ordered the others, in the nicest way possible, to come to my home turf, my office, where it'd be even more obvious who ruled. My client and I held all the cards.

At precisely 4 P.M., Cal Orlando arrived with Lester on a leash. I've often subscribed to the saying that people choose pups who resembled them, but not so in Cal's case. Lester, the basset hound, had long, bedraggled ears and wonderfully woeful eyes. Cal was cool—optimistic, upbeat, and obviously fit, the kind of chap who, when not working, spent all his waking hours at a gym. Nothing bedraggled about him, and he smiled often to reveal his straight white teeth. We strategized for a short while in my office, then headed to the bar–turned–conference room.

I wasn't exactly an electronics whiz, but I'd learned a lot about presentations thanks to my years of courtroom performances. As a result, I ensured that I had everything ready, so when Mignon announced that the other parties were present, I started the show: a life-size projection of the damning video right on a bare wall.

Jerry and his client, the self-proclaimed bite victim Sheldon Siltridge, entered the room just as the video Lester bounded up to that very same Sheldon, the vicious neighbor who'd strewn his own mail on Lester's turf. In seconds, as the others took seats around the conference table, Sheldon—skinny and scowling and an all-around miserable character—was seen striking Lester with a rolled-up newspaper.

"Hello, gentlemen," I said, proud that only a hint of satisfaction slipped from my tone. "First, I'd like to refer you to page forty-six of the transcript of Mr. Siltridge's deposition. There's a copy at each of your places at the table."

Jerry Ralphson had a buzz cut and bow tie—both of

which might have set him apart before a jury, but neither appeared particularly snazzy here. I watched as his superior and slyly confident gaze stuck on the video on the wall, and then moved uneasily down to the depo. He turned to the page I'd designated, blanched, then bade his client to read what he'd run into.

"I trust you saw the website even before you got here today?" I asked Jerry. He nodded nastily. "And are you now paying attention to the part of the depo in which Mr. Siltridge says he never baited Lester by tossing things into his yard? And that he absolutely never struck the dog, whether with a newspaper or anything else? Of course the stenographer administered the appropriate oath before we began our deposition. Can anyone here say 'perjury'?"

Jerry Ralphson sat up straight and glared at me, as if I were the one in the wrong. "My client never consented to be photographed, Ms. Ballantyne."

"These were taken with a security camera aimed only on my client's own property, Jerry. For his peace of mind and safety, and all that. Don't bother posturing."

But my admonishment fell on ears that had elected to stay deaf. "And whatever this film shows," he continued, "which is unclear, very poor quality, it had to have been taken after the deposition. Long after the dog bite at issue. And after your client gave Mr. Siltridge the idea of acting in such a way. He'd never have done so before, but the bite, and these proceedings, have been hard on him. He—"

"Forget the sob story, Jerry. And stop cluing your client on how to testify. Here's what we want. Your client drops the suit and pays Mr. Orlando the amount of my fees plus expenses, plus another five thousand dollars for Cal's pain and suffering, they sign a settlement agreement in which Mr. Siltridge admits no wrongdoing but promises never to enter Mr. Orlando's property again for any reason—mail, female, or neutral—or to get within fifty feet of Lester, and we're happy as basset hounds."

Jerry glanced at Sheldon Siltridge, whose white face seemed stricken. Sheldon only stared back at Jerry.

"A moment alone with my client," Jerry commanded.

With a smile at Cal and Lester and a crook of my head toward the door, we assented.

Ten minutes later, we held a formal handshake with the opposition, temporarily sealing the deal until the settlement papers were signed.

WHEN I PICKED Lexie up before pet-sitting rounds later, I related briefly to Darryl how my day had been, starting with the good stuff—the settlement—and ending with the bad—my ongoing ambivalence about Jeff, his relationship with Amanda, and his innocence.

He gazed over his glasses at me and slowly shook his head. "Sorry things are rotten again on the relationship front. Any chance of salvaging it?"

I sighed so loud that Lexie, who'd been sniffing her playmates goodbye a few feet away, darted over and leaped sympathetically on to my lap. "I doubt it."

Darryl gave me a hug. "You need a vacation, Kendra."

"I need a life."

LEXIE AND I stopped for Rachel Preesinger before hitting the road for our evening pet-sitting patrol. She was excited and animated, telling me her dad's trip was delayed till tomorrow.

When we returned to my rented-out house, Rachel said, "I can't think when I've had so much fun, Kendra. Are there any other pets you sit for?"

"Maybe," I said. I'd asked Darryl to slow down on referrals due to my reduction in time, but with her assistance I might order him to rev it up again. Maybe even for daytime walks now and then, which I'd forgone to avoid exiting my law office or even court midday for a visit to a client of a canine kind. "If you're serious. And if you can work out access to a car. I'll have to add you to my insurance. And we'll both probably need to get bonded one day. But if you really want to become my assistant, we'll set things up like a real business, and I'll pay you a generous percentage of what I bring in for the work that you do. Think about it."

"Cool!" she exclaimed, just as her dad exited the big house with Beggar in tow—or vice versa. She told him concisely what was so cool, and the two invited me to share their pizza dinner—Lexie, too.

When I headed for bed much later that night, my mind was a vortex of visions of films of furtive neighbors leading to lucrative settlements, a possibility of an accelerated pet-sitting business, the excellent time I'd shared with Rachel and her attractive dad, Russ . . . and the sound of a macaw singing a particularly familiar cell phone ring.

And the resulting argument.

And the certainty that the usual call I received at bedtime when Jeff was on the road wouldn't come tonight.

I wanted, for Borden's sake—and my own rejuvenated legal career—to work things out for T.O., and to dig into the other cases Ezra had left which were assigned to me.

But mostly, I still wanted to solve the two murders and pray my key suspect would not ultimately be Jeff.

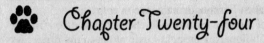

Chapter Twenty-four

THE NEXT MORNING, my ego still tasted a touch of triumph over the resolution of one of my pet-related cases—even if that same ego also sat in the toilet mourning the other issues in my life.

As a result, after easing Lexie off my arm and pep-talking myself out of bed, I called Rachel and asked if she could be ready to accompany me pet-sitting half an hour earlier than I'd originally told her. She eagerly agreed. Ah, youth. With someone else bearing all burdens of the business, my young associate could bask worry-free in the pleasure of pet-tending.

As I dressed in a rust-colored sweater and cargo pants, then tended Lexie, I considered the course of my pending day.

I wanted to massage the good emotions engendered by my success and cast aside the regretful ones. But the only other pet-advocacy issue I was involved in looked as dire as my murder investigation, my representation of T.O. . . . and my nonrelationship with Jeff.

I'd already called to tell Irma Etherton about my interview of Walt Shorbel's estate attorney, Dennis Kamura, and his take on Walt's stubbornness in deciding on the contents of his will.

I needed a new angle here, one that stood a chance of success when I argued Irma's case in court.

When I'd ended escorting Rachel and pets on our morning constitutionals, I brought Lexie along to my office. As was now my habit, I asked Mignon where Gigi was. Today, Elaine had taken the bird to her turf. After settling Lexie under my desk, I visited Elaine's office, glad when Gigi didn't warble out Jeff's melody. Instead, Elaine and the macaw managed to appear at peace with one another. Gigi sat uncaged on her large perch in the center of the office, and all looked well.

"Hi, gorgeous girl," I said as I popped my head in. "You, too, Gigi." As I anticipated, that engendered a giggle from Elaine.

When I returned to my office, I patted Lexie, then called Irma. "I'd like for us to meet," I said when she answered. "To discuss strategies." I drummed a pen on a legal pad as I prepared to make notes. "I'll dig into legal research today so I can draft a complaint with enough substance that the suit won't appear frivolous, but I have to warn you again, before I throw much time into it, that our chances of getting a court to order anything similar to Walt's stated wishes are slim to zilch."

Especially since attorney Dennis Kamura could testify that such stated wishes might not be what Walt wanted when he first executed the will. Kamura had advised him then that his bequest could fail and his kids would then take all. At least the wording of Walt's later codicil suggested he'd intended the will to work. Since the codicil was all in his handwriting, a court would likely consider it the equivalent of a holographic will, so it could be valid despite the lack of witness signatures. Enforceable? That was another legal dilemma.

I'd at least run my ideas by Elaine Aames, since her legal specialty was estates and trusts.

"We have to try," Irma asserted into my ear. "When I think of that poor pup Ditch, I could cry. I was going to call you today, Kendra. I left word with a neighbor of Myra Shorbel's to keep in touch, to let me know how Ditch is being treated. She called me early this morning saying that she thought Ditch was left outside all night, tied on a cold, hard patio."

I glanced down at Lexie, who cocked her head soulfully and stared back. The idea of a dog left outside without shelter on a chilly January night, even a dry one, caused my skin to shudder.

But still . . . the law might provide for care of mistreated pups, but it didn't provide that one could inherit a million dollars. At least not directly. "I'm concerned that if we report abuse to the authorities now, Ditch might be put into Animal Services custody, not necessarily yours. We need to go about this carefully so the court will buy into our arguments. If we try to get Ditch his full million dollars plus your custody, his kids will argue that you're only fighting their claim to get your hands on all that money. What if we ask for something less, like—"

"Ask for a lot less, as far as I'm concerned. Like *nothing,* as long as I get Ditch to take care of."

My sense of possible settlement suddenly went on full alert. "Are you serious, Irma? I mean, are you willing just to adopt Ditch and let Walt's kids keep all the money?"

"Of course."

"I'll call their attorney," I said. "We'll set up a conference. Soon."

UNFORTUNATELY, THE SHORBEL siblings' lawyer, Gina Udovich, was out of town, or so I was informed by her secretary. It was Thursday now, and she was not anticipated to return to her office until Monday.

At least that gave me the opportunity to probe into the research I'd planned anyway, to give myself an edge and scope out whatever leverage I could provide.

Over that weekend, I also spent time on my T.O. matter, researching approaches that other attorneys representing developers had taken against vocal and vehement antidevelopment property owners.

Talk about precedents and ingenious endeavors, they were prodigious in the L.A. area, especially these days when environmentalists, pseudo and real, were eager to slam lids down durably on developers' dreams to change still-existing open space into private homes and commercial areas.

One constructive component of the Vancino situation was that the bitterly disputed block was already built out into commercial structures. T.O. intended to increase the density of the use—like, they would sardine scads of prosperous people into upscale high-rise apartments, while adding offices and chic stores as well. But no additional endangered species would be forced to flee their habitats—unless one included obsolescent, antiprogress property owners like Millie Franzel.

Also during the weekend, I spent more time rooting Rachel in the ins and outs I'd learned about pet-tending. I even had an unanticipated opportunity to take her to meet one of my favorite charges, Pythagoras the ball python, who welcomed us with open coils . . . after his owner, Milt Abadim, called and mentioned he'd be traveling to see his mother again soon, and he'd love for me to keep an eye on Py.

I enjoyed the company, during those days, not only of Rachel, but also her dad. Russ's trip had been delayed yet again, until early next week. All of us strolled with Lexie and Beggar. I came to feel included in their incomplete family.

And I definitely sensed that Russ was interested in me as more than his daughter's quasi-employer and substitute big sis.

And me? I made a damned fine effort to keep Jeff Hubbard as far from my frazzled mind as the moon was from the earth. Only I realized that analogy was apt in too many ways, for the earth's gravity didn't let the moon sail off into space . . .

He didn't call me. I didn't call him.

But I amazed myself by calling Detective Ned Noralles. I wasn't surprised, and felt a smattering of relief, when he wasn't accessible. And no wonder. It was Sunday. Only, I assumed that L.A.P.D. detectives' days on duty could occur anytime. I left a message suggesting that he and I speak soon. What would I tell him? I wasn't sure. I wanted more from him than I intended to relate. But if he insisted, I'd give him the benefit of my so-far unsuccessful investigative work. Most of it.

I'd keep Gigi's song to myself. After all, it was unlikely to have any significance.

Monday finally meandered around, and I heard back from attorney Gina Udovich. She hadn't a moment to spare until Wednesday, which was when we scheduled the all-hands meeting regarding the case that, if I had to file a complaint, would be known as *Etherton v. Shorbel et al.* I was pleasantly surprised when Gina agreed we could confer on my turf instead of hers, giving me a kind of home court advantage. Or was that only to patronize me and put me off guard so she could swoop in and clobber me in front of her clients?

Oh, yes, all the old slimy litigator tricks were still simmering in the back of my brain. They might have slipped there to curl up into a cold little unused ball while my law license was lifted, but now they were unfurling, stretching, warming up, and making sure I grew reacquainted with every one of them.

Which turned out to be a good thing, since it became clear by the grand finale of our settlement conference that this case was going forward.

WE CONVENED AT one o'clock in the Yurick firm's handy-dandy bar–slash–conference room. Gina Udovich appeared to be vying for the title of superchic attorney of the year, clad in a short leather skirt over black stockings, and boots with amazingly high, skinny heels. My feet ached just observing them. On top, she wore a black vest over a silky peach blouse. In all, it was a good thing that the only guys around this office were old enough to be her grandpa. Not that William Fortier and Borden Yurick didn't ogle her as if they were forty years younger.

In the beauty department, she was upstaged by her pretty client Myra Shorbel. Myra wore a vest, too—a knit one—over her ordinary blue blouse. Her makeup was lighter than her lawyer's. Her slacks were black denim and she'd donned sports shoes that nearly matched her brother Moe's.

Moe hadn't worn clothes that might concede he had come to a business meeting. His grungy T-shirt had torn-off sleeves, which I noticed immediately as he took off his equally dirty denim jacket. His bony knees knobbed their way through the holes in his jeans.

Irma, about the age of most of my firm's attorneys, had donned a dress for the occasion. Her hands fluttered nervously when we all took seats at the conference table, but she wisely shoved them into her lap to keep them still. The bouffant style of her dyed black hair had deflated a bit, but on the whole she appeared prepared for the impending ordeal.

And me? Well, I'd dressed in a regulation pantsuit that I could wear equally well had we headed for court. I'd checked in the mirror before meeting up with everyone here, and my shoulder-length, still ordinary brown hair hung neat and professional. My makeup was neither over- nor underdone. Most important, I was psyched.

"Okay," I said after I'd ensured that everyone who wanted any had gotten coffee from the carafe on the bar. "Listen up. We have a situation here, and before Irma files an action against the Shorbels regarding Walter Shorbel's estate, we wanted to see if there's any possibility of compromising on the issues." I wasn't about to blurt right out that Irma had already determined to forgo the funds if she got custody of Ditch. Let them stew a bit, then make it appear that Irma was making a colossal concession. Which she was.

Gina Udovich stretched her arm out over the table and idly drummed long red nails that looked anything but lovely on the wood. "We're here because my clients aren't interested in being sucked into a frivolous lawsuit. Their father was quite obviously in his dotage when he made such an absurd will. His dog can't inherit his estate. Even if the court attempts to impose a different interpretation, we have a diminished capacity argument. The will must be disregarded, and Mr. Shorbel will be deemed to have died intestate." Exactly the arguments I'd have asserted had I been in her uncomfortable boots.

Calmly, I said, "Interesting theory, counselor. I've got some of my own that I won't share with you just yet. We'll wait for the trial, if it comes to that. But we have a proposition for you, plus some teeth to back it up."

Gina's grin displayed *her* teeth, which were so white that I figured she bleached them nightly. "Ah, yes. I've done my homework, Kendra. I'm sure you're bringing up teeth because you take on cases about dog bites."

"And get them settled, too, since I find creative ways to

make the plaintiff grovel. Did that show up in your research?"

Ah, yes, it was back—my litigator sting! Always presented with a smile, of course.

"Well, there won't be any groveling here. But go ahead and try to convince us to settle."

Her clients observed her with apparent adoration. I'd fix that fast by turning the talk back to them.

"Fine," I said. "Now, as Mr. Shorbel's alleged heirs, they have taken custody of his dog, Glenfiddich, who was the intended beneficiary, correct?"

"Purportedly." Gina pushed herself back and studied me with her snide crocodile smile.

"Our first action, if we must go to court, will be for a TRO"—a temporary restraining order—"to stop your clients from mistreating that poor dog. We ourselves observed his quarters—locked away in a storeroom. We also have an eyewitness who'll testify as to how the animal is abandoned outside in foul weather, left on an unenclosed patio all night."

"It's just a dog," shouted Moe Shorbel, his pale brown eyes clamped on me in an evil glare.

"You mentioned dog bites before," interjected Myra Shorbel in a much more modulated voice. "I've been worried that Ditch will bite my young daughter Ellie. I can't just let him run loose in the house."

"He doesn't bite!" Irma raced into the fray before I could restrain her. "There's no reason to treat the poor thing like that. Shame on you. Your father was right, leaving everything to the dog instead of horrible children like you."

I could hear an imaginary judge in my mind if an outburst like that occurred at trial. "Control your client, counselor."

I didn't wait for Gina Udovich to suggest the same. "You're right, of course, Irma. But let's try to resolve this amicably." I returned my litigator's unperturbed attention

to Gina. "Ms. Etherton is prepared to make a most generous offer of settlement. First, she wants immediate, permanent custody of Glenfiddich. If that's agreed, she will
reduce her claim on the estate on behalf of the dog to two
hundred thousand dollars. The estate amounts to a million
or more, and the remainder may be retained by your clients
Mr. and Ms. Shorbel."

I half anticipated an onslaught of objections by the
sour siblings surrounding us. Instead, I noted a sly smile
insinuate itself onto Moe Shorbel's face as his sister hazarded a glance at him that suggested admiration. What
was going on?

"We discussed this possibility in advance, Ms. Ballantyne," Gina Udovich purred. "My clients are willing to
convey custody of the dog to your client as long as she
makes no claim at all on the rest of the estate."

"I'll need to discuss with my client whether she is willing to lower her settlement amount to a hundred thousand
dollars," I said, "but she clearly is entitled to some com-
pensation on behalf of Glenfiddich. She will need money
to care for him—food, veterinary bills, and so forth, for the
rest of his life. He is now six years old and can live another
six years or more."

"Nothing," Moe Shorbel stated. "She can have the mutt
but no money. And if she doesn't agree, we'll keep the dog,
too. And if you think he's been mistreated till now—"

"Enough," Gina said in an attempt to shut up her client.

But Irma had extracted from that exactly what I had.
"Did you start abusing that poor animal so I'd agree to take
him quickly, without claiming any of the money dear Walt
didn't want you to have?"

This time, Moe stayed discreetly silent. But his slimy
smile said it all.

"Forget settlement!" Irma stormed. "Kendra, I want
Ditch out of that house now, so get that restraining order
first thing. Then I want to sue them for the entire amount of

the estate on behalf of Ditch. I won't care if they spend every cent of it on attorneys' fees, as long as they don't get any use of it."

Gina didn't appear upset in the least about that idea. "Moe, Myra, I think this settlement conference is over."

"No," Myra said with a sigh as she stood. Her pretty face appeared pained. "The dog shouldn't get the money, of course, and I'm willing to fight in court about that. But I don't want Ditch around and neither does Moe. Forget about that restraining order stuff. You can have custody of Ditch right away, Irma, as long as it's understood that we still don't agree that the damned dog should inherit our dad's estate."

Irma beamed. "I'll come right over for him."

"And I'll draw up the necessary document to ensure there's no modification of the resolution of this issue," I added. "And now, please excuse me a moment while I confer with my client." I motioned for Irma to follow me out the door.

I scooted her into the nearest empty office and whispered, "You got what you wanted—the dog. Do you want to continue this fight over the money?"

"Yes, damn it," the sixty-year-old hissed. "Those miserable children purposely mistreated the dog their dad loved to get me to cave and let them keep the money. I meant it. I'll fight them forever over it, since it's what Walt would have wanted."

Maybe, if the handwritten codicil was the key. "I have to warn you that they have a good shot at winning. And then you'll not only fail to get the million, you'll be out all the money you pay to me."

Irma's smile was wry. "Honey, I don't need Walt's mere million dollars. And my own heirs are well provided for even if I spend a million to keep those kids from getting Walt's. I started my own brand of canned soups about forty years ago and sold my secret recipes for a fortune five years back to one of the majors. It's a matter of principle, though. I loved Walt, and he loved me, and now his damned ungrateful offspring are going to pay."

Which meant this formerly suspended litigator was finally returning to her favorite surroundings very soon. *Hello, court. Here I come!*

Chapter Twenty-five

I USHERED THE Sorbels and their not-so-smug attorney out the door, then said farewell to Irma. "I'll get the settlement document about Ditch done right away," I assured her, "then prepare a complaint to file in court to claim the money."

As Irma strolled down the Yurick offices' sidewalk toward the street, I was slightly surprised to see Detective Noralles approach. I'd planned to pop in on him at his office at the North Hollywood Station. My intent hadn't been for him to insinuate himself here.

Well, I was the one who'd maneuvered this meeting, so why not make it convenient? I'd need to be careful, though, about what he heard. "Hi, Ned," I said. "Come in. We'll talk in the conference room. There's coffee there from my last meeting."

"Sounds good." The good-looking African-American cop was clad in one of his characteristic suits, this one tweed with tones matching shades in his multicolor tie. "I'd like to use your washroom first."

"Fine."

He greeted Mignon, and I directed him toward the men's room. Unnecessary, I realized, for me to tell him where to go—at least in this sense. After the multiple murder investigations he'd been here to conduct, he probably knew the location of every nook and cranny a lot better than I did.

While Ned was otherwise occupied, I stuck my face into Borden's office as a courtesy, to inform him the police were present. Same with Elaine, since as a former lady friend of Ezra's, she doubtless still teetered near the top of the cops' suspect list.

"Thanks, Kendra," Elaine replied after I told her. She sat at her desk, and Gigi perched on her pole.

"Bottles of beer," Gigi countered, lifting her beautiful blue wings in a quasi-shrug and causing me to laugh.

"What's so funny?" asked Ned from behind me.

Uh-oh. I'd loitered too long. Before I could turn and usher him in a different direction, he'd pulled open the door and edged in around me.

"I'm just happy that Gigi's doing so well," I responded rapidly. "Come to the conference room. We'll talk."

"Sure," he said to me, but instead of accompanying me, he sauntered toward Elaine's desk. "I don't suppose you've recalled exactly when you first met Corrie Montez, have you, Ms. Aames?"

Elaine appeared unperturbed as she dug in at her desk chair and folded her arms. She'd removed her suit jacket, and today she wore a pearly gray shirt that complemented her short silver hair. "Trying to catch me in a fib, are we, Detective Noralles? I told you already that I can't recall, but even though we only recently became close, I knew Ezra for ages, from a law firm where we both worked long ago. I visited him occasionally at Jambison & Jetts. I could have run into Corrie there sometime, though I don't remember meeting her till recently, when Ezra and I both started discussing coming to work here. He mentioned he might invite a young paralegal named Corrie to join us and introduced us then."

"So you still maintain you'd have no reason to harm either Mr. Cossner or Ms. Montez?" Despite the obvious insinuation in his words, Ned's voice remained as deadpan as his face.

"As I said, stop trying to rile or confuse me. You have my statement. That's all I'm saying." Elaine didn't sound confused, but Noralles had unmistakably sparked the riling part. Her voice was raised, and so was her body as she stood and shot him an angry glare.

The tension in the room must have gotten to Gigi, too. She started to squawk in her familiar rhythmic chant effectively designed to drive humans nuts.

Startled at first, I turned toward her and raised my hands in a placating pose. "It's okay, gorgeous girl. Everything's fine." I intended my tone to sound soothing. At least she hadn't issued an uncanny shriek. But there were other sounds she might make that Ned Noralles shouldn't hear. "We've upset her," I said. "Why don't we leave, Ned. I want to tell you—"

And then, there it was. Jeff's cell phone song, sung in Gigi's inimitably hoarse rasp.

"Gorgeous girl," I prompted more loudly.

"Hang on," Ned said.

I wished I *could* hang on. To Gigi's large black, menacingly barbed beak, to shut her up. Or to Ned's arm, to arrange for him to exit this office with me, pronto.

"Isn't that—hell, yes!" He looked at me, a gleam of excitement emanating from his dark brown eyes. "That sounds like part of Hubbard's ring tone."

I knew Noralles had heard that cell phone sound at least once, right here in the Yurick offices when he'd regrettably run into Jeff here. Even so, I said, "I don't think so. I suppose you could read a resemblance into it if you stretch your imagination, but the notes and rhythm are really different. Besides, Gigi hasn't the ability of an African Grey when it comes to aping sounds. Macaws have lots of talents, but—"

"I've done some reading about birds in the parrot family," Ned said, his gaze pinning me motionless like a stuck butterfly.

I hazarded a helpless glance toward Elaine, but this time the confusion she had avoided before seemed pasted all over her scrunched-up face.

"You're right, Kendra," Ned said. "Some birds are better than others at repeating things they hear under emotional duress. But how often is Hubbard around here?"

"Not often," I said. "And to teach macaws to say things or sing songs, repetition is the key."

"Twice could do it. Say, two visits with a lot of duress each time? With the same cell phone ringing in the background."

"Who would call in the middle of a murder?" I demanded.

"Someone who didn't know what was happening," he replied, so smug I could slug him. "Maybe even you. And then when you realized what had happened, you felt stuck. You cared for the guy—note the past tense. In our interrogations of him, he's seemed pretty bummed out about your relationship. Maybe you are, too. And that's why you happened to invite me here today and lead me to the macaw, so I could hear her sing Hubbard's song—allowing you to add another nail into his post-lethal-injection coffin. Assuming, of course, that we get a murder conviction. Thanks to you, we've another bit of evidence to add to his bloody jacket."

With effort, I lured the overly confident cop away from the off-key macaw. I wished the office's bar was still stocked with booze. *I* needed a good, stiff belt, and maybe a nip would turn Ned's certainties about Jeff back to mere unsubstantiated suspicions.

Bending his bored ear while we sat in a booth, I disclosed more than I ever had before with this detective. I lavished on him my own inquiries and investigations over the last few days. I let him know I couldn't buy the too-expedient openness of Bobby Lawrence's admissions of no alibis. I chose not to spew the same about Millie Franzel. I loathed even the small likelihood that she could have killed anyone and chose not to sic the detective on her further without certainty.

I slipped in a stab at statistics—and how many people, even solely in L.A., had cell phones that could sing similar tunes—not mentioning the uniqueness of Jeff's.

And Ned's reaction to my tidy tap dance?

He leaned over the table between us and looked me earnestly in the eye. I tried to ignore the gleam of satisfaction in his oh-so-innocent gaze. "You're having second thoughts about having handed me this last piece of evidence against Hubbard, aren't you, Kendra? I understand. You two were really tight for a few months. But you're a lawyer—an officer of the court, as they say. You should feel damned proud for helping bring a murderer to justice."

"I do feel proud," I assented. "And don't forget I found you *two* murderers—those who framed me and my tenants. Now I'm hunting whoever's been framing Jeff, and you should be, too."

Any pleasantness departed from his demeanor. He stood and shot me the evil eye as he stared down at me. "Stay out of it now, Kendra. I warn you, if you do anything to get in the way of Jeff Hubbard's conviction—"

"Like find the real killer?" My mood had segued from fear for Jeff to fury with this egotistical cop with the single-track mind. Justice? He was letting retribution for old gripes against Jeff get in the way of good cop sense.

I had no reason to suspect the rest of the L.A.P.D. was as incompetent and vengeful as this nasty Noralles. If I had time, I planned to contact his superior in this investigation, Detective Schwinglan, and lodge a huge complaint.

But right now, I was more concerned with undoing my part in Jeff's mess.

Fists clenched as if he'd love to flatten me, Ned instead let his big cop's body tower over me menacingly for an utterly unnerving moment. "Like I said," Ned spit as his parting shot, "don't get in the way, Kendra, or you'll be sorry."

I waited till he was way out in the entry, with Mignon and other staff around providing safety in numbers before I shot back, "I'll be sorrier if I don't help get things right, Ned. See you around."

BACK IN MY office, I faced a frisky Lexie, who clearly had something on her mind: lovingly chewing out her hopeless owner for being untrainable.

As I consequently walked her, my mind converted itself into a computer. I brought up the screen on which I'd inserted all my possible murder suspects in order of lethal likelihood. I reordered them, then rejected that and reshuffled again. I'd need to refer to the real thing, to ensure that I hadn't inadvertently omitted any possible people.

I did just that when Lexie led me back to our daytime digs. While she curled up beneath my desk on the Berber rug, I pulled my list up on my genuine electronic computer and edited it much as I had in my mind.

I ensured that Borden and Elaine were down at the bottom. Not that I believed that either was guilty any more now than I had before, but for the moment I elected not to remove anyone from my musings.

Just above them was Jeff. I hated to slip any credence into Ned Noralles's flimsy rationale and his dogged determination to bring Jeff down for these killings. Still, Jeff's alleged involvement made slightly more sense than the aforementioned elderly Yurick firm attorneys. He had been

heard arguing with Ezra. Ezra had threatened his liveli-
hood, claiming he could cause other attorneys to avoid en-
gaging Jeff's P.I. and security services. Not that I believed
Jeff would find Ezra's bombastic bullying credible.

As a P.I., Jeff could probably purchase spare handguns
without a problem, and could have underground resources
so no one would be the wiser. Not so, necessarily, with ordinary, apparently law-abiding attorneys.

Then there was that other annoying little question: Why
was Gigi singing Jeff's ring tone?

Move on, Kendra, I cautioned myself, staring at my fingers now resting on my keyboard. Otherwise, I might bog
down right at this spot on my little list—and I was damned
if I'd give Detective Noralles the satisfaction.

Okay, then. Back to my tell-all computer screen.

Above Jeff, I kept Millie Franzel. As open and above-
board as she was about her gun-toting and lack of alibi, I
couldn't help thinking that she used her honesty as a
shield. She'd hated T.O. and therefore its attorney for trying to force her into selling her beautiful pet boutique business. Was that a credible motive for murder? Certainly.

Same went for broker Bobby Lawrence. With him, the
motive could also have been monetary. I doubted he'd kill
over losing a single sale: Elaine's aborted offer on a Vancino home. But I'd learned that he'd coveted the representation of T.O. in future property purchases, and Ezra had
vetoed that potentially lucrative possibility. Could a broker
get his greedy hands on some guns? Why not?

I kept my consideration centered on Ezra instead of
Corrie. My mind was mired in the concept that the paralegal's death was the direct result of something she saw or
knew about Ezra. Right? Wrong? I'd keep my befuddled
brain open to an alternate scenario.

Beneath my desk, Lexie lifted her head and sighed at
me. "You're right, girl," I replied. "It's nearly time for us to
go pet-sitting." That generated a happy tail wag as she

stood in anticipation of departure. "Five more minutes," I bargained. A biscuit would have sealed it, but my office cupboard was bare. Lexie stood on both hind legs and began to dig at my forearm with her front paws. "I promise," I told her with a pat to the head. She settled back down a little sulkily, I surmised. "Spoiled puppy," I said in a tone suggesting more praise than insult. I smiled as she wagged once more. Her Cavalier moods never remained glum for more than a moment.

Okay, I said to myself. Back to the list.

I'd done little so far to investigate or eliminate my top three contenders: VORPO president and property owner Flint Daniels, Ezra's former law partner Jonathon Jetts, and Jetts's new wife who was formerly Ezra's lady friend, Bella Quevedo-Jetts.

Daniels was problematic as a person to seek out on my own, since he was representative of an opposition party in ongoing litigation. As a result, I lifted my phone and called VORPO's counsel, Michael Kleer.

Whose name I incidentally added to my suspect list. He'd been among those who knew and opposed Ezra. To what extent did he despise him?

"Hi, Michael?" I said when I got him on the line. "Could we set up a meeting tomorrow morning—you and Flint Daniels and I? I'd like to discuss the lawsuit and VORPO's willingness to look at alternate dispute resolution. Yes, I'll try to bring Brian O'Barlen."

Brian, too, was available for the meeting.

Brian, too, was a card-carrying, lower-level member of my suspect list.

And then I called to set up a session with Jonathon Jetts for the afternoon. He wasn't thrilled, but when I told him our confidential topic of discussion was the apparent dissatisfaction of some of his former clients with the Yurick firm, he sounded a heck of a lot happier to oblige.

Hey, cops were allowed to tell lies to suspects to get

them to confess. I was simply appropriating one of their sleazier techniques.

"Okay, Lexie," I finally said. "Time to go. And I know you'll have more fun tomorrow. You'll spend the day at Darryl's doggy resort."

And me? Would I enjoy tomorrow's contrived confrontations with some of my most suspicious suspects?

You bet!

Chapter Twenty-six

IN THE OLD days, I'd leapt into litigation with the greatest of gusto. Law and motion was my meat and potatoes. Courtroom drama was my dessert.

But during the days my law license had been suspended, the pet disputes dropped on my apartment doorstep, mostly by Darryl, had required the most creative of approaches—ones that didn't smack of practicing law without a license.

As a result, I'd assumed a sort of pet mediation posture, alternate dispute resolution with pizzazz.

That was the attitude I assumed the next morning, while sitting beside Brian O'Barlen across the table from Michael Kleer and VORPO pres, Flint Daniels.

None needed to know my ulterior motive for this meeting.

Because we were on Kleer's home turf at his offices in Warner Center, I let the baby-faced barrister in the beige shirt and blue striped tie kick off the meeting. He greeted us all grandly, then pontificated for several malicious minutes on how his client VORPO would kick my client's butt when we stood before a jury of their sympathetic, dead-set-against-development peers.

I didn't have to look at squirmy and chunky Brian O'Barlen beside me to know how brutally he was biting his tongue, but I anticipated blood flowing down his extra chin if I hazarded a glance. It would contrast with the pink shade his cheeks became when he was irate, but would go stunningly with his flowing silver mane. He had come alone, as requested. I figured that if his sycophants were genuine suspects in the murders, it would be because O'Barlen bade them to commit the crimes. His attitude was what I aimed to learn.

"Very interesting," I said in a bored tone slightly short of a yawn when Kleer had concluded his tirade. I sat up straighter then in the swivel chair that matched a dozen others around this big firm's massive conference table. "Now, let's stop posturing and start solving our mutual problem." I grinned at Kleer's perturbed expression as a result of my put-down. "Yes, I know we've spoken about the parties' respective positions before, but now it's time to get serious—unless both sides are really ready to start hemorrhaging legal fees. The reality T.O. needs to face is that there are a lot of property owners around the key block in Vancino who have concerns about their development."

Only then did I turn to behold O'Barlen. No blood on his chin, but irritation was obvious in his pink-tinged expression.

I pivoted back to face Kleer and Daniels. I was pleasantly surprised to see that the latter, whom I'd only seen dressed down in the most casual of clothes before, had also donned a button-down shirt and tie—even if both glared in garish hues of green and orange. He didn't look much older than Kleer, and his gray eyes glowed with surliness mirrored in his straight-lipped scowl.

"And the reality VORPO needs to face," I said to the two of them, "is that T.O. does own most of the pertinent property. Maybe they can get the rest, and maybe not. But even if they don't, they're going to develop the portion they do have, one way or another." This time, the opposition turned red and irate. "So, the reason I called this meeting was to suggest that it's way past time for both sides to end the posturing and really propose what's most important to them, with the hope we can carve out a compromise now to avoid a lengthy and costly court battle that's otherwise bound to start soon. Unless you're all thrilled about the idea of ensuring that Mr. Kleer and I grow rich?"

The strength with which Michael Kleer clenched his legal pad suggested he'd like to fly across the table and use his hands to commit mayhem on me. It was a position I'd seen a lot of lately, and it failed to faze me.

"What do you suggest, Ms. Ballantyne?" demanded Daniels.

"As I said, tell me what's most important to your group, and Mr. O'Barlen will do the same. Nothing will be binding since this is a settlement discussion, but let's see what you might be willing to give up to achieve what you really want."

To my delight and surprise, the session turned at least partly productive. Per Daniels, VORPO members detested the idea of high density in a small space, which could lead to terrific increases in traffic and crime. Plus, they liked the quaintness of their cute business center. And per my client O'Barlen, T.O. needed enough density to ensure the development earned oodles of income for its investors. It remained willing, though, to allow limited input in the architectural design—which they had already anticipated would keep the community's quaintness while allowing a more efficient use of space above street level.

"I suggest we not wait any longer. The next meeting should absolutely include T.O.'s designers and architects, and appropriately knowledgeable VORPO sorts," I said. "See if they can work out a compromise on building design and concentration of people. Michael and I can make ourselves available, but why not try it without incurring legal fees? If you start squabbling, call us to come in and argue on your respective behalfs at our high hourly rates."

This elicited a laugh from both the business sorts, and a bitter titter from opposition counsel Kleer.

"So if all goes reasonably well, Flint," I said, "do you think your company will sell its piece of property to T.O.?"

"Maybe. If all really goes reasonably well," he reiterated with a resolute nod. "And for the right price."

This last extracted a snort from O'Barlen, which he covered up with a cough.

"Reasonability is the key," I reminded everyone. "And what about Millie Franzel, Flint? Can she be convinced to sell?"

He shrugged. "I'm not sure anyone can convince Millie of anything, but if we're satisfied, we'll give it a try."

"That's the best anyone can do." And now it was time for my ulterior motive for calling this meeting. "I only wish Ezra Cossner were here to see this," I said sadly. "He'd have been so pleased that both sides are at least talking."

The air suddenly grew so still that I anticipated the remainder of the hurricane to swoop down full force.

"That bastard?" rumbled Flint Daniels. "No way would we have made any progress. It's just as well he's dead."

I surreptitiously skimmed the other faces about the table. No one seemed to disagree. All looked equally ambivalent about Ezra's demise. But no smoking gun suddenly shot out and showed me who'd murdered Ezra and Corrie.

"Do any of you have an idea who might have killed him? I've talked to the cops often, and they're still not sure." I chose my first target: my own client. "Brian, you were angry with Ezra about his representation at the time. I don't suppose you decided to do something violent about it." I'd blown client confidentiality if he really was guilty, but hell, if he'd done it, he'd have to hire a criminal attorney to defend him, and that wasn't me.

O'Barlen looked as eager to silence me as Kleer had with his clenched fingers earlier. "What the hell kind of question is that, Ballantyne?"

"I just wanted to toss you off balance and see if you'd confess," I responded with a smile. "How about you, Flint? After the VORPO meeting that night, you were pissed with Cossner. Did you decide to silence the opposition mouthpiece?"

"No!" he shouted, and methought the man didst protest too much—or at least too loudly. But since William Shakespeare wasn't in the conference room to help dissect this particular tragedy, I couldn't rely on that as evidence.

"Then what about his paralegal, who was doing all the research about VORPO and its members? Did you decide to deal with Corrie Montez, Flint? And do you have someone who'll verify your alibi for both nights?"

"I don't have to take this, do I?" he demanded of his attorney.

My turn to make a demand on that same man. "I don't suppose you decided to rid yourself of a difficult opposition attorney, did you, Michael? If so, I'll bet you think it's a bad decision now. You're now opposing me instead, and here I am promoting a settlement that'll take money from your pockets. Where were you that night? Can someone swear to your whereabouts? How about the night Corrie died and someone shot at *me*?"

"We're through here," Kleer asserted acidly. "You'd better go." He turned to his client. "After these accusations, are you sure you want to attempt to resolve this matter out of court?"

"What, and have to face me again?" I asked. "I'll bet all parties would be delighted to settle to avoid ever having to be in my accusatory company."

"I'll say," O'Barlen barked.

"But I really hoped to get a confession," I said as the men prepared to exit the conference room. "I think you're the most likely culprit, Michael." Not true, but I still needed someone to react suspiciously enough for me to grow certain of his guilt.

"Go pound sand, counselor," Kleer said and trooped out, Daniels behind him.

"What the hell were you doing?" O'Barlen appeared royally peeved. The former rosiness of his complexion was now angry red.

"Just what it looked like," I answered him. "I don't suppose you care to confess to the murders."

"You're a weirdo, you know, Kendra?" He collected the paraphernalia he'd pulled out for the conference and crammed it haphazardly into his briefcase. "But I have to say you done good today. Maybe we really will get this fiasco settled." He moved to plant his portly self in front of me, and his glare was anything but pleasant. "As long as you stop with this confession nonsense. Did you really think someone at this meeting killed Cossner? Well, if so, it wasn't me."

Well, if not, who was it? I absolutely was not done investigating.

Chapter Twenty-seven

CALL IT A gut feeling, but I couldn't get excited about either Kleer or Daniels as the two to tango at the top of my suspect list. Not O'Barlen, either, although it wasn't because of his denial.

Though each was clearly peeved by my pushing on the subject, none struck me as hiding something hugely major—like, "I'm the murderer, so what do you think you're going to do about it, Ballantyne?"

Not exactly evidence of innocence. The L.A.P.D.'s Scientific Investigation Division wouldn't make book on it. But I felt reasonably definite that I had to drape my accusations around more credible suspects.

Kleer's Warner Center office was mid-Valley, and I now had to travel south to Century City to see Jonathon Jetts and his wife, Bella.

I headed south on the 405 Freeway and made my way once more to the Avenue of the Stars. I was prepared this time for the Jambison & Jetts shrew of a receptionist. When she peered over her haughty puggish nose as if she despised my deodorant, I scrutinized her severely, then shook my head. "Sorry to mention it," I whispered, "but you might want to go look in the restroom mirror. There's something in your hair." Like the scrunchy that held the black mass straight back off her face, but I didn't mention that. Instead, I felt a guilty sense of pleasure as she grew pink and squirmy.

"Thank you," she managed with a weak smile. "I'll let Mr. Jetts know you're here."

A few minutes later, after I'd sat alone in the reception area thumbing through law journals containing articles by-lined by names of Jambison firm attorneys, Jonathon Jetts appeared. "Please come this way, Ms. Ballantyne," the short and stocky, man intoned heatedly, as if he'd had to burn his way through icebergs to come out and get me.

"Kendra," I said as I followed him down the hallowed, art-decorated hallways of the firm.

"Pardon?"

"Call me Kendra, Jonathon. Might as well keep things informal."

He sneered as if he'd rather dive under those icebergs than play nice with me, but I simply smiled.

He showed me into an office a few doors down from his wife's, where I'd hung out the last time I'd been here. His was equally vast, and also contained a matched row of decorator file cabinets. His desk was more traditional than Bella's modern one, a wood reddish in tint, carved in design, and polished in finish. His sitting area furniture sported fabric of deep green rather than primly appointed white.

Instead of inviting me to get comfy in his conversation pit, he motioned me to a high-backed, starchy-seeming chair facing his desk, then took his own comfortably upholstered seat behind it.

"So you want to talk about returning some of our clients to us, Ms. Ballantyne," he intoned, ignoring my earlier invitation to put us on a first-name basis.

"Perhaps," I said. "But only if that's what they want, of course. And I'll have to advise them whether I consider it in their best interests." I paused for effect, tossing him a guileless grin. "That's why I'd like Bella to join us in this conversation. She's a much nicer person than you, so I want to make sure she's prepared to handle any cases we send back this way."

Jonathon Jetts appeared utterly outraged. His brown eyes bugged apoplectically. "Are you a nutcase, Ms. Ballantyne?"

"Absolutely, Jonathon. Aren't you?" I kept smiling sweetly, not moving my gaze from his. "Shall I call Bella, or will you?"

His response was to lift his phone receiver and press a couple of buttons. "Can you come in here?" he ordered someone, presumably his wife. Sure, he'd phrased it as a question, but I doubted the person he'd directed it to would take it that way. "She's coming," he said as he slammed down the phone.

He was right. Bella Quevedo-Jetts appeared in the office less than a minute later. She glanced quizzically from her husband to me, then back again. "Hello, Ms. Ballantyne," she finally said, holding out her hand.

"I'm Kendra, Bella," I said. She was probably a nice enough person to react more favorably to my friendly overture than her harrumphing husband.

I'd already risen from my less than comfy seat and eagerly gave her proffered hand a slight but professional pumping. She wore all white today, a silky dress whose paleness emphasized the silver streak in her smooth black hair.

She smiled uncertainly. "What brings you here today, Kendra?"

I gave her the same song and dance about defecting clients that I'd given Jonathon. "Now that Ezra's gone, we've been working to convince them all to stay with Yurick & Associates, and I'm sure some will. But they were really Ezra's clients."

I looked for some reaction on the faces of husband and wife. Husband stayed scowling. Wife seemed a smidgen weepy.

"You knew him pretty well before, didn't you?" I directed my question to said female spouse.

She nodded slowly, hazarding a sideways glance at her obviously unhappy hubby. "He and I were close for a while," she said sadly.

"I know he wasn't always the easiest person to get along with," I encouraged. "But despite his gruff ways sometimes, he seemed to me to have a good sense of humor. And deep down, I gathered he was quite kind."

That obviously got to Bella, who teared up and slouched down in her seat, which appeared unusual for this elegant and poised professional. "Yes. At least he was kind to me, most of the time, even though he could put on airs and become difficult and demanding. But he especially loved Pinocchio, my Amazon parrot. That was why he adopted his Gigi, you know."

"Why was that?" I inquired, even though Polly Bright had made a similar statement.

"Ezra and I saw a lot of each other for nearly a year, and I think he cared for Pinocchio even more than he cared for me. When I told him we couldn't see each other anymore on a personal basis, he seemed all torn up. And angry. And when I actually married Jonathon, he made it clear he'd decided to outdo me and get a bigger and better bird. A macaw."

"Gigi?" I asked.

"Gigi." She nodded affirmatively without disarranging a solitary hair in her perfectly coiffed do. "She was an adult macaw and moderately well trained, and though she was not the most expensive bird he could have found, I'm sure he attempted to outdo me in that department as well. Ezra tended toward ostentation in his spending habits even when he wasn't attempting some subtle revenge."

She glanced at Jonathon, and so did I. His conservative and styleless suit looked economical enough to have come off the rack at Sears. He doubtless drew down a hefty salary as a name partner at this prestigious firm. Perhaps he squirreled it away for the day he'd cease earning acorns here. I'd once seen the word "husbank" as what appeared to be a misprint on the dedication page of an excellent mystery novel, although as I'd considered the word, I'd wondered whether it was intended to genuinely describe the financial association between the author and her spouse. I doubted it in that situation—but I suspected that one reason Bella selected Jonathon over Ezra was for his superior *husbank* potential.

"I see," I said to encourage Bella to keep speaking. "So he acquired Gigi in a game of one-upmanship?"

"Yes, especially because he then made it clear that his bird was bigger and better than mine. Gigi could beat poor Pinocchio in a parrot fight any day. Despite Gigi's prior training in civility, he at first egged her on when she nipped with that big beak of hers and started squawking."

"That's nasty!" I exclaimed. "No wonder the poor bird had control issues even when Ezra was alive."

"He encouraged her to be like him," Bella said with a sad laugh. "Ezra believed in approaching every challenge by intimidation. That's one of many reasons I eventually broke up with him. Not that I took him seriously. Only people who didn't know him well wouldn't know that he was all talk, but little action—despite what he fomented in Gigi. And he soon rued what he'd allowed her to get away with. He needed to retrain her without knowing how. He asked me, maybe hoping I'd step in and visit him at home to help. But I wouldn't have been much assistance. That's when I introduced him to Polly Bright. I'd met her at some meetings of bird fanciers I attended. Since I liked what she said in person and in her books about training members of the parrot family, I got her to teach me how to work with

Pinocchio. She really knew her stuff—and wasn't afraid to brag about it!"

Having met Polly, I laughed along with Bella.

And then I continued with my inquiry, keeping my tone light despite the heaviness of the answers I sought not so subtly now. "So when you dumped Ezra, he decided to settle the score by outdoing you in the bird ownership department. And when he left here, he took a paralegal and a bunch of clients. Sounds as if he really got you good. I don't suppose you decided to get him back . . . ?"

"All right," Jonathon finally interjected. "I have work to do, and I'm sure you do, too, Bella. Are you here to see if we're willing to resume the business of some of the clients Ezra stole, Ms. Ballantyne? If so, I'm sure you already know the answer is yes. If not, please stop your ugly innuendoes and state your business so we can finish this little session."

"All right," I said, "forget the innuendoes. I'm actually here to ask one important question." I aimed an apologetic glance toward Bella. I'd already made up my mind about her, kind of. I only hoped I wasn't wrong.

Her *husbank* was another story.

"What I'd really like to know is which of you killed Ezra Cossner and your former paralegal, Corrie Montez."

As I'd anticipated, my impudent inquiry elicited a roar of rage from Jonathon. "You're way out of line, Ms. Ballantyne. You'd better leave, or I'll call building security to eject you."

I studied his unattractive face for a sign of fear peeking from behind the outrage. I did likewise with his lovely and poised wife.

"I'll leave," I said, standing as if to prove it. "I figure that my reputation has preceded me. Did you know I've solved three murders in the last few months? If you're guilty in these two, you can be sure I'll find out and prove it." I turned to Bella Quevedo-Jetts. "I really hope *you're* not involved," I told her. "Thanks for seeing me."

"Good luck, Kendra." She sounded sincere, which kind of convinced me of her innocence—and that she considered her husband not guilty as well. Of course, she could be wrong about that.

Other than his being a *husbank,* I didn't see what she saw in Jonathon Jetts. And if I had to select a guilty suspect, he'd be way at the top of my useful little list.

WHEN I ESCAPED from Century City, the afternoon was well on its way toward being over, but I still had time to visit my office before commencing the evening's pet-sitting. As I drove, my mind twisted over and over around my suspect inventory.

Who done it?

Saying a hasty hello to Mignon after reaching our building, I hightailed it into my own digs and shut the door. I didn't have time to engage in amenities with others at the Yurick firm. I had too much to do.

I first spewed my notes from the T.O.-VORPO settlement conference onto my computer to ensure I'd have an ongoing record. Everyone there might despise me, but I was still hopeful I'd been instrumental in causing them to band together in their mutual dislike of me. Maybe they'd hammer out mutually agreeable terms to cease their ongoing overt animosity. Bye-bye courtroom and lucrative legal fees, hello compromised development. Everyone a winner except this firm and my paycheck. Oh, well.

And then I turned to that list that inevitably loomed in my mind. I tweaked it so Jonathon Jetts swam up to one, while his wife Bella sank to the bottom.

I considered all the suspects I'd managed to see today—I'd visited with nearly everyone I considered viable. Except Jeff. But I still didn't want it to be him.

As I had with the settlement meeting, I pecked out notes on my computer keyboard about all I'd said and heard, and extracted from everyone I'd spoken with and essentially accused of murder.

When I was done, one particular statement stood out.

I mused over it for several long minutes.

And then the answer came to me. Or so I surmised.

If so, it could explain everything! But I had work to do if I intended to be certain.

Chapter Twenty-eight

THAT NIGHT, WHILE Lexie and I lay alone in our apartment bed, I figured out how to fix things. A bit dramatic, but I'd been known to pull no punches when acquiring a killer's confession.

I commenced my preparations for the anticipated event the next day—and night, when I returned to the offices once again after everyone had left.

The following day was Saturday, and as I wasn't yet ready, I resorted again to the same routine.

Sunday, I considered a visit to Darryl's resort, since Lexie was being left home alone an awful lot, mostly at odd hours. I did the obvious thing and asked my pet-sitting protégée Rachel to care for my Cavalier. Both acted elated.

And me? Yes, my horrendous schedule was becoming a habit, but there was no help for it.

Although I expected that the end was in sight. And I felt surer of it late Sunday, when the breakthrough I'd been betting on finally occurred.

That meant that I made several calls, come Monday. And then I was ready to rock and roll . . .

"GORGEOUS GIRL," I crooned to Gigi near the middle of Monday night.

I'd moved her into the bar, the better to enjoy her company as I waited for what was to come.

I heard a knock at the door to the office building, and I took a deep breath beneath my oversized white sweater. Or tried to, considering how constricted I felt by the proceedings I predicted.

"Show time," I said, sticking my hands down deep into the pockets of my pink denim slacks.

"Aawrk," Gigi squawked in response.

I hoped she remembered her role. And then I went to admit the person I'd grown positive was the murderer.

Not that I truly needed to, since the killer had a key.

"Hi, Kendra," said Polly Bright when I opened the door. As always—almost—the celebrated parrot psychologist was clad in flowing garments of garish shades—orange and purple and green this evening. A huge tote bag swung from her hefty shoulder. "How's poor Gigi? I'm sorry to hear she still hasn't settled down after all the terrible things she experienced."

"Me, too," I responded ardently. "Come in. I really hope you can help. I remembered what you said about startling her and shifting her environment to earn her attention, so I've relocated her to the conference room."

Confess now, I ordered nonverbally as I preceded Polly into the former restaurant bar. Naturally she didn't blurt out that during two of her most recent visits, she'd shot people to death in this very building and also aimed at me.

Gigi was calm and stood serenely on her large wooden perch, surveying the two of us via one gleaming eye, then the other.

"She looks all right to me." Polly appeared puzzled. She drew closer and eyed Gigi up and down from below, since the top of the evil bird expert's head, crowned by her strangely shaded red-hued hair, was shorter than Gigi on her perch.

"Appearances can be deceptive," I intoned. "The thing is, I had a visit from Jeff Hubbard today, and she became so nervous that I thought she would fly off her perch and nip someone. Namely me."

"Oh. I see." Polly nodded knowingly, and I nearly asserted my accusations when I noted the delighted twinkle in her ordinary brown eyes. I still hadn't cinched it, but my certainty mounted that my theory was true.

"No, I'm not sure you do see," I said with a sad pseudo-sigh. "Jeff and I were an item for a very short while. I really came to care for him, so I didn't want to believe he could have killed Ezra and Corrie. But all the evidence seems to point toward him."

"That's what I gathered from the news," Polly said solemnly, sinking her pudgy body onto the seat of the nearest booth. "What evidence have the police found?"

"A couple of things," I answered evasively, sitting on the edge of the seat opposite her. "One of the things I wanted to talk to you more about is the ability of macaws to repeat things they hear during an emotional moment. Your books say they aren't as good as, say, African Grey parrots at doing that. But you told me it is possible, right?"

"As I mentioned to you, every bird has a different personality," she preached, her expression solemn, as if she imparted invaluable information to a sycophant who'd begged for facts. "My books also point that out. Most macaws don't pick things up that fast, but obviously Gigi is different."

An interesting observation, considering that the news vultures hadn't been informed about that particular piece of purported evidence. Nor had anyone else.

Polly could have inferred my meaning, of course, but I hadn't expressly mentioned Gigi while inquiring about emotional macaw repetitions. In fact, I had intentionally posed my inquiry to be nonspecific.

So how would Polly know that Gigi was so different?

"I see," I said contemplatively. "You know, I'm not sure I believe you. I've read a couple of your books, and they appear to be drivel to me. I mean, how can a fraud like you make a living pretending you're a parrot expert?" I smiled snidely at her. "You seem to change the facts to meet the situation. I don't believe that Gigi picked up Ezra's dying scream, 'Stop it, Hubbard,' the moment before he died."

Polly's pudgy brow pursed, and her double chins wiggled. "That's not what she picked up. I mean—"

My wicked grin widened. "No, it isn't. It was the sound of Jeff's cell phone. How did you get Gigi to repeat it, Polly?"

She stood and stared furiously down at me. "How did you know?"

"I read your books and asked you questions. I worked with Gigi myself. And I believe now that even if macaws sometimes pick up sounds they hear once, they're more likely to repeat things taught over and over. But when did you play Jeff's cell phone ring to her?"

"Mornings," she spat. The brightness of her cheerful demeanor and clothing now seemed awfully ominous as she loomed over me. "Very early mornings when the cops weren't here and no one else had arrived yet. I had to get up even earlier than the birds, so to speak, but fortunately only a few times. Gigi is, in fact, pretty good at picking things up fast."

"Dare I ask your reason for teaching her that tune?"

She gave a shrug that set her colorful robe swaying. "I was here the day Jeff Hubbard started his investigation of everyone who was around this office even occasionally. I had to turn things around on him to get him to stop. He'd gotten a call on his cell phone, so I knew what it sounded like. I downloaded it from the Internet onto my digital music player—I couldn't find it as a ring tone. I took Elaine Aames's set of office keys from her purse one day when I was here, had them duplicated, and put them back the next time I was around. And each time I came on my own, I played that damned tune over and over again till Gigi finally started repeating it. I just needed the cops to understand the implication, even from a macaw. They don't reproduce sounds exactly, you know."

I nodded. "You got your wish," I told her. "The primary detective on the case understood what it meant."

"Detective Noralles? Yes, I made sure he knew. He called me in as an expert to help with Gigi, you know."

"Yeah, I figured," I flung at her.

"Ah, but did you know you gave me the idea to teach Gigi that cell phone ring? That day you asked whether birds can repeat things they heard in moments of emotion—well, it started me thinking."

Damn! I'd have to tell Darryl . . . "And you recognized Jeff's sports coat so you ensured he'd be implicated in Corrie's murder, too, by decorating it with a dab of her blood."

Polly nodded. I noticed that one of her hands had disappeared into her oversized tote bag. A bad sign. Was she fumbling for a weapon?

I had a trick or two of my own up my slightly less massive sleeve, but I still had to stay observant. "All this is interesting," I said, "and somewhat as I surmised, but what made you decide to murder Ezra in the first place?"

She stopped scrounging and stared down at me with sadness in her small eyes. "I'd done such a fine job for his friend Bella Quevedo—Mrs. Jetts now. Her beautiful Amazon parrot, Pinocchio, was such a dream to teach. When Bella, who was so nice, referred me to her friend Ezra Cossner, who'd just adopted a macaw, of course I had to try to help him out."

I wriggled back in my booth when Polly's expression turned thunderous.

"He was mistreating poor Gigi, encouraging her to do terrible things, like screech and bite," Polly stormed. "I tried to be professional in the way I criticized him for causing her problems, and at the same time I tried to teach them both what was right. But Gigi is stubborn and smart."

I nodded. I'd experienced her obstinacy firsthand.

"When she didn't respond right away and behave better," Polly continued, "Ezra yelled at me. Threatened to expose me as a fraud so I'd never be respected as a parrot expert again." My neck was growing cramped, yet I still nodded. I'd heard a little of Ezra's attempt at intimidation. "He said he'd do all he could to see I never was invited to speak again or work with parrots anywhere in the world, and that I'd never sell any more books. He was a lawyer. People listened to him. I was afraid he'd ruin me. And so . . . that awful night, when Gigi was so upset, he ordered me to come back here even though it was late. He yelled at me again, even as Gigi shrieked and bit at us, and, well . . . I somehow grabbed the gun from my purse and shot him."

"Oh, yes. The guns. I know the cops used them to assist forming their conclusions that Jeff was guilty. A P.I. would be aware of places supplying weapons with no questions asked. But a parrot person?"

"I am highly aware of security issues," Polly replied primly. "I visit people in their homes at all hours, alone with them except for their birds. In my many travels, I've gained access to weapons of self-defense from others who understand the need for discretion. I was sorry to have to leave them behind, but that was ever so much better than having them found on my person, with all the questions that would engender, even after I'd only used them as they were intended—in self-defense."

"How—" With the self-righteous way she regarded me, I

bit back my angry inquiry about how she'd convinced herself of that insane conclusion. I even forbore from retching
at that ridiculous interpretation of reality. Instead, I said
softly, "You needed more than one gun to protect yourself?"

"Why, yes," she responded smugly. "I'm a great be-
liever in belt and suspenders in duplicate, triplicate, and
more. But now, sadly, there are two missing guns from my
collection. I will need to replace them."

"You knew enough to eliminate your fingerprints," I
stated, still keeping my criticism to my outraged self.

She nodded slowly, appearing exhausted now that she'd
confessed her first crime. "I love those TV shows about investigating crime scenes. I figured that it was okay if my
prints were around otherwise, since people knew I came
here to help Ezra train Gigi."

"What about the ammunition?" I asked. "No prints
were found on bullets or casings. If the killing wasn't
premeditated—"

"I certainly wasn't going to let anything so nasty come
in contact with my skin," she interrupted with a grimace. "I
always use gloves when I load."

I recalled her use of her own cup when visiting here,
and other acts of eccentric primness, like personal preparation of parrot treats, which proved she was probably telling
the truth. "And Corrie? Why did you kill her?"

Again Polly's features contorted into a furious frown.
"She knew Ezra had called me to come in that night. She
suspected what had happened and came to my very own
home to accuse me. She said she'd been planning to give
up her career as a paralegal, and I was providing her with
the perfect opportunity—or I would, when I paid her not to
tell what she knew about me."

"Blackmail." I nodded knowingly. I'd suspected something like that but had hoped Corrie wasn't really that kind
of person.

Of course, a lot of people are opportunists, even accomplished paralegals.

"I went along with her the first time, figuring that would be that. Only that *wasn't* that. She wanted more. I still had my office key, so I sneaked back in that night when she expected me, only later. And I did what I had to, to shut her up."

"And shot at me!" I couldn't help exploding.

"Only when you looked out the window. I was wearing ugly and drab, dark clothes, so I doubted you would recognize me, but even so . . ."

"And that's also when you took advantage of Jeff's jacket being abandoned here."

She nodded. And then she drew a scary-looking silenced handgun from her handbag.

My heart started hammering so hugely that I was afraid it would get bruised beneath my rib cage. I swallowed, then said, "So how do you think you'll be able to blame this one on Jeff?"

"I don't know yet," she said with a deep sigh. "And I've hated having to deal with all that blood. I know from the shows that there's likely to be some residue in my car no matter how much I scrubbed it, though I was careful to dispose of my clothes from those nights by burning them. At least no one has suspected me. I think I may have to wreck my car, though, and buy a new one. And here goes yet another gun."

"What a shame," I snarled.

I shuddered in anticipation, yet even at that I felt surprised at the suddenness of her move. She drew the gun up and aimed it, even as I attempted to shoulder my way away from her and the bar booth.

Pudgy Polly was fitter than she appeared, and her strength, partly born of desperation, was enormous. I threw one hand up in a gesture of defiance . . .

And suddenly a loud siren screamed throughout the room.

"No!" Polly wailed as, startled, she failed to stop me as I shoved her out of the way.

I reached into my pants pocket and pulled out a pistol of my own, as the siren continued—rather raspily, emanating from the mouth of the beautiful Blue and Gold Macaw. I ensured that the safety was off and aimed it at the cowering parrot shrink.

"Gorgeous girl," I gasped to Gigi, who had come through with the sound I'd instructed her on over the last few nights.

Only then did two male humans insinuate themselves into this latest crime scene—also with weapons at the ready.

"It's about time you showed up," I shouted shakily to Detective Ned Noralles and his temporary partner of this night, Private Investigator Jeff Hubbard.

Chapter Twenty-nine

I WAS WIRED, of course, and I'd worn a bulky protective vest beneath my big sweater.

I'd had to practically tap dance to convince Detective Noralles to participate in what he called my latest "hare-brained scheme." But he knew that, as a pet-sitter, I revered all species of domestic animals and therefore didn't mind—much—being compared with a hare. I had, after all, tended bunnies near the beginning of my pet business.

He'd at least listened to me as I'd laid out my suspicions, and much as he hated to admit it, he saw where they'd started from and couldn't completely discount them.

Ned had always acted fair to me—except when he'd considered me his main murder suspect—so even though, if I turned out to be right, he'd lose his big chance at avenging himself on Jeff for besting him way back when in L.A.P.D. history, Ned went along with me.

Jeff, too. He was harder to convince, since he asserted how much he abhorred the idea of my putting myself in so much danger. But with the borrowed vest and firearm, I'd felt pretty much protected.

Now, after Polly had been Mirandized and taken into custody by a couple of local L.A.P.D. detectives, including Candace Schwinglan, the three of us sat in the same booth where I'd been with Polly. Despite how late the night was now, Ned wore his typical suit. He didn't appear particularly uncomfortable in it. In fact, I'd come to think of suits as part of this dynamic detective's persona.

Jeff, on the other hand, had shown up in snug jeans and a denim jacket in a different shade of blue. He looked damnably luscious in them. Too bad we weren't talking to one another.

"So you figured it was Ms. Bright how?" Ned demanded. I'd given him only pieces of the puzzle when I'd phoned and pleaded for his participation tonight.

"It was last week, when I met with Bella Quevedo-Jetts. Bella liked Ezra, even though she admitted he took great enjoyment out of threatening people, particularly regarding their livelihoods. Of course, Bella said that those who knew Ezra well knew better than to take him seriously."

"But why Polly Bright?"

"Weren't you listening to this?" I gestured toward the gadget they'd stuck on me to record the conversation.

He nodded.

"Well, then, you know. Bella mentioned how much Polly prided herself on being considered an expert. Polly didn't know Ezra well. And I don't know how thickly Ezra laid on his threats, but even I heard him threaten Polly's future. She'd been around this office enough to get to know the players here, including some of our occasional visitors, like Jeff. Jeff started to get nosy when his own nose was on the line as a possible suspect, so to get him off her case, Polly decided he was the perfect person for her to frame. She stole Elaine's keys one night and had them copied.

And who better than a parrot person to train a macaw to make an unusual sound?"

"Damn," Ned said. "We interviewed her, of course, but she appeared to lack motive and opportunity. And the means, guns—who'd have thought this crazy civilian would have a collection?" He ran his fingers through his short, dark hair, and stared at me, then smiled. "Hey, counselor. And Ms. Pet-Sitter. Care to take on a third career as an L.A.P.D. detective?"

I laughed, knowing full well he wasn't serious. Was he? "I'm busy enough with two, but thanks, Ned."

"Thank you, Kendra." He stood. "Only, since you refused my offer, how about staying away from murders from now on?"

"Amen," I answered fervently . . . while I wondered whether I meant it.

When he was gone, I was left in that same booth with Jeff. He reached across and took my hands in his, and it felt too damned good. I let mine rest there for a few moments, then gently pulled them away.

"Thanks aren't adequate, Kendra, for all you did. But . . . thanks."

"You're welcome." I sensed wetness welling up in my eyesockets and scowled. "So now that I don't have to feel sorry for you anymore, I think it's time we made it official. Goodbye, Jeff. Have a good life—you and Amanda."

And with that, I stood and stalked off, figuring he could find his own way out.

LEXIE WAS NATURALLY waiting for me in our apartment. She seemed sleepy but pleased to see me. Not frantic, so I figured Rachel had done a good job tending her this evening.

"It's over, girl," I told her. If she'd spoken English, I knew she'd ask *what* was over, so I explained the whole murder scenario, with Jeff as suspect. "And now that I've cleared him, I figured I didn't need all the confusion in my life. I'm still a mess about picking men," I ended with a sigh.

Lexie wasn't in my life when I'd made the miserable mistake of sleeping with Bill Sergement at my old law firm. I'd hoped I'd made a better choice when I'd fallen—hard—for Jeff Hubbard, but now I knew the sad truth about that sexy fiasco, too.

"Who needs a relationship anyway?" I asked Lexie when I was in bed and she'd nested at my feet. "I'll settle for some good, no-strings sex again one of these days, and that'll be enough."

Or it would be when I finally erased Jeff from my system.

THE NEXT MORNING was Wednesday. I knocked on the door to my main house, and Rachel responded, ready to go pet-sitting at my side. I brought Lexie along, and after we'd visited and cared for all of my charges, I dropped Rachel back at home.

"My dad's here," she said. "Why don't you join us for dinner tonight?"

"Okay," I said, only slightly reluctant. I liked Russ. Maybe I'd target him for that no-strings sex one of these days.

The Yurick firm was abuzz with rumors about last night's arrest of Polly Bright. It had hit the news, too, but fortunately my role in it hadn't been found out by the media vultures. At least not yet.

But Corrie's body would soon be released for burial. Unlike with Ezra, we'd all be given the chance to say good-bye. Whether or not she'd become a blackmailer by opportunism, she hadn't deserved to die.

"You're okay, Kendra?" Borden demanded.

"I sure am. And I owe an awful lot to Gigi."

That beautiful macaw was back in Elaine's office. I told

her what a brave bird she had, and the older attorney smiled. "I think she's settling down now, don't you? I'll try taking her for rides soon, and then I'll see how she does at my home."

"As long as you bring her here often for visits. She's part of the firm family now." I approached Gigi and grinned. "Gorgeous girl," I said.

Which was when Gigi started shrieking her new noise: the siren that I'd taught her by repeatedly playing the sound of a toy police car to her at night.

Elaine covered her ears. "Thanks a lot, Kendra," she said with a laugh.

"Any time," I replied and escaped from her echoing office.

In my own, I found a message from Brian O'Barlen. "You did it!" he exclaimed.

"Well, it wasn't just me, but the police—"

"What do the police have to do with it?"

That got me realizing that our ramblings were on different topics. He wasn't calling to congratulate me on my part in Polly's arrest.

"Let's start over," I suggested. "What did you call about?"

It turned out that the T.O.-VORPO discussions I'd suggested had come to pass and had turned out better than either side had envisioned. They'd come to an agreement about how dense the density would be, how beautiful and abundant the buildings would be, nearly everything. And all pieces of property would be part of the development.

"So no more legal fees on this one," he said with a self-satisfied chortle.

"Well, a lot fewer," I agreed. "You still need to have the settlement agreement written to memorialize your accord. That way both sides can review it in black and white to ensure they've got a true meeting of the minds."

"Yeah, yeah," he said snappishly. "Go ahead and deal with the details."

"Sure will," I said. I called Michael Kleer. "Have you heard?"

"On the news?" he said. "Oh, yeah. You're one brave lady, Kendra."

He sounded admiring, but I didn't want to take time to preen. "No, I mean about the T.O.-VORPO accord."

"No. Really? They've reached a settlement?"

"Sounds that way. Go ahead and check with your client. Oh, and is it okay with you if I call Millie Franzel? I won't push her, of course, but I'm eager to find out if she's been included and voluntarily agreed to sell her site."

"Go ahead," he said, and I did.

"Oh, it's wonderful, Kendra," Millie said when I had her on the phone. "I'll be provided a temporary, rent-subsidized shop across the street in one of the empty stores. Then, when the project is built out, I'll lease another, prettier store at a low rent for years. Plus, I'll live in one of the penthouse apartments—also at a low rent. I'm so pleased. Thank you. Come to my shop, and I'll give you a special treat for Lexie."

I beamed as I hung up. There was even a pet-happy ending in my non-pet law litigation matter. And I'd helped to end Polly Bright's reign of macaw-involved mayhem. I rocked!

MY DINNER THAT night with Russ and Rachel went well. Rachel's dad had bought her a new, used car that day, so my pet-sitter protégée now had wheels.

"I've got an audition for a small role in a play tomorrow, Kendra," Rachel said with an overjoyed glow in her big brown eyes. "But whether or not I get the role, can I do some pet-sitting for you on my own? I mean, now that I'll be able to drive, I can do all the work for some of your customers. And you'll be able to take on more, if you'd like."

"Sounds like a plan," I replied with a smile. I swiveled

my head so that smile landed smack on her dad. "Thanks, Dad," I told him.

"I had a method to my madness," he said. "If I can free up some more of your time, maybe you and I can go out for dinner ourselves now and then. Take in a movie."

"Or Rachel's play," I said, which made Rachel's wide grin grow even greater. Where was the pout that had defined her face when I'd first met her?

I was definitely delighted that it had disappeared.

And I purposely left the response to Russ's question hanging.

Question: Why was it I couldn't get as excited about this nice, slightly older, and absolutely attractive man as I did about Jeff?

Answer: Because I'm a perpetual flop in the select-the-right-man-for-a-relationship department.

Question: Would that ever change?

Answer: Damned if I knew.

While Lexie and I climbed the stairs to our apartment at about 7 P.M., my cell phone rang. I noted the number.

Jeff.

I thought about letting it tumble into voice mail. Hadn't he gotten *my* message, when I'd handed it to him face to face? Or at least face to back. Like, we're history, Hubbard.

Well, obtuseness wasn't this P.I.'s middle name, but obstinacy might be. I decided to answer.

"Kendra? Could you come over here? I'm going out of town on an emergency assignment and I'll need for you to take care of Odin, okay?"

"Now? Tonight?"

"You know I prefer your staying here when you pet-sit Odin. And I always pay you extra for it."

I considered saying no. But hey, I liked Odin. If I kept on pet-sitting for him, I could ensure everything stayed on a strictly professional basis.

I hoped.

I PACKED AN overnight bag and Lexie's breakfast, then we were on our way.

We were soon on the flat Sherman Oaks street where Jeff lived. I didn't park behind his Escalade but would pull my Beamer into the driveway once he'd departed.

I rang the bell and heard Odin's responsive bark. That set Lexie prancing.

The door opened, and there stood Jeff. Looking every bit as good as last night.

"Thanks for coming, Kendra." He motioned me to come in.

Which was when I saw Amanda sitting in Jeff's sunken living room, looking as much like a slender, gorgeous fashion model as she ever had—not that I'd been informed of what the bleached blonde's genuine career was these days. She was clad in a sexy form-fitting sweater and equally tight slacks—and looked about as thrilled to see me as I was to see her.

Somehow, I must have missed her red car outside.

"What's going on, Jeff?" I demanded. "I thought you wanted me to stay overnight with Odin."

"And me," he said aloud—loud enough for Amanda to hear it.

She rose rapidly and hurried toward us.

Jeff turned toward her. "I wanted to make things clear to Kendra, Amanda. You and I are history. Our only relationship lately has been as customer and security consultant."

"Right," I said. "Like on those nights when she provided you an alibi."

"Tell her the truth, Amanda. When was the last time you and I slept together?"

"None of her damned business," Jeff's ex spat from behind a sneer.

"I wanted to give you this right in front of Kendra." Jeff

reached into his pocket, then handed her what appeared to be a business card. "This is the contact information for a friend of mine who's also in the security business. I've told him to expect your call and explained about your stalker. He'll give you a discount on his fees, as a professional courtesy to me. But from now on, you talk to him, not me, if you need protection. Got it?"

She didn't reply—verbally. But talk about vicious looks. And hers was aimed solely at little old me. She turned her back and without another word stalked from the house.

I smiled inside as I watched through Jeff's front window to be certain she drove off. Sure enough, her car had been parked several doors down.

And then I hazarded a glance at Jeff.

His look was absolutely lustful.

"Er . . . I think Lexie and Odin need a walk," I stammered uneasily, even as my own hormones started hustling up heat from way inside. "Care to come along?"

"Sure," Jeff replied huskily. "We'll take the dogs out for their last fun of the evening. And then we'll come home and take care of *ours*."

Terrible taste in men be damned, at least for tonight. I hurried into his arms for a long, luscious, lascivious kiss. Then backed out of them, using the eager dogs as an excuse. But later . . . well, later would come, and I'd enjoy it for now.

If real life was like a romance novel, I'd assume that we'd live happily ever after—together.

The reality was that tonight I'd settle for a superb session of making up in bed. And tomorrow?

Well, men can be so naïve. Jeff didn't really think he had ended things with Amanda so easily, did he?

I'd learned to rely on my gut feelings, and I had one way deep down as we walked.

Amanda would be back.

What would I do then?

On that, my gut stayed silent. For now.

Lexie must have sensed that my thoughts were on something besides her walk. She leapt up on my leg for attention.

Not to be outdone, Odin stood up on my other side.

And Jeff put his arm around my shoulder.

No murders left to mull over . . .

It was going to be a damned good night.

Meet Kendra Ballantyne.

Former high-powered litigator.
Hollywood pet-sitter.
Crime solver.

Sit, Stay, Slay

By

Linda O. Johnston

Canned from her L.A. law firm, Kendra Ballantyne is now a freelance pet-sitter. When her clients start getting murdered, Kendra fears she's being set up. Aided by sexy detective Jeff Hubbard, she's got to find out why, and fast, because this killer's animal instincts are downright dangerous.

"Brilliantly entertaining."
—Dorothy Cannell

0-425-20000-0

Available wherever books are sold or at
penguin.com

pc992

Nothing to Fear but Ferrets

By
Linda O. Johnston

Attorney-turned-freelance-pet-sitter
Kendra Ballantyne has found a corpse in a
client's apartment, and it's up to her to prove
the innocence of the obvious suspects:
her client's furry ferrets.

0-425-20373-5

**Available wherever books are sold or at
penguin.com**

The Dog Lovers' Mysteries
by
Susan Conant
Featuring dog trainer Holly Winter

The Wicked Flea
0-425-18885-X

The Dogfather
0-425-18838-8

Bride & Groom
0-425-20074-4

Stud Rites
0-425-20250-X

Praise for the Dog Lovers' mysteries:
"Hilarious." —*Los Angeles Times*

"A real tail-wagger." —*Washington Post*

Available wherever books are sold or at
penguin.com

NEW YORK TIMES bestselling author
Lilian Jackson Braun

"Her storytelling voice...is filled with
wonder and whimsy."
—*Los Angeles Times*

First Time in Paperback

The Cat Who Brought Down the House
0-515-13655-7

Actress Thelma Thackeray is organizing a
fundraiser revue starring Koko the cat. But
Thelma's celebration takes an unpleasant turn
when her brother is murdered and Jim Qwilleran
is the suspect. Can Koko put aside stardom
to lend a helping paw in the case?

"Most detectives do their legwork on two legs.
A few, however, do it on four!"
—Associated Press

B147